ALSO BY JOHN McMAHON

A Good Kill

The Evil Men Do

The Good Detective

HEAD
CASES

HEAD CASES

A NOVEL

JOHN McMAHON

MINOTAUR
BOOKS
NEW YORK

First published in the United States by Minotaur Books, an imprint of St. Martin's Publishing Group

HEAD CASES. Copyright © 2024 by John McMahon. All rights reserved. Printed in the United States of America. For information, address St. Martin's Publishing Group, 120 Broadway, New York, NY 10271.

www.minotaurbooks.com

Designed by Omar Chapa

Library of Congress Cataloging-in-Publication Data

Names: McMahon, John, 1970– author.
Title: Head cases / John McMahon.
Description: First edition. | New York : Minotaur Books, 2025.
Identifiers: LCCN 2024025745 | ISBN 9781250348296 (hardcover) |
    ISBN 9781250348302 (ebook)
Subjects: LCGFT: Detective and mystery fiction. | Novels.
Classification: LCC PS3613.C5843 H43 2025 | DDC 813/.6—dc23/
    eng/20240621
LC record available at https://lccn.loc.gov/2024025745

Our books may be purchased in bulk for promotional, educational, or business use. Please contact your local bookseller or the Macmillan Corporate and Premium Sales Department at 1-800-221-7945, extension 5442, or by email at MacmillanSpecialMarkets@macmillan.com.

First Edition: 2025

10 9 8 7 6 5 4 3 2 1

For my mother, Margaret "Betty" McMahon.
Her strength, joy, and ability to love . . . are like a beautiful hurricane.

It is better to be lucky. But I would rather be exact. Then when luck comes, you are ready.

HEAD
CASES

CHAPTER ONE

RIDDLES. THOSE ARE *MY* SPECIALTY. THAT IS, WHEN I AM not studying patterns. Or decoding enigmas. Some might say that solving puzzles is all I'm good for. That leaving my desk in the Jacksonville office of the FBI to interact with real people is not the best use of my time or talent. And I would agree with them.

I stood beside my rented Toyota Avalon and stared at the yellow one-story ranch home.

"Hella impossible," a voice came from over my shoulder.

I glanced at my partner.

Cassie Pardo is a petite five foot three but has the propulsive energy of a thousand suns. She also uses the slang of a nineteen-year-old.

"Nothing's impossible," I said.

Cassie closed the manila folder that her head had been buried in since we left DFW Airport. As we drove here, she had been handicapping the odds on what we were about to see. One in a million . . . one in two million.

A deputy walked over. He was fortyish with a comb-over the color of wheat and an Adam's apple that protruded fourteen millimeters from his larynx.

"Ryan Hollings." He reached out his hand.

I stared at it. Over two hundred bacteria thrive on each square inch of our palms. "Gardner Camden," I said, shaking. I'm not OCD. I just know things like this.

I pointed at the yellow house. "Your victim," I said. "How exactly was he found?"

"An employee from Ashland Gas was checking the meter," Hollings said. "Glanced through the slider and saw blood. Called us."

Cassie popped a piece of chewing gum in her mouth. She was twenty-nine and wore a tailored black jacket over gray slacks. "And you ran the man's prints," she said. "Saw Agent Camden's name?"

Hollings nodded, and we followed him across the lawn. "I googled you two as I waited," he said. "Saw you were the ones who found that six-year-old in those caves down in Sonora. That was big news here in Texas."

The case he referred to had been solved thirteen months ago, with Cassie and me at the helm.

"Not sure if you remember how crazy that was," Hollings kept up. "Folks were setting up phone banks and doing grid searches. You two came along and *bam*—"

"There were traces of an anhydrous carbonate on his father's shoe," I said.

Hollings scrunched up his face.

"The kid rescued from those caves," Cassie clarified.

"There are only nine places in the U.S. where that mineral has been mined," I said. "Only one in Texas."

"Well God damn, man." Hollings shook his head. "That's what I'm talking about."

The deputy had a deep voice, and I pictured a book. *A Study of Laryngeal Prominence*. Page 52. Right side. An illustration of an Adam's apple, along with a statistic about baritones.

We got to the front door, and Cassie took out two sets of purple nitrile gloves. She snapped a pair over her olive skin and retied her brown hair into a tight ponytail.

"No one's been inside?" she asked, handing me the other set of gloves.

"Just me and medical," Hollings said.

He pushed the screen door open with the steel toe of his boot, and I studied him. Two inches shorter than me and stocky. I have more of an athletic build. Six foot one with curly brown hair and blue eyes.

Cassie pointed at the open door, her lips forming a smile. "Age before beauty."

I evaluated the statement. Then walked exactly five feet inside and stopped.

The place had an open floor plan with an island situated in the center of a combined kitchen and living room. A pool of blood spilled out from behind it.

A man was crouched there, a disposable crime scene coverall wrapped around his wide frame. "You two must be the federals," he said. He weighed roughly two hundred and eighty pounds, and his hands went first to his knees and then his hips as he stood.

"Terry Ward."

"Dr. Ward?" Cassie asked, confirming we were speaking to the medical examiner.

"That's what they call me."

The doctor had blinked when Cassie asked the question, and my eyes moved to his medical kit on the kitchen counter. It looked like a cleaned-up tackle box, once used for fishing. Shoved into it was a pair of forceps, bent at an angle, with only one loop, on the grip side.

I took in the wrinkled skin around Ward's knuckles. He was sixty-five or seventy.

"Ashland doesn't have a full-time ME?" I asked.

Ward narrowed his eyes, and Cassie glanced at me.

"Cervical biopsy forceps," I said, motioning at his kit. "I assume you were an obstetrician."

"That's very perceptive," Ward said. "I'm retired. Came here as a favor."

"And we're glad you did," Cassie said. "We always appreciate local cooperation, don't we, Agent Camden?"

I made eye contact with Cassie. "Yes," I said to Ward. "Yes, we do."

I crouched a foot from the dead man, who lay face down on the tile. Without touching the body, I could tell it had achieved rigor by late last evening and was now coming down the other side, the muscles softening in what's called secondary flaccidity.

But Cassie was staring at something else.

The victim's shirt was bunched around his sides, as if unbuttoned in the front. Cassie lifted the edge of it. There were blood drops on his left sleeve that moved up instead of down, defying gravity.

"Did you flip the body?" she asked.

"I had to," Ward replied. "I had to confirm he was dead."

The blood under the man's legs formed a meandering oval that ran under the refrigerator. I studied the dark liquid. The average adult body holds five quarts of blood, and there were at least four on the floor.

"I put him back, though," Ward said. "Exactly as I found him."

"Yes. Thank you," Cassie replied. Her brown eyes connected with mine, and her lips turned up.

I smiled back. Ward had turned the body to inspect the man and then laid him back down, redunking him in his own blood.

I placed one hand on the victim's shoulder and the other on his waist. Pushed him until I had his body up on its side, like a book on a shelf. Stared at a face I knew all too well.

Ross Tignon.

A man I had hunted years ago. I had only *stopped* hunting him because he turned up dead . . . years ago.

The screen door clicked, and Hollings took two steps inside. "So you knew the guy?" he asked. "The dead fella's got a history with y'all?"

Statistics filled my head. The three women Ross Tignon had murdered back in March of 2013. The precise depth in centimeters his knife had plunged into their skin.

"'Cause the computer spit out his name when we took his prints," Hollings went on. "Then we saw the confusion with him being listed as dead already."

Confusion was the wrong word.

"Seven years ago," Cassie said, "Ross Tignon was the primary suspect in three murders in Florida. Then a fire broke out in his home."

An image formed in my head. Ross Tignon's wife, Beverly, being pulled from the blaze, her face soot-covered and her curly blond hair singed a charcoal color. But her husband did not appear to have such good luck. I remember examining the stretcher that ferried Ross Tignon's burned body out to the coroner's van.

"I'm not following," Dr. Ward said. "Your suspect—he was in that fire?"

I pictured the stretcher, Tignon's body atop it. "There is a pose the human body takes when it has been scorched," I said to Ward. "The muscles constrict, hands drawn close like a boxer about to throw a punch. 'Pugilistic' is the word coroners use. But that expression is unnecessarily dramatic. The posture is simply based on the constriction of muscles as the body is burned at temperatures over two hundred degrees."

As I spoke, creases formed along Ward's forehead. First confusion. Then disgust.

"You thought your man Tignon was dead?" the doctor said.

Which brought an immediate question to mind. If Ross Tignon had been killed yesterday here in Texas, whose body had we found seven years ago in the Florida fire?

Cassie took out her iPad. "You interview the neighbors?" she asked Hollings.

"A real estate agent owns the place over there," he said, pointing in the direction of the cul-de-sac. "He said the victim moved in two years ago. Didn't call himself Ross Tignon at all. He was Bob Breckinridge to the neighbors."

Tignon had set up a false identity. Bought property with it. Lived here in hiding.

A second question arose. *Why kill a man who was already presumed dead?*

"Any sign of a blond woman?" I asked. "Late sixties? Tignon's wife?"

Hollings shook his head. "No, this guy lived alone."

I glanced down. The victim's dress shirt was unbuttoned and spread open, revealing the source of the blood. A cavity had been carved between his xiphoid process and his waist.

My eyes moved up to Tignon's chest.

Something was marked there. Carved into his skin six inches above the area where he was cut open. But when Dr. Ward had flipped the body, blood had smeared across Tignon's torso.

"The deputy took pictures," Ward said, following my gaze. "From before I laid him back down. We figured that's why you're here."

We were here because Cassie had received a text from our boss, Frank Roberts, at 5:03 a.m.

> I've got you and Gardner on the 7:30 from Jacksonville to Dallas.

But Frank had only received word about Tignon's fingerprints popping up on a body in Texas. Nothing more. This is why Cassie had been handicapping those odds on the drive here. She was estimating the chance of two different men with the same prints.

But this wasn't that. This was the same man. My suspect from 2013.

I walked toward the door. Deputy Hollings had moved only two feet inside, as if keeping his distance from that oval of blood would ward off something evil.

Death has a smell, I thought.

It is more than the acrid odor of rotten eggs. Or the stink of blood and urine as they leave areas in the body designed to hold blood and urine in place. This smell is something invisible, something that comes from those who look on. From coroners, lawyers, and cops. From the imaginations of men and women who see bodies like this and entertain thoughts like, "If it could happen to him, it could happen to any of us."

I don't get these thoughts. When I was younger, my mother told me that my mind "just worked differently than others'." That my affect was simply "a bit lower than normal." And that this could be a good thing. It would offer me clarity when others became reactive, scared, or angry.

But there were other effects, too.

Things my mother had not described. Things you had to live through.

Last week in the office, I had been inside a restroom stall when two agents came in to wash their hands. "When he's on a case," the first man said, "it's a wow. I mean, a real wow. But in social situations . . . well, I think we're not supposed to say the r word anymore, right?"

"No, we're not," the second man said. "You mean retard, right?" He laughed. "Whoops, I said it."

When I emerged from the stall and saw the agents' faces, I knew they were speaking of me.

I approached Deputy Hollings. Ten minutes ago, he had been giddy to see us. "Fan-boyish," Cassie would say. But now his face looked green.

I remembered a piece of advice that my mother taught me years ago. To add bits of information at the starts of conversations. To be perceived as more likable. Emotional.

"I'm sorry this is happening here," I said. "Ashland seems like a beautiful town."

Hollings nodded in appreciation. "Thank you for saying that."

"You have pictures from before Dr. Ward flipped the body?" I asked.

The deputy retrieved a phone from his back pocket. He showed me a wide shot of the kitchen. Then a close-up of Ross Tignon, lying on his back.

"I need a sponge," I said, turning to the doctor.

Ward fished through his kit. Handed me what appeared to be a brand-new construction sponge. Yellow and rectangular. Three inches thick. Three dollars and eighty-nine cents at the nearest Home Depot.

After wetting it at the sink, I leaned over the body. Used the corner of it to slowly clean Tignon's upper chest.

The numbers 5 and 0 were carved into his skin, two inches high and an inch apart, right between his nipples.

"The number fifty mean something to you?" Ward asked.

In my head I combed through every detail from the three murders Ross Tignon had been accused of in 2013. His victims' ages were twenty-six, twenty-nine, and thirty-two, and each had been knocked unconscious, the depth of their stab wounds 4.2, 5.3, and 6.1 centimeters past the chest wall.

My mind cycled through a half dozen other variables.

The number fifty . . . meant nothing.

CHAPTER TWO

SEVEN YEARS AGO, A WOMAN NAMED DAISY CARABELLE had been abducted from a parking lot near The Beachcomber in Sandstone, Florida, where she worked as a bartender. Daisy was twenty-six, with no boyfriend or ties to the community. By the next morning, her body was found in a stolen Chevy Astro van on the side of Highway 60.

Seventeen days later, another woman was killed, and a day after that, a third.

The FBI pairs young with old. And in March of 2013, my partner Saul was three months from retirement when we were invited in by local police. And so the case was mine to lead: my first time in charge at the FBI.

We arrived in Sandstone on a Tuesday afternoon. By Thursday night, we had narrowed our suspect pool to one man: Ross Tignon, the man who owned that stolen Astro van. As I interviewed Tignon, I'd found a thread that local police had missed in their initial questioning, and I kept pulling. By late that night, I woke a judge up, got an arrest warrant signed, and called in support from SWAT.

But as we arrived at Tignon's house, the place was engulfed in flames, and we were lucky to get his wife Beverly out.

The next day the case was over, and the result deemed a success. A serial killer was dead, all without the expense of a trial.

Or so it seemed.

I glanced at Ross Tignon's body on the kitchen floor. Then stared into the sink, two feet away. A hard plastic container bore the words "Magic Bullet," the remains of something blended visible inside.

"What are you thinking?" Cassie asked.

"Soft food," I said, recalling a detail that helped us identify the body in the fire in 2013. "Cass, check if the victim is missing teeth. A molar on each side."

Cassie crouched by the body. She reached a gloved hand into Tignon's mouth and scuttled around. Lifted out a pair of partial dentures.

Below where the dentures had been—on each side of the victim's mouth—was a black gap toward the back.

"Savage," Cassie exclaimed. It was an expression she used in three different ways, more often than not to describe the craziness of her twenties. Her "savage days," as she called them. But today, I knew to interpret the word more literally.

The body in the 2013 fire had been charred beyond all recognition, the skull bashed in from a fallen beam. But we had found a pair of molars, loose at the rear of the mouth. An FBI forensic odontologist had extracted DNA from their pulp and verified that the molars had come from Tignon.

"So he yanked out his own teeth back then?" Cassie said.

"Then hid them in a stranger's mouth," I replied.

When one thing is not as it seems, look for more.

I stared at a small mark between the numbers 5 and 0 on Tignon's chest. A cut? A sharp but tiny slice?

Using a gloved finger, I pressed on the area. A bead of pus bubbled up through the hole, forming a small dot between the numbers. Blood may have come earlier, but now the body was drained of nearly every liquid.

"Five-oh," Cassie said. "Like cops?"

I took out my phone. Frank had sent us here because I was the lead on the case seven years ago. The FBI wanted someone to visually verify if this was Tignon.

But these days I work for a unit in the FBI called PAR, for Patterns and Recognition. There are four of us in the group, and we are brought onto cases only after others in law enforcement have hit an impasse.

Our job is to identify peculiarities in cases that have stalled. To solve puzzles and highlight new theories. Then we hand the cases off, either to a team in Virginia or to a field office. We do not travel. And we do not interact with local law enforcement or the public. Making this morning's trip unusual.

I brought up the messaging app on my phone to text Frank.

> It's Tignon

I hesitated, staring at the 5.0 on his chest, my mind itching at some thread that I couldn't grab. Something was wrong with this scene. I felt it. But I kept typing.

> Back from the dead. And now dead again.

> What do you want us to do?

CHAPTER THREE

FRANK TOLD US THAT AGENTS FROM THE DALLAS OFFICE would arrive to take over, so we focused on the four primary considerations in solving a homicide: preserving the scene, inspecting the body, securing evidence, and identifying persons of interest.

By 10:30 p.m., two Bureau investigators and a coroner's assistant had shown up. We handed off the body and said goodbye to Deputy Hollings.

"You two wanna grab a drink on the way out of town?" he asked. "Talk a little shop?"

"No," I said, answering quickly.

Cassie jumped in, her eyes on me. "We have somewhere to be."

"Next time we're in Ashland, though," I said, forcing my lips into a smile.

"Rain check for next time." Hollings pointed at me.

Outside, Cassie and I got in our rental and headed northwest for thirty miles. To Woodrell, Texas. Population 12,100.

I parked in a visitor's lot beside a brown three-story building downtown, but left the car running.

"You sure you don't mind waiting?"

Cassie shook her head, her wavy brown hair loose around her shoulders. "TikTok." She held up her phone.

In the lobby, a man in his fifties looked up from a security desk. His face settled into a gentle smile.

"Agent Camden."

The man was Black and wore a gray uniform with two red angled bars on each shoulder. More white hair was in his sideburns than the last time I'd visited.

I pulled a carton of Marlboro Reds from my work bag. Placed it onto his desk.

"You're a class act," he said.

I glanced around the empty nursing home. A pair of couches faced an interior garden that let in natural light during the day.

Talk about regular things.

"Your wife is well?" I said. "Glenda?"

"Glenda is just fine." He waved his hand. "Go on now. Visiting hours don't apply to you."

I took the stairs to the third floor and emerged into a carpeted hallway. Opened the door to number 302.

My mother looked up. Her adjustable bed was in TV mode, her body upright.

"Well, for crying in a bucket," she said, using a remote to flick off the TV. "I would've put on makeup."

"For your son?" I smiled. "C'mon, Mom. I was in the area."

My mother rolled her steel-blue eyes. She was tall like me, but her hair, once dyed weekly by a stylist in Charleston, had gone bright white. "You were just passing through *Texas*?"

My mother has a South Carolina accent. It is different than the drawl you hear in Georgia or Alabama, formed by a mixture of dialects—African and European—all jumbled together.

"You come unexpected, baby, and I know something bad happened around here. Sit down. Tell Momma about your case."

"It's not *my* case," I said.

My mother scowled. She wore a black V-neck made from the same material as hospital scrubs, along with what she called "beach trousers." Which were loose-fitting white pants with a shoestring for a tie.

"Sweetie, I know you got pictures on that phone of yours."

"The pictures are too bloody, Mom."

"For me?"

My mother was a psychiatrist for twenty years. And not just any shrink. Before she'd retired and moved west, she was on retainer with the Charleston Police Department. There, she consulted on dozens of investigations, including a particularly infamous strangler case where a man had been abducting prostitutes from the First Ward and killing them out in rural areas.

"One photo," she begged.

I bit at my lip. *Didn't fathers and sons who were lawyers discuss the complexities of interesting legal cases?*

"Stop thinking all the time, Gardy," my mom said. "Just act."

Gardy. No one else called me that.

Pulling out my phone, I showed her the two photos I'd received from Deputy Hollings.

My mother stared at the carvings on Ross Tignon's chest. In the last year, the skin around her jaw had become puffy and wrinkled.

She studied the mark between the numbers that looked like a period. "Five-oh?" she said. "Like cops?" The same question Cassie had asked.

I hesitated. I didn't want to get my mother worked up.

"Would you consider that a reference to yourself?" she asked. "Or just local guys?"

"I think most people lump all of us together," I said. "Call us all five-oh. Plus, there's a dot, Mom." I motioned at the photo.

"Ah, a dot," my mother repeated, her eyes sparkling. "Well, there's a spice called five-*point*-oh, Gardy. A great rub."

"There are cars called five-point-oh," I said. "The Mustang, for instance."

My mom and I had played these games since I was a kid. The back-and-forth volley of the mind. The riddles.

"Dolby sound," my mother said. "They used to call that five-point-oh."

"There was a Google Chrome extension called five-point-oh."

"A Midwest rock band," my mother countered. "Late nineties. They went by the name Five Pointe O."

I had three other five-points-ohs lined up, but I caught myself and smiled. "You win, Mom."

A vertical indent had formed between my mother's forehead and her nose. "Of course it could be a dash, Gardy," she said.

I leaned over the phone, surprised I had not noticed this. Five-dash-oh meant something completely different.

"The score of the baseball game," I said, remembering Ross Tignon's alibi for that first murder, the killing of Daisy Carabelle. Tignon claimed he'd driven to a Marlins spring training game in Jupiter, Florida, seventy-three miles from Sandstone. A game that ended in a score of five to nothing.

There were few cameras in the team's spring facility back then, and Tignon had provided his ticket to the game. He reported that he'd made the journey in his wife's car, not his Astro van, which had been called in as stolen that night.

When questioned, Tignon had described every play in intricate detail. The bounce of every ball. Every base stolen and error made in the third through seventh innings, right at the time of Daisy Carabelle's death. By the end of the interview, only two possibilities emerged: One, he was innocent. Or two, he had an eidetic memory, just like mine. I suspected he had left the baseball game early, driven home, and abducted Daisy. Then he listened to the play-by-play on the radio in his van as he cut her up. After all, the man didn't own a TV. Didn't have a DVR to record the game.

I glanced down at my phone and saw that my mother had swiped to the next photo.

"So he's lying on his back," she said. "Where?"

"In his kitchen."

"Was he drugged?"

"The agents will get that information from toxicology," I said. "But we noted an injection mark on his neck."

"Who's 'we'?"

"Myself and my partner," I said. "Cassie Pardo."

My mother put the phone down. "Tell me you didn't leave her in the car, Gardy."

"No," I said. "I mean—she had stuff to do. TikTok."

My mother's squint was skeptical. But she let it go.

"So the injection mark," she continued.

But I was stuck back on her question. *Should I go get Cassie? Bring her up here?*

I pointed at an area on my own neck, below my right ear, where we'd noticed the needle mark. "There were minor defensive wounds, Mom. I suspect Tignon was alive when he was cut up."

"So someone drugs the guy," she said. "Maybe with a paralytic. He becomes disoriented and falls over. Catches himself with his hand and his face."

"Precisely."

"Then your suspect cuts him open. Why? How?"

"And who?" I asked. "We don't know, Mom. He was presumed dead seven years ago. The house was bought under a false name."

My mother's forearm twitched with a muscle spasm, and I recalled a lecture from her doctor about blood pressure and stress. "We don't need to worry though, Mom. It's not our case anymore. It's not my job to be out in the field."

My mother started coughing. A plastic pitcher stood on a counter near the door, and I poured her a glass of water. As she wrestled with her posture, I began opening wardrobes, looking for a pillow to prop her up. In the second closet, I found an oversized one in a clean pillow-case. Turning, I started toward the bed.

"Oh, what a surprise," she said.

"You didn't know there were pillows in there?"

"My Gardy is here," she announced, as if I'd just arrived. "Were you in the area?"

I froze. Thought of a quote I'd read about fools and hope.

Because I had been caught thinking that the problem was gone. *It's a good day again. Her mind is clear.* Then, quick as a lightning flash, the day was like so many others when I'd visited recently.

"Hi, Mom," I said, with a concrete smile.

And suddenly all I could think of was that smell of death. Because as much as I rarely felt fear, if this disease could attack my mom . . . if she, who was once brilliant and still had spells of it, could lose all her thoughts in a flash, then it could happen to any of us. It could happen to me.

"You're in the area because of a case," my mother said. "Tell me about it."

I hesitated.

Two people in the world can make my heart sink. My mother is one. The other is seven and a half years old and lives with her grandmother in Miami. I visit on the weekends.

"No, Mom," I lied. "No case. Just a social call."

My phone pulsed as I said this, and I found a text chain with four other people on it. An agent on my team named Jo Harris had texted:

> Who's point on the new investigation?

Then an answer from Frank.

> Gardner takes the lead on this and all related cases unless I say different

Related cases? I had only been off email for an hour.

Pouring myself a drink of water, I opened my message app and typed.

> Is there another body?

The response came from a number without a contact name attached. Someone Frank had added to the text chain.

> Rawlings, New Mexico

A message from Frank appeared next.

> You guys studied Barry Fisher at the Academy, right?

Barry Fisher was a killer. He had served thirty-one years for multiple murders back in the nineties, before being paroled this week as an old man. There had been news coverage of him leaving prison in Otero, New Mexico, twenty-four hours ago. He was frail and connected to an oxygen tank.

> Fisher's body was found in Rawlings, NM

I put my fingers to the phone.

> Cassie and I were headed home. Are we regrouping at the office in the morning?

Frank responded quickly.

> Negative. Head to New Mexico. I'll send you an address.

I blinked. This morning Frank had sent us to a crime halfway across the country. Now he was telling me I would head to New Mexico and oversee a multicase investigation, a first for me at PAR.

I began typing.

> Seal Fisher's place. Don't let anyone in or out. Our people included. A local doctor in Texas contaminated Tignon's body. Cassie and I will need an hour for travel. And a jet at DFW Corporate.

I put my phone away and turned back to my mother. She had fallen asleep, and I switched off the light by her bed.

When you realize as a child that you are not like others, you are faced with a choice. Instead of leaning more into who I was, my mother encouraged me to iterate into someone better, even if I could only make minute changes.

I kissed her on the forehead and turned. Headed out.

When I got to the car, Cassie was not on TikTok. The dome light was illuminated, and she was reading Tignon's file again.

"Fisher and Tignon," she said as I put the rental in reverse. "That's big-time."

I nodded, thinking about the two men. They had operated in different decades and in different states. Ages apart, really.

But even though they were unrelated to each other, there was a pattern.

A serial killer was murdering serial killers.

CHAPTER FOUR

THE CORPORATE AVIATION FIELD IN DALLAS FORT WORTH was one mile from the main airport, housed in a low-slung tan building with a curved overhang reminiscent of airline terminals from the 1960s.

A woman from the rental car company dropped us off, and we made our way inside a glass waiting room. Out the window, a Gulfstream was parked on the tarmac, the alphanumeric string G-650 on the jet's wing.

Traveling by private jet is not protocol at the FBI, unless you're at the director or deputy director level. But Cassie and I had to be in New Mexico by dawn, and it was already 1:33 a.m. No commercial flight would get us there on time.

"So this is how the other half lives, huh?" Cassie said, staring out at the jet. "Pretty Gucci. I could get used to it."

My lips formed a slight smile. "Try not to," I said. "I haven't been on a plane like this in years."

A man in his twenties popped his head into the room. He was tall and underweight, his skin the color of overmilked coffee.

"Mr. Camden?" he said. "Ms. Pardo?" He wore a black suit with a pressed white shirt. "I'm Travis, your cabin attendant." He took our bags. "We'll be in the air in fifteen minutes. You're welcome to board now, and we'll keep the lights low. You can catch some shut-eye."

Cassie and I followed him outside, heading up the steps to the jet. The new Gulfstreams could do Mach 0.85 and came with fully functioning executive kitchens. "Fly and fry" was the headline I'd seen in an advertisement.

Inside were six reclining seats with fold-up tables between them. Beyond that, a lounge area with a couch. On a side table was a bucket with an open bottle of white wine, fresh fruit, and four bottled waters.

Cassie inspected the fruit, and I grabbed two waters.

"Is it just us?" she asked.

When Travis nodded, she grabbed the whole fruit plate. Dropped into the aisle across from me, her eyes moving around the tan interior of the small craft.

I was older than Cassie by several years, and in my first few at the Bureau, we had regularly traveled this way. That was before Congress heard of it, and the practice was moved to urgent use and higher-ups only.

"First time on a small plane?" I asked.

Cassie nodded, her dark eyes big.

I avoided relationships, even friendships, with other agents. But Cassie was different. "It's a short flight," I said. "I wouldn't worry."

Cassie just made a chuffing noise and flipped open her laptop.

"It's interesting you mention flight time, Gardner," she said, tying back her long brown hair, "since that's the main cause of the misnomer about air travel being so safe."

I turned to face her. In terms of analysis, Cassie Pardo is the closest at PAR to my own skill set, except her point of view is slanted more toward numbers. By trade, she is a mathematician.

"Car fatality rates," she explained, "are measured per one hundred million miles traveled, while air fatalities are measured per hours of flight time. But no one wants to compare the two. I'm not sure if you've studied this, Gardner?"

I had done no reading on the subject, but Cassie kept talking, at ninety miles an hour.

"See, if you take an average speed of fifty miles an hour," she said, "you'll find that car travel translates to 1.1 deaths per two million hours. Compare that to flight time and you see a different picture."

"A bad picture?"

"It's not bad if you're flying commercial." She shrugged. "But limit your flights to small planes like this? You'll find that private air travel is nineteen times more dangerous than the family sedan."

Travis came down the aisle as she finished. "Cocktail?" he offered.

"Two." I put up my fingers.

Thoughts about Tignon and Fisher filled my head, but I needed rest if I was expected to be productive in three hours. I took a blanket off one of the seats and folded it behind my head.

"Are you gonna sleep?" Cassie asked.

Travis brought us two Glenlivets, and I took a strong pull on mine, hoping the alcohol would push my fatigue over the edge.

"Absolutely," I said.

I pushed my seat back until it lay flat. The leather smelled of bleach and tanning agents. I estimated the jet at less than six months old.

Closing my eyes, I began counting in my head to accelerate REM sleep.

Prime numbers.

2, 3, 5, 7, 11, 13, 17, 19, 23, 29, 31, 37 . . .

A bump woke me up. From the digital display on the seatback in

front of me, an hour and forty minutes had passed, and we were eight
miles south of Roswell.

"Snack?" Travis asked. He held up a plate with watermelon slices,
each speared with a sprig of mint.

"No," I said. I glanced over. Cassie was out cold, her highball glass
empty. Her right hand lay across the smooth skin of her neck, her fingers touching an ornate beaded necklace.

Travis informed me we would be descending into Las Cruces in
fifteen minutes and left a business card on the open seat beside me.

I checked my cell. Frank hadn't sent the update he'd promised. This
was par for the course for the boss. When anyone complained about it,
the answer was always the same. *Bias avoidance.*

"Y'all understand the power of bias, right?" Frank would say. He
was from Austin and had worked eleven years as a profiler. "Lotta sorts
of biases, people. Innate. Learned. Systemic. Prejudiced."

This logic was why most case files he emailed simply came with the
words "give this a gander" in the subject line.

The jet shimmied through an air pocket, and Cassie stirred.

"We're landing?" she murmured.

I nodded.

As the plane hit the small runway in stride. I got out my phone and
texted Frank.

Still on to meet?

His response came back fast, listing the address of a café twenty
miles away.

A half hour later, our Uber slowed next to a handicapped spot in
front of Dino's All-Nighter. The sun was cresting the horizon, but the
New Mexico desert was cold. Forty-three degrees at 4:42 a.m.

As I got out of the car, I scanned the diner. Frank Roberts sat at a booth near a window, his head buried in a file. Frank is six foot one, and every day he wears a suit, always with a vest. He's Black with short-cropped hair, and he glanced up as we entered. Frank was old-school. Yellow legal pads. Pens that clicked. Both of which were on the table in front of him.

"Welcome to beautiful New Mexico," he said.

"Morning, boss," Cassie replied.

Even at five in the morning, Frank didn't have a curl out of place. Since I'd first met him, the same went for his physique. Not too slender. Not too muscular. I'd call him perfect, but that title is taken by his wife, who is five years younger than Frank and a former Miss North Carolina.

We slid into the booth across from him. The diner was lit by weak fluorescent lights and smelled like coffee grinds and pie crust.

"Cassie, you look chipper," Frank said. Turning to me, he hesitated. "Gardner, you look slightly above average."

I caught my reflection in the window. My brown hair was tufty and stuck up in places, and my eyes were bloodshot. Frank's description was accurate.

I stared at the boss. Too many unanswered questions, too early in an investigation.

"So what are *we* doing here?" I asked. "Shouldn't there be a local Marriott full of agents from the Albuquerque office, raring to go?"

"Or local PD," Cassie added, "working the scene first?"

A waitress swung by and refilled Frank's coffee. She lifted the pot at us.

"Yes, puh-lease," Cassie said, getting a mugful. I shook my head.

Frank waited for the woman to walk away, and I noticed a knife scar, six centimeters long, cresting the back of her neck.

"Well," Frank said, "y'all haven't been to the crime scene yet, but I think it's fair to say that it's above the pay grade of the local PD."

So the FBI had been invited in by Rawlings Police.

"Why PAR?" Cassie asked. "The powers that be don't think dead murderers rank high enough to put a *real team* on this?"

Frank's head tilted to one side. "I might take offense to that 'real team' business, Cassie. There's still people who think that PAR contains four of the best ten minds at the Federal Bureau of Investigation."

This back-and-forth was fun for Frank, who was full of Texas wit and loved to talk. For me, it was time spent inefficiently. I had to lead the case.

"Has Gardner caught you up on Tignon?" Frank asked Cassie.

"I caught myself up," she replied, producing the manila folder.

Frank tapped a similar folder in his open briefcase. "I was just reviewing it," he said. "Reading about this witness who went fishing with Ross Tignon two days after the last murder." Frank turned to me. "Tignon bragged to this guy about hooking catfish with human liver?"

I nodded. "Those statements were overheard by the boat captain who hosted the fishing trip. Seven years ago, I drove overnight to speak to that witness. But by the time I got to Orange Beach, Alabama, he had disappeared."

"The boat captain didn't know his name?" Cassie asked.

"Nope."

"And you and Saul thought what back then?" Frank said, referring to me and my old partner. "That *Tignon* disappeared the guy?"

"That was our working theory," I said. "Tignon was already our prime suspect in three murders, and each victim was missing a liver."

"And now?" Frank asked.

"Now I suspect this witness was more than just Tignon's fourth victim," I said.

"He was the body in the fire?" Cassie said.

I nodded. "Tignon must have abducted him after the fishing trip. Drove his body back to Florida. Burned him up."

"So where does that leave us?" Frank asked.

I laid my phone down, spinning it so the picture of Ross Tignon's chest faced Frank. I explained about the 5–0 baseball score—something I hadn't yet shared with Cassie.

"This information about Tignon's alibi and the baseball game," I said. "It was never released to the public."

Frank took this in. "So even if someone knew that Tignon fooled us with that body in the fire—"

"Only the FBI and local police knew about his alibi and that score," Cassie finished.

"Exactly," I said. "So how did someone *know* to carve five to zero on Tignon's chest all these years later?"

"Only two options there," Frank said. "Tignon told someone. Or our killer's law enforcement. Has access to the same files we do."

I had been considering this theory since my mother noticed the mark was a dash. "But why now?" I asked. "Tignon got away years ago."

"That—I dunno." Frank shrugged.

I thought about the number I didn't recognize on the text chain from last night. "Who's the 760 area code?"

"New guy," Frank said.

Strange. PAR hadn't added an employee in eighteen months.

"Last Tuesday's staff meeting," Cassie said, "you said there was a budget freeze."

"Got unfrozen," Frank said. "This new kid requested PAR. Requested to work for *you*, Gardner. When's the last time you trained someone?"

Never, I thought.

"Straight out of Quantico?" I asked.

"Number one in his class," Frank said. "He's here with Shooter. They're headed to meet us right now."

Joanne "Shooter" Harris had grown up in Alaska, hunting from a young age. She'd been part of an Olympic shooting team before she became an agent, competing in both the twenty-five-meter pistol and the fifty-meter rifle. Then, five years ago, when she was with the ATF, she grew frustrated with their lack of funding. In the decades following 9/11, Congress had funded double- and triple-digit increases for every branch of law enforcement except Alcohol, Tobacco, and Firearms. Supporting them was tantamount to taking a side in the gun control debate.

So what did Joanne Harris do? She used her fast-draw skills to write F-U-C-K-C-O-N-G-R-E-S-S across a series of targets at a federal gun range, each letter in perfectly formed letters made from bullet holes.

Unfortunately for her, a senator from Massachusetts was visiting the range that day.

This was the start of a career slide that would land her, like me, in PAR. All of us had a story like this, something a new kid straight out of the Academy would not. But logistically it made sense to add someone. A team member had retired in October, causing Frank to be paired with Shooter for the last two months, rather than overseeing the group.

"They're in New Mexico?" Cassie asked. "This new kid and Shooter?"

Frank glanced at his watch. A Shinola Canfield with a blue dial and a stainless steel band. "As we speak."

"So I guess we'll just have to wait a bit longer," I said, "on whatever you're holding back. Why PAR was assigned."

Frank took a swig of his coffee. "I guess you will."

I examined the boss. Some people see the withholding of information as betrayal, but to me, it is simply part of Frank's style. He wants his agents to experience things fresh. Draw their own conclusions.

Plus, he was never unkind. Never raised his voice. And he never treated the personality traits that made me different as anything other than a positive for PAR. He also never cursed, other than the word "bullshit." Some say *that* was why Frank hadn't been promoted more. There were those at the FBI who didn't trust a man who didn't curse.

Then again, statistically speaking, it could've been because he was Black.

"Have you been to the house where Fisher was found?" Cassie asked.

"I have," Frank said. "I was standing in the kitchen, making my initial assessment. Then I stopped. Our team lead sent a text. Told me to get out."

That was *my* text. The note I'd sent to seal the place up, even from "our own people."

"What's Fisher look like?" Cassie asked.

"You tell me when you see him."

Classic Frank.

"Forced entry?" I asked.

"Nope."

So Fisher let the person in. Maybe even knew them.

"How far away is this place?" I asked.

"Ten miles," Frank said. "It's a rental house, by the way. Owned by Fisher's younger brother, Kenny. The brother stopped renting it a few months ago, knowing Barry was coming out of Otero Prison."

"Is the squad coming here?" Cassie asked. "Or are we meeting them at the house?"

The squad. Cassie had a knack for making us sound cool.

"Here," Frank said. He threw down a twenty for his pie and coffee. Collected his two pads and three pens and dumped them into his ten-year-old briefcase.

The worn leather case was the one accessory that looked out of place with Frank's perfect wardrobe. But the ten-year-old bullet hole in one side told the story of why he kept it. It had saved his life.

"Why aren't *you* leading the investigation?" I asked.

"Because when that body was found yesterday in Texas," Frank said, "the director of the FBI himself asked who that smart agent was who figured out Tignon was using girls' livers as fish bait down near the Alabama border."

Cassie put out a fist for me to bump. "Director of the FBI," she said. "Hashtag goals."

I kept my focus on Frank. "Director Banning doesn't remember what happened after? With me and the Bureau?"

Frank pursed his lips, a dismissive look. And then he lied straight to my face. "Ancient history, Gardner."

I nodded as if I believed him. But the Bureau wasn't one of those workplaces that forgave and forgot.

Still, I didn't want to focus on everything that had gone wrong back in 2013. I didn't want to think of the reasons I wasn't allowed to travel for the Bureau or interact with the public.

"Maybe the director's forgetful," Frank added. "I heard something about that. Remember y'all, a year ago November was his last month officially. Director Banning had retired. He was out of the bureau for a year. Private citizen."

We knew the rest of the story. The deputy director under Banning was promoted, but within a few months this successor had a heart attack and died. So the president himself asked Banning to come back and help groom a new director—one the administration liked. A guy named Craig Poulton.

"This week marks the end of month six," Frank said. "Everyone is waiting for Banning to retire again. In the meantime, Deputy Director Poulton doesn't want anyone countermanding Banning's orders."

So bureaucracy was keeping the case with us. That, and no one cared about victims who were once killers.

"What about press?" Cassie asked. "HQ trusts us to handle that?"

"Well." Frank lowered his voice. "Nobody knows who Ross Tignon is except us. Folks in Ashland knew him as Bob Breckenridge."

"Sure," I said. "But that was in Texas. Here in New Mexico with Fisher . . ."

Frank shook his head. The media hadn't been notified of Barry Fisher's death, he told us.

"What about Fisher's brother?" I asked. "He's not talking?"

"He's not too keen on it being announced in the news," Frank said. "Him as the brother of a serial killer and all."

"He said that to you?"

"I dunno." Frank smiled. "Maybe *I* suggested it to him. The conversation was fluid."

"So no media on either case?" Cassie said.

"At least for a few days."

Still, none of that answered the question of why I was leading the investigation. I wasn't sure I believed Frank's given reason. I scrutinized him. Frank had been passed over so many times for a promotion that I didn't think he even cared about politics anymore.

The door to the diner jingled, and we looked over.

Joanne "Shooter" Harris was thirty-five with green eyes and a head of wavy strawberry blond hair. Out in the field, she'd tie it back in a ponytail, but at the moment it was loose at her shoulders. Tight black jeans, a white pullover, and the duffel bag slung over her shoulder rounded out her athletic look.

"Hey, gang," she said. "Looks like somebody gave us a get-out-of-jail-free card."

"What's up, guns?" Cassie said.

"Just the facts," Shooter replied, their usual back-and-forth introduction.

All eyes moved to the new guy, standing next to her. The kid could pass for nineteen as easily as twenty-six. He was five foot nine with a slender frame and an Italian look. Olive skin and an angular face with high cheekbones. His dark hair was spiked with product, and his suit was too expensive for his pay grade.

"Richie Brancato," he introduced himself.

"Welcome aboard," Cassie said, smiling.

And we were, in fact, a welcoming group. Small. Insular.

Unknown.

In that moment, I realized—no one had applied to work at PAR before. Ever.

I looked to Frank, but his eyes were firmly on the checkered floor, avoiding questions of why this kid was suddenly part of our team.

A snake pit. A border market full of thieves. There were so many less political places to work than the Federal Bureau of Investigation.

CHAPTER FIVE

IN THE FIRST FIVE MINUTES OF THE DRIVE TO RAWLINGS, little was said.

I sat shotgun in Frank's rented Suburban and scanned an FBI bulletin that listed recent graduates from the Academy. Directly behind me was Cassie; to her left sat the rookie and Shooter.

"Richard Neal Brancato," I said without turning. "Do I have that right?"

"A hundred percent," Richie said.

"You got a nickname?" Cassie asked.

"Just Richie," he replied.

A moment of quiet.

"Not Rich?" Shooter asked.

"Nope."

"Huh," Frank and Shooter replied, almost in unison.

The kid looked young. *Did he even shave?*

"Richie's the name of a guy you play cards with," Shooter said.

"A guy named Richie gets you a great mortgage rate," Frank said. "A great deal on a boat."

Shooter flicked her eyebrows. "Richie sets you up with a girl who knows how to have a good time with—"

"What prompted you to request PAR?" I asked, turning to make eye contact.

"I studied math at Michigan," Richie said. "Data mining. Machine learning. Predictive analytics as a basis for—"

"Cluggghhh." Shooter made a snoring noise, as if she'd just woken from a long nap. "Whu happened?" she said. "I fell asleep. Did somebody say something?"

Cassie snorted, but I waited for Richie to finish. If anyone cared, hazing was still alive and well in the twenty-first-century FBI.

"I did a project while I was at the Academy, Agent Camden," Richie said. "Punched in the Bureau's coldest cases between 2016 and 2020. Looked at which ones got solved. And which agents touched them. Kind of a personnel study of how many people it took to—"

"Oh my God," Shooter interrupted, her strawberry blond hair shaking as she talked. "Did *Gardner Camden* win your contest? That's why you asked to work for him? He worked the most cold cases?"

Between smarts and physicality, few people are better balanced for our job than Shooter Harris. Still, in nearly all FBI circles, she is known as a hardass. A ballbuster. And that's from people who like her.

"I wanted to work with *all* of you," Richie said. "Not just Agent Camden."

Smart. And a politician.

"They said I'd be placed in PAR for a month," Richie continued. "After that, it'd be up to Agent Roberts."

I looked to Frank, but his eyes were on the road. We were rounding the corner into a starter neighborhood that looked like it was built in the 1970s. The rental house owned by Barry Fisher's brother had wooden siding in a baby-blue color. But more paint had fallen off the wooden planks than was on them.

A black-and-white was parked at the curb, and Frank nodded to the cop as he turned the SUV into the driveway.

"That study you did," Shooter said to Richie, gathering her hair and tying it into a tight ponytail. "Did it take into account . . . other variables?"

"Sure," Richie said. "I considered how cold the cases were. Their geography. Also, how—"

"I mean about PAR," she said. "When you requested to work on the team, did you do any recon on *us*? Find out why PAR sits in a crime hot spot like Jacksonville?"

Three horizontal lines formed across Richie's forehead.

"We've got a pretty superb view of the parking lot," Shooter continued.

Richie looked to me, then back to Shooter. "I guess I *didn't* ask too many questions, Agent Harris," he said. "Then again, I'm on a murder case my second day on the job, while all my peers who requested LA or Miami are working healthcare fraud."

Richie opened the door, and Cassie reached out a finger to Shooter's shoulder. "Burn mark," she said. To which Shooter nodded, smiling.

The rookie was polite, but he gave back as good as he got.

I stepped out and surveyed the house.

The angled wooden siding had been repaired with caulk instead of nailed in place. Eleven horizontal planks were tilted, off angle by four to six percent. Around the perimeter of the property, the lawn had given up its fight against crabgrass. Long strips of weeds grew wild, six and eight feet long, like knob-and-tube wiring in a 1930s attic, waiting for a fire.

"Your case," Frank said to me.

I approached the front door. But before I grabbed the knob, I turned to the group.

"You may have assumptions," I said. "About why we're here. You might even be thinking that Frank's holding something back."

Everyone stared at the boss, but he said nothing.

"Forty-two percent of PAR's cases come to us because some investigator got tunnel vision on day one," I said. "Don't be that guy. Keep an open mind."

In my head, I knew it was the right thing to say as case lead. But I was thinking of layers, too. Of patterns. Of things that made sense— and things that didn't.

PAR out in the field, investigating for the first time together as a team.

Me in charge, instead of Frank.

A new kid, right out of the Academy.

Too many new things layered atop each other.

Compartmentalization. It's an advantage to the way I naturally operate. I put all these thoughts aside and grabbed the doorknob.

"Go time," I said.

CHAPTER SIX

THE SMELL HIT ME FIRST. THE STING OF BLEACH, ACRID IN the air.

But inside wasn't some bloody scene like at Ross Tignon's. The place looked clean. Too clean for a crime scene.

I walked into a small, tiled entry, and the others filed in behind me.

To our right was a living room. Spartan and carpeted with a tan, worn-down low pile. A sagging kelly-green couch sat against the wall. In front of it was a coffee table sprayed with black lacquer and a twenty-eight-inch TV on a rolling cart made of wood laminate. Furniture you could find in an alley.

Ahead of us was a ten-by-twelve kitchen. The wooden cabinets were painted white, but you could see red oak through the brush streaks. A yellow refrigerator—so likely from the 1970s—stood along the north wall.

To my left, a hallway opened up, and I followed the smell of bleach toward a bathroom.

The tub was filled two-thirds of the way. But there wasn't an empty bottle of Clorox in sight. Or even a sign that a messy cleanup job had been performed.

I moved into an empty spare room. Then to the master. Nothing in either, except made beds.

Soon I had circled back to the kitchen and covered the entire place. It was an efficient fourteen hundred square feet. Two bedrooms. One bath. Zero bodies.

"You spent an hour in here last night," I told Frank. "I could keep looking for a body—or do you just want a drumroll?"

"I do love a good drumroll, Gardner."

It was usually better for everyone if Frank was happy, so I used my two hands to batter out a beat on the counter.

Frank took two steps across the kitchen. "Fisher's brother Kenny came by yesterday to visit," he said. "But he didn't see his brother. He figured Barry had gone out, so Kenny decided to grab a beer and wait."

Frank opened the refrigerator. Inside was a single box of baking soda and two dozen clear bags. Through the plastic, I could see red fluid.

I picked up one of the bags with my gloved hand. Felt something tubular squishing around, shrouded in ten or twelve ounces of blood.

The tub had been a temporary workplace. A filling station. The bleach, the cleanup effort after.

Back at the diner, Frank had told Cassie to see what Fisher looked like for herself.

I looked more closely at the clear sack. Floating free in the bag's red liquid was a white label, two inches long, printed with the kind of machine you'd buy in an office supply store.

ESOPHAGUS, it read.

What the hell was this?

CHAPTER SEVEN

AS IT TURNED OUT, EACH BAG CONTAINED A FLOATING BODY part, surrounded by chunks of fat and dark blood.

"Handy, huh?" Frank said, holding up a bag. Inside, the shiny white strip read KIDNEY. "Laminated for your legibility."

I flipped open the freezer compartment. Another twelve bags, these with ice crystals shining amidst frozen red chunks.

But no head. No hands. No feet.

I moved back to the fridge, pushing around the other twenty-four bags laid out on the three plastic shelves.

Experts in physiology will tell you there are seventy-eight organs in the human body. But what constitutes an organ is not a cut-and-dried scientific fact. Some doctors will argue that tissue groups "are in," bringing the total closer to a hundred. As I glanced at the labels floating in each bag, I saw the mainstays: Gallbladder. Kidney. Brain. Pancreas. Lung.

Frank pulled out his phone and showed me a picture of a smaller bag.

"This one had an index finger in it," he said. "I sent it to the Albu-querque office last night for identification."

I inspected the photo.

"Results should be in within the hour," Frank said. "But at first blush . . . guy leaves a finger to print? You got a game player on your hands, Gardner."

The compressor on the fridge kicked on, and a rattling noise vi-brated off the kitchen walls. I had taken apart home appliances as a child. Either the compressor piston was jostling loose or one of the rubber feet at the bottom of the unit had come free.

"The killer had a vacuum sealer with him," I said. "And a label maker." I pointed toward the bathroom. "Cleaning supplies. Bleach. I don't see any skin. Where's the rest of Fisher? Where's the murderer's equipment?"

Shooter walked into the kitchen, and her eyes took in the bags. "Jesus, is that him?"

"We're checking on that," Frank said.

Cassie walked in behind her, with Richie in tow.

Shooter pointed at the fridge. "Our vic."

"Wow." Cassie examined the bags. "A little extra, don't you think?"

"It's a small detail"—Shooter motioned back toward the bedroom—"but there's a blood smear on the dust ruffle of the master bed. Two reddish paw prints on the carpet."

Frank nodded. "I had the local cops take a puppy out of there. White shih tzu, mouth covered in blood. I figure the little guy hid under the bed with a piece of Fisher. Maybe during the cutting."

As Frank spoke, I made a mental composite of the organs I'd seen so far, searching for a pattern. But they came from multiple systems, from circulatory to digestive to respiratory.

"I guess the killer didn't give a shit tzu about who was gonna take care of the puppy," Shooter said.

"Doggone right." Frank chuckled.

Being funny, I thought.

A hard task for me. Still, I could try.

"At this point," I said, "with organs in bags, anything is poss-ible." I pronounced the last word slowly, in parts.

"True," Shooter said.

"Paws-ible?" I repeated.

Frank and Shooter glanced at me, but didn't laugh.

"I need ten minutes to get organized," I said, moving past my failed attempt at humor. "Then I'll have assignments for each of you."

I circled back to the front door, then walked slowly from room to room.

The master bedroom barely looked lived in. Unsurprising, for a man who had been out of prison just two days. Three outfits in the top dresser drawer. Two more, dirty, in a white plastic laundry basket in the corner. The bed was made with a perfect hospital tuck. You could bounce a quarter off the top sheet.

The rest of the house lacked any mementos or personalization. The spare room contained a twin bed and one dresser, but nothing was in it.

Moving back to the kitchen, I opened every cupboard but found them all bare, except for two containers of salt, one of pepper, and a box of Safeway-brand coffee filters. Off the kitchen, a sliding glass door led out to a back lawn made of white rocks. Exactly six diminutive dog turds lay among the stones.

I turned to Richie and Shooter, the latter of whom was using a gloved hand to move the bags on the top shelf around. The others were elsewhere in the house.

"You took anatomy, right, Richie?" I asked.

"It's Rich," Shooter said without looking up.

I ignored her remark. "Take an Uber to the closest hardware store. Pick up some five mil plastic sheeting and the heaviest folding table they sell."

"Got it," Richie said.

"Video every bag as you take it out." I motioned at the refrigerator. "Then set up the table right here." I pointed at the middle of the kitchen. "Tape your sheeting down and start laying out the organs relative to where they'd be in the body. I want to find out what's here, what our suspect took with him, and what the dog ate." I turned to Shooter. "That dog . . ."

"You want his stool?" Her eyes glimmered. "I know how you feel about stool."

"Have Animal Control quarantine the dog and get it for you," I said. "I want you out at Otero." The prison that had been Fisher's home for the last decade. "See who visited this old guy in the last year. Relatives. Parents of victims—"

"It's been almost four decades since the murders," Shooter said. "Most of his victims' parents have gotta be dead or elderly."

"Statistically, that sounds accurate," I said. "But I'm sure he got visitors. Maybe it was the kids of victims. Brothers and sisters. Murder groupies."

"Got it," she said, turning to grab her stuff.

I found Cassie in the living room. "Can we talk outside?"

"Sure," she said, following me out to a spot on the unkempt lawn.

"When's the last time you read up on Barry Fisher?"

"Not since the Academy."

For Cassie, that was nearly six years ago. She'd logged two years in data science at Quantico, then worked two in the field in Denver before something went awry with a supervisor. She had never told us what happened.

"You never checked the file out as a side project?" I asked, knowing her proclivities for research. "Perused it when you were bored?"

"No," she said.

"Me neither. So that's a circle of two. That's our trust circle."

Cassie squinted at me. "You want to know every agent who checked out Tignon and Fisher?"

"I do."

"Have you proven the two are connected?"

"We've proven nothing," I said.

"Pffft." She blew air up toward her bangs. "You think it's someone at the FBI?"

"You're getting ahead of yourself," I said. "Coordinate with the EAD for Tech and use my name." This was Marly Dureaux, the executive assistant director for Science and Technology in Quantico. "I want a list of every agent who looked into Tignon and Fisher in the last two years. And that information is for you and me only."

"Gardner," Cassie said, "Barry Fisher's file is one of the go-to projects for NATs at BFTC. There's gonna be four hundred names on that list."

BFTC, or basic field training course, was a nineteen-week testing period that every new agent trainee, or NAT, had to go through.

"I acknowledge it might be a long list," I said. "I need it anyway."

"Heard," she said. "What else?"

I thought for a moment about my role in the investigation. Why the director had picked me to lead it. Was it as simple as what Frank had said?

"Fisher's file." I was sure Frank had it in his briefcase, but for reasons I could not explain, I did not want to ask him for it. "I need the full abstract on Fisher via email. And fast."

"Easy," Cassie replied. "But lemme clarify something on the search for who checked out both files. When you say 'a trust circle of two' . . . you mean three, right? You, me, and Frank?"

"Cassie, you've known me for two years," I said. "We've been partners for one. So you know I always mean exactly what I say."

"Gotch," she said. "Just me and you." Cassie pulled her hair back from her forehead and her lips grew thin and pale. I knew her well enough to see that my request had caused her anxiety. "You want me to set up a base camp?" she asked. "A hotel nearby? Somewhere I can actually do this work?"

"Can you?" I asked. "Get six rooms. One for each of us, and an adjoining one to mine as a meeting space for the team?"

"Donezo."

"And interview Fisher's brother."

Cassie balked. "I thought Frank did that last night."

"He did," I said. But I wanted to leverage a particular persistence Cassie was famous for. "Do it again, please."

Shooter came out of the house then, her work bag under her left arm. She was talking on her cell with Animal Control and headed for the SUV.

"I'm hitching a ride with you," Cassie said, jumping in.

Shooter backed out, and they left. I turned to the rental home, three questions moving through my head.

First: how had someone located Tignon and Fisher, both of whom were living off the radar? Second: who wanted them dead? And third: were the cases really connected?

Inside, Frank loitered between the kitchen and the living room.

"Everyone else seems to have a job," he said, raising one of his perfect eyebrows. "What about me, boss man?"

"You and I are going to brainstorm," I said. "There are some holes here. For instance, until we get that ID, we're not absolutely sure that's Fisher in the refrigerator. Or that this crime and the one in Texas are connected."

"What's giving you pause?" Frank asked.

"The knife work," I said. "Here, it's precise. In Tignon's murder, the cuts were messy. Amateurish. Hurried."

"So you're not convinced it's the same killer?"

I hesitated. It wasn't about being convinced.

"I just ID'd a body in Texas that I declared dead seven years ago, Frank," I said. "Until we're a hundred percent, let's keep an open mind. Call everything a working theory."

"Sure," Frank said.

"Fisher's brother." I cocked my head. "He tell anyone he was putting the ex-con up here?"

Frank shook his head. "Incognito. Why?"

"Something feels wrong."

"Well, you pointed out the differences with the knife cuts," Frank said. "But the two cases have other things in common. Both men's whereabouts were unknown. Both were white, both were male, and most importantly, both were serial killers."

I thought of Frank's weekly speeches on assumptions and bias. Now that I was the lead, was the shoe on the other foot?

"You ever hear the story Nabokov told about coincidence?" I asked.

Frank shook his head.

"A man loses a cuff link in the ocean. Twenty years later, on the exact same day of the week, on a Friday, he's eating this enormous fish. You know what he finds inside?"

"The cuff link?" Frank asked.

"Fish meat," I said. "No cuff link."

Frank stared at me.

"I'd put it at sixty-three percent," I said, "that the cases are connected. But until that ID comes in—"

"Everything's a working theory," Frank finished. He shook his head,
the corners of his mouth turning up. "I'm gonna use that story, Gardner. Maybe on Richie. Definitely on the wife."

"Consider it yours."

We heard the front door open, and Richie was back. He carried a
folding table gripped in one hand, and a roll of plastic under the other
arm. Ready to lay out the organs.

Frank's phone buzzed.

"Albuquerque," he said, holding it up. He made small talk before
asking the question. Then hung up a moment later with a nod.

"The finger belonged to Barry Fisher?"

"DNA confirmed it," he said.

"All right." I gestured to the front of the house. "You ready to talk
this through?"

"Absolutely."

"Let's start with Fisher," I said. "But we'll go through both crimes
in parallel."

We headed to the front, and I opened the door, turning so one way
gave me a view out to the street, the other toward Richie in the kitchen.

"Someone comes to Fisher's door," I said. "Let's say it's a stranger."

"Most likely scenario for a guy who's been in prison for the last
thirty-one years," Frank said.

"'What do you want?' Fisher asks."

"I'm selling something," Frank said. "Candy. Pest Control. Cable TV."

"I don't want any of that. I'm old. An ex-con."

"Something's broken," Frank offered. "TV antenna. Gas meter.
Water pipe."

I thought of Texas and Ross Tignon. Cassie and I had gone through

the same exercise before the Dallas agents arrived. In Texas, we'd suspected the killer had come prepared with something in a needle to
subdue Tignon.

I pointed at the front entrance. "Let's say Barry invites the killer in.
If he gets incapacitated right here, someone's gotta move him twenty
feet around that corner to the tub to cut him up." I glanced at the path
from the front door to the hall bath. "It takes size to drag size. How big
was Fisher?"

Frank brought up a photo on his phone, taken at Otero on January
10, the Friday before Fisher's release. The man in the photo had wavy
white hair and a thick beard.

"Five foot six," Frank said. "A hundred and fifty pounds."

An easy drag.

"I'm going to collect a sample of the bleach in the tub," I said,
leading us into the bathroom. "Then let's drain this."

Frank grabbed my kit and handed me two gallon-size bags and a
small cup. We filled one of the bags, sealed it, and placed it in the sink.
Frank peeled back an evidence sticker and attached it to the bag's side,
writing a notation with the date, time, and his signature.

The tub held twenty or thirty gallons of bleach. Had no one seen
a person going in and out with a few dozen bottles of Clorox? Had no
neighbor heard a saw going as Fisher was being cut up?

Something heavy thudded in the kitchen.

"I'm okay!" Richie hollered.

I glanced at Frank with questioning eyes. Did we need a rookie?

"Be patient, Gardner."

Getting on my knees, I leaned over the tub. Pulling the stopper, I
drained the rest of the bleach. Ran two gloved fingers along the side of
the porcelain, above and below the waterline.

I held them up. "If this was where someone chopped up Fisher, and this bleach is a countermeasure, they scrubbed the inside real well before dumping it in." I thought of a UV test, to check for the telltale blood smears of a cleanup operation.

"You got a theory yet?" Frank asked. "For all these interesting unknowns?"

I hesitated. With the body in bags, establishing a time of death would be challenging.

"Ross Tignon was killed between eleven a.m. and one p.m. on Sunday," I said, standing up. "Six hundred and fifty-one miles from here."

"Check," Frank said.

"If the two crimes are committed by the same person, then the suspect either flew or drove here from Ashland, Texas. But you'd also imagine the killer would want to sit on this house for at least a half day after arriving in New Mexico. See if anyone's coming or going."

"Especially if he's about to spend this much time inside, cutting Fisher up," Frank said.

"So in a one-killer theory, let's say our suspect left Texas immediately after killing Tignon."

"Sunday afternoon?"

"By plane, it's a short flight," I said. "One hour and forty minutes to El Paso, plus the drive. You also pick up one hour going west. If you drive, it's nine hours less the one."

"So if he flies, he's here by Sunday early evening. Call it six p.m.," Frank said. "Monday morning at one a.m. if he drives."

I pictured a horizontal timeline, with colored dots populating key moments. At the far right was Fisher's brother Kenny discovering the body. Tuesday, 12:30 p.m. To the left was our estimated TOD for Tignon in Texas: Sunday, between 12 p.m. and 2 p.m.

Forty-eight hours in between.

"If it's the same killer, and he flies, he has to procure equipment here in New Mexico," I said. "Gear to cut up a body. To bag it. Clean up afterwards. That could take hours and produce a lot of receipts. A lot of witnesses."

"You're betting he drove?"

"If it's one guy, yes," I said. "Less paperwork. And easier to bring tools you're familiar with."

"With either method of transportation, we're talking about someone being in here all day," Frank said. "But if he drives, he's cutting that time even shorter. Including time to case the house."

"It's a lot of risk," I agreed. "Coming into a strange town. A house owned by a relative."

Plus, the killer had moved quickly. Travel to arrival to bagging in under forty-eight hours.

"You thinking it's too much for one person?" Frank asked.

I thought of the time frame, hour by hour. *The killer had to sleep. Eat. Did he stop along the way from Texas? Did he get here later on Monday than we imagined?*

"Breaking down the body is a six-hour job, minimum," I said. "The cut, gut, and bleed-out is two hours. The skinning, two. And that's if you're experienced with animals. Quartering the body. Bone breaking. Grinding. The smaller cuts."

"Don't forget the bagging and labeling," Frank said.

I glanced at the tub again. The pristine tub.

I was guessing I might already have the full abstract on Barry Fisher via email from Cassie. It would offer more background on the victim. Still, a theory was percolating.

"What is it?" Frank asked.

And for the first time in four years, I lied to Frank.

"Nothing," I said. "I have to go through each room. One hour. Part of my process."

Frank stared at me, leaning against the bathroom door. *Was he reading my mind?*

"Leading a case isn't something small that you tack on to other work, Gardner," he said. "Oversight and leadership take time."

"I know."

"So you *assign* process now. *You* check on Richie. *You* call my boss tomorrow morning and report in. So would you like *me* to spend an hour in each room?"

Frank was right. But he was also too skilled an agent to be inventorying a mostly empty house. A place that Fisher had only moved into two days ago. Especially when I had a theory rattling around my head.

"No," I said. "Richie can do that. Why don't you crawl under the house?" I grabbed a pair of coveralls from the kit and held them out. "Take apart the drain pipe beneath the tub. If this is our kill site, something's down that trap."

Frank glanced down at his two-thousand-dollar suit. Then at the coveralls.

"Of course," he said. "Not a problem."

"When you're done under there, and there's less natural light coming in these windows"—I motioned around the bathroom—"can you set up a UV light above the tub? See how clean this place really is."

"You got it."

I headed out to the back patio. Laid my laptop on the lawn chair by the white rocks. I closed the sliding glass door that led out from the kitchen, blocking out the noise of Richie arranging the bags that contained Fisher's organs.

I sat down and opened the file Cassie had emailed me about Barry Fisher.

And I began reading about one of the most gruesome killers in FBI history.

CHAPTER EIGHT

THE OFFICIAL FBI ABSTRACT ON THE CRIMES OF BARRY Fisher was twenty-nine pages long, delivered to me via secure download from Marly Dureaux at Science and Technology.

I started at the beginning, reading a one-page summary of the events that sent Fisher to prison.

Between August 1984 and May 1986, three Latina women went missing in San Diego County in California. The women were all in their thirties and vanished after meeting friends at a restaurant or bar for cocktails.

Within forty-eight hours of each disappearance, a relative of the women made a similar panicked call to the police. They'd discovered a human organ in a sealed, gallon-size Ziploc bag inside the missing woman's apartment. There were no signs of the women.

When police arrived on each scene, they discovered the organ was a heart, neatly cut from the body with a surgical scalpel.

The three women's blood types were matched to the organs, but that was as close to confirming identity as 1986 forensics could do.

After the third woman went missing, the FBI was invited in, but came up with nothing new.

The glass door slid open behind me. Frank had changed into coveralls to undo the plumbing that ran beneath the tub. He headed around the house's east side, a monkey wrench in hand.

I continued reading.

The big break in the Fisher case came on the evening of June 21, 1986. Off-duty Detective James Riordan had come out of a Costa Dorada restaurant and interrupted what appeared to be an altercation between a couple in the parking lot.

Detective Riordan was from Oceanside PD, thirty-five miles north of San Diego, and was not part of the missing persons case. Still, as he stepped outside, he noticed a man lifting a woman's body in a fireman's carry. Riordan was instantly on alert, his hand moving to rest atop his service weapon as he approached.

The man carrying the woman explained that his girlfriend had had too much to drink. But the off-duty cop noticed that the man's pickup truck had what Riordan called a "tonneau cover" on its back. This was a molded vinyl covering that protected cargo from weather or would-be thieves. It could be folded back in thirds, until the entire truck bed was exposed, but Riordan noticed that only the closest third was folded back. To the detective, it looked like the man was about to slide the woman's body under it, placing her in the truck bed. An odd location to put your inebriated girlfriend.

Riordan pulled his badge, and the man dropped the woman and took off down the street. But Detective Riordan was a track athlete in college. He caught the man in a hard tackle near the I-5 freeway on-ramp, holding him while the manager of a nearby 76 station called police.

When Riordan got back to the Costa Dorada, a special agent from the FBI was waiting. The agent had heard of the crime on the police band, and the two interviewed the woman the man had been carrying. Angela Vasquez was bruised, but alive.

Vasquez ID'd Barry Fisher as her attacker. She also explained the ruse he'd used: he claimed he was a resident of the adjoining apartment complex and was looking for his Chihuahua. If she went around one side of a vehicle, he would go around the other, and the dog would run to one of them. But as she got down on her knees to look under the truck, she saw no dog. The last thing she felt was Fisher's hands around her neck in a chokehold.

I looked up from my reading. The sun had moved across the New Mexico sky, and I shimmied my chair back into the light. Flipped to the part of the file that described how Fisher had been adjudicated.

San Diego District Attorney Sheila Donahue slow-played the 1987 case to give police as much time as they needed to connect Fisher to the three missing women or locate the rest of an actual body. But nothing was found. The incident looked like an attempted abduction of Angela Vasquez in the Costa Dorada parking lot and nothing more.

Then a week before trial, the FBI discovered Fisher owned a self-storage unit in Mission Beach, registered under his mother's maiden name. Inside was a massage table covered in heavy-duty plastic, along with a set of surgeon's tools and two bone cutters. The place also contained a flyer for a dating event with Denise Gonzalez's picture on it. Gonzalez was victim number 1.

The evidence gave the police confidence, but legally the case was still circumstantial, a fact reinforced by the lack of bodies. The defense was prepared to argue that the organs could belong to anyone, that the women had simply gone missing, and that none of it was related to Fisher's "misunderstanding" with Vasquez in the parking lot.

And so, as the trial approached, the district attorney rolled the dice on a brand-new technology called DNA analysis that had led to a conviction in Florida just months earlier. They tested the three human hearts against comparable DNA from the women, then matched the DNA to a single spot of blood found inside the storage unit. Victim number 2's blood, as it turned out.

The trial got underway, and six weeks later a jury sentenced Fisher to forty years in prison.

I looked up from the file at the sun, dropping over the fence line, and tried to imagine what it was like to reemerge into today's world after almost four decades in prison.

And then someone comes for you a day later.

In Marly's email, which accompanied the file, she clarified that Fisher had never admitted wrongdoing or reversed course on any testimony. At two separate parole board hearings in the 2010s, Fisher was offered leniency in exchange for telling the families of his victims where the rest of their loved ones' bodies were buried, but Fisher refused to speak. After decades of good behavior, he was paroled out of Otero.

Flipping down my screen, I walked around to the crawl space Frank was exploring. A metal grate, two feet by four, was laid out on the nearby rocks.

"Everything all right?" I hollered.

"Not plum, but pert near," Frank yelled back.

This was a Frankism. It meant things were workable.

Frank promised to lock up the place when he and Richie were done, and I took an Uber to a nearby Homewood Suites, where Cassie had secured our rooms. I checked into mine, then opened the door to the adjacent one, which we'd use as our meeting space.

I ordered dinner from a place called Inky Joe's BBQ, which the front desk recommended. I even got a few salads and veggie sides, since Shooter texted that she was now a vegetarian and would expect broccoli and barbecued tofu. I was pretty sure she was screwing around, but I got the food anyway.

It was time to hear what everyone had found. Time for my specialty to take over. My ability to assimilate information, to connect dots unseen by others. Because if my theory was right, Barry Fisher wasn't going to be the last one to die in this case.

CHAPTER NINE

EIGHT QUARTS OF MEATS AND SIDES COVERED THE SPECK-led Formica counter in the suite's kitchen. I borrowed two chairs from my room and rolled them over, my eyes fixed on the food.

"Yo," Shooter said, arriving first. She'd changed from the white pullover she wore like a uniform to a white long-sleeve shirt.

I moved the boxes that held proteins into one group, the sides into another.

"You okay?" she smirked, watching me arrange the boxes into a perfectly straight line.

"Of course."

The others arrived a minute later, with Cassie getting there last, double-fisting hotel coffee in cardboard cups. Everyone grabbed food, and I pulled up my laptop as a signal it was time to get going. Shooter hopped up on the counter in the suite's kitchen, her iPad on her lap, while Frank leaned against the far wall, no food in front of him. I'd rarely seen the man eat. Richie sat on the arm of the small couch, a plate balanced on his knee.

When we met back in Jacksonville, we always started with victimology, but today I had divided up assignments by person.

"Okay," I said. "Completed reports by eight a.m. But for now, let's go around the room and see what cross-connections come up."

Everyone stared at me, and I felt what Frank must feel every day. All eyes on him. The expectation of leadership.

I turned to the rookie. "Richie, what's the update on the organs?"

He put down his food. "Right, so, from the head down, I've got bags that contain brain, pharynx, larynx, trachea, heart, spleen, and liver."

Deliberately, I placed my tri-tip aside.

"Lungs, gallbladder, kidneys, pancreas. In the miscellaneous category, some joints." He consulted his notes. "Large intestine, small intestine, bladder, and the penis. I've photographed all these."

"With your work phone?" Shooter asked.

"Uh-huh."

"So you got dick pics on your work phone? This is the new FBI, rook. You can't have dick pics anymore. I got rid of all mine." She nodded convincingly. "Big collection."

Cassie smirked, but said nothing. Richie took off his suit jacket and rolled back his dress shirt to the elbows.

"And the cuts?" I asked.

"The cuts appear to be made with a blade that's flat, not serrated," Richie said. "They're smooth and clean. I can perform some tests to replicate them, but I'm thinking a surgical instrument or an Exacto blade."

"The labels?" Frank asked.

The rookie held up his laptop to show us a picture. His arms were muscular under his dress shirt.

"I believe they're from a Brother P-touch label maker," he said. "I matched the built-in font and the size of the strip. Judging by the width of the bags, I'd assume the vacuum sealer was commercial. Probably a twelve-incher."

Shooter snorted.

"And the rest of the body?" I asked. "Did you make a reverse list—of what's missing?"

Richie shrugged. "A lot more is gone than is here, Agent Camden. Muscle groups, skin, joints, bones, cartilage, skull, tissue, eyes, ears, hands, feet. A couple dozen other organs."

I waited.

"I'll make a formal list," he said.

"Good. Who's next? Shooter?"

Shooter put her food aside. Her plate was piled high with barbecued pork. Not a chunk of vegetables or tofu in sight.

"All right," she said. "I spent the day at Otero Prison in beautiful Chaparral, New Mexico. Home of the Fighting Lobos, in case anyone's wondering." She looked down at her iPad. "Barry Fisher had six visitors in the last year. But I got three to run by you, Gardner."

I took a single bite of pulled pork and again put my plate aside, shifting over to my laptop to take notes.

In large federal and state prisons, the process of visiting an inmate is highly regulated. You cannot simply show up and see the incarcerated without being on their list. There are limits on the number of visitors at one time, as well as the total visits each day, month, and year.

"First, I got a victim's daughter," Shooter said.

"The daughter of someone murdered back in the eighties?" Richie asked.

"Exactly," Shooter said, pointing at him with her plastic fork full of pork.

"Which victim?" Frank asked.

"Janice Salcedo. The daughter who visits is Aileen Salcedo. She was nine when her mom was killed."

Janice Salcedo was victim number two. In 1985, she was separated, and her daughter, Aileen, was living with her dad.

"Apparently Aileen makes a trip once a year from her home in Hemet, California, to Otero Prison. Each year, she and Fisher spend an hour in the prison visiting room. She asks him to admit what he's done wrong and tell her where the rest of her mother's body is buried."

"And what does Fisher do?" I asked.

"He sits in silence. She prays for him, then leaves."

A couple decades of road trips from the San Jacinto Valley in California were not nothing.

"Aileen's last visit was the day before Fisher got out," Shooter added.

"And did the old dog tell her anything?" Frank asked.

"The warden put one of his best guards on detail this year," Shooter said. "He made a couple laps around the table where they were sitting. Eavesdropped. Fisher's mouth never moved."

But what was this woman's connection to Ross Tignon? After all, wasn't our working theory that the same killer took down both men?

"Why is she an interesting visitor?" I asked. "I'm sure there are other family members who—"

"Because this year Aileen moved to New Mexico permanently," Shooter said. "She rented a house a half mile from here. Keep in mind, that's not her moving near Otero Prison. Otero's a half hour away. She moved to Rawlings. Two miles from Fisher's brother's house. Even though supposedly no one knew that his brother was putting him up."

"Interview her tomorrow," I said, making a note on my laptop. "Find out if there's a connection to Tignon. If not, move on. Now, you said three visitors. Who's the second?"

Shooter pulled her shirtsleeves back to the elbows. The material was made of the same waffle mesh used in thermal underwear. Below it, her tattoo of the Olympic rings was visible on a freckled forearm.

"Second's a writer," she said, looking down at her notes. "Jonas Goldstein."

"He's writing a book about Fisher?"

"I don't think so. I went through his social feed." Shooter held out her iPad, which displayed two images. One was a selfie of a man, taken alongside a life-size statue of Superman. The other displayed the same man, standing in a lobby with angled contemporary pillars, on which movie images were projected. "It's HBO," she said. "Their new building in LA."

"So this writer's trying to get a deal with HBO?" I asked.

"After his prison visit, Goldstein tweeted that he locked down some exclusive story, hidden away for four decades," Shooter said. "A tell-all documentary. We gotta assume it's about Barry Fisher."

"Pin down how big this project is," I said. "If what this writer wants is HBO's best ratings ever . . . and he's trying to make it happen by giving Fisher a dramatic ending . . ."

"Understood," Shooter said.

"And who's visitor number three?"

"Number three might be something or nothing. A priest visited Fisher two weeks ago Friday."

The rules at most institutions didn't count visits by clergy against a prisoner's number. Still, the religious had to register.

"You get a name?" I asked.

Shooter blew a gust of air that moved her reddish-blond bangs out of her eyes. "Maurice Merlin."

She held up her iPad, which showed a photo of a white man with a scruffy beard and unkempt sideburns. The photo was taken at Otero Prison as part of their check-in procedures.

"Odd thing is, Maurice Merlin wasn't on Fisher's visitation list."

This meant that Merlin had showed up without notice. At that point, it was Fisher's choice to see him or not.

"And Fisher met with him?"

"Uh-huh." She nodded.

Normally all three of Shooter's leads would interest me, but we had two murders to contend with. Which meant we needed a connection to Ross Tignon, too. Otherwise, how did someone know to pluck Tignon from hiding?

"Tomorrow I'll run down all these clowns," Shooter said. "By the end of the day, I figure I can eliminate one or two of them from involvement in both murders." She took her plastic fork and stabbed one of the chunks of tofu in the untouched box. Winked at me and swallowed it.

"Okay." I looked around. "Cassie, why don't you go next? Did you follow up with Fisher's brother?"

"Kenny Smith," she said, standing up from the love seat. Cassie had changed into black tights and a pink V-neck tee that bore a long chemical equation: $C_8H_{11}NO_2 + C_{10}H_{12}N_2O + C_{43}H_{66}N_{12}O_{12}S_2$. It was a science-geek shirt; the chemicals listed were commonly known as dopamine, serotonin, and oxytocin.

Put together, the three were the formula for love.

"I talked to Kenny by phone," she said, pacing as she talked. Cassie was petite, but muscular. "I also set up a time in person to chat. Tomorrow morning, breakfast. You, me, and him, Gardner."

"But you found something?"

"Hells to the yeah," Cassie said. "I mean, at first he gave up nothing. We shot the shit, and I'm being patient, you know. Chitchatting. Small talk. Warming him up."

Frank smiled, still leaning against the wall. Cassie didn't chitchat. She asked questions. Relentlessly. At two hundred miles an hour.

"About a half hour in, Kenny suddenly remembers he showed the house to someone."

Frank's body came off the wall, and his smile disappeared. The boss had done the initial interview with Fisher's brother and come up with nothing.

"Apparently, little brother Kenny got a call," Cassie said. "Sounded like one of those schemes where they're just dialing for dollars, you know? Seeing if you're in distress or your mortgage is about to default. The caller says he'll pay top dollar for your house."

"This is Kenny's place here in Rawlings?" Frank confirmed.

"Yup," Cassie said. "But the brother *wasn't* in default. In fact, his loan was paid off years ago. But the guy said he was paying above market. Kenny thought he'd hear him out."

"He took the meeting in person?" Frank said.

"Oh yeah." Cassie smiled. "A white guy, he told me. Brown hair."

"So the brother met this guy at the house where Fisher was murdered?" I asked.

"Not just that. The brother gave the guy a tour of the place. Kenny's like a human Zillow, Gardner. A walking Redfin." She imitated the brother, saying, "'Two bedrooms, one bath, fourteen hundred square feet, pool-sized backyard.' And get this, Kenny even mentioned that if the guy wanted to make an offer, he'd better do it quick. Now go ahead, Gardner. Ask me why."

"Why?" I said.

"Because Kenny told him he was about to let his brother stay there after he got out of prison."

"Oh for God's sake," Frank said. "He told a stranger that Barry Fisher was about to live there?"

Cassie grinned, pleased to have found a detail the boss had missed.

"Did he get this investor's name?" I asked. "An email or phone number?"

"Only a name," Cassie said. "Creighton Emwon. I looked it up, b-t-dubs. No such guy, at least locally. The boys in Albuquerque are checking further."

"So someone came here to Rawlings on January second," I said. "Toured the house."

"Unless we've got tunnel vision, that's gotta be our killer," Shooter said.

"It may well be," I said. "We just need the connection to Tignon's murder in Ashland."

Frank adjusted his posture. "It does address the question you and I were debating earlier, Gardner, about how a killer got to work so quickly in the house here in New Mexico. Without worrying about casing the place."

"Sure." I nodded. "He'd been given a tour a week earlier."

Cassie picked up her barbecue, a sign that this was all she had to tell us. As she did, I noticed her meat was on a separate plate from her rice. A third plate held her veggies.

"All right," I said. "Frank, how was the crawl space?"

"Dusty," he said. "But I undid the drainpipes from the tub with a monkey wrench. Three guesses on what I found in 'em?"

"Blood evidence?" Richie said.

"Nope."

"Fragments of bone?" Shooter guessed.

Frank shook his head again. "Gardner?"

"Fish meat," I said.

It was a reference to my story about Nabokov. Everyone except Frank looked confused.

"Exactly," Frank said. "Nothing in those pipes at all. Which I'm guessing our case lead here already figured." He smiled curiously. "Maybe even lied to me about earlier?"

"I needed positive confirmation," I said, using Frank's words. "Confirmation without bias."

"Well, I took out eleven feet of pipe, Gardner. That's a lot of confirmation. There was even this curved trap." He made the shape of a U with his hand. "The kind of junction where little pieces of bone would drop with gravity. Stay there for years as water flowed above them. No bone in there."

"And the Luminol?" I asked. "Did you spray the bathroom with—"

"The bathroom was clean," Frank said. "No blood smears. No blood at all."

Just as I'd suspected, the tub *hadn't* been the place where Barry Fisher's body was chopped up.

Richie was squinting. "So *nothing* happened in the house?"

"Barry Fisher had a kill site in the eighties," I said. "Far away from where he was abducting those women."

"So whoever did this murder is copying that," Shooter said.

"Yes," I said. "Cutting Fisher into pieces somewhere else, then bringing him back to the house in bags and sticking him in that fridge."

"And the bleach in the tub?" Cassie asked.

"A misdirect," I said. "This guy is playing games with us."

"If you've got a theory," Shooter said from where she sat on the counter, "I'm not clear on why you're holding it back from the team."

"A fair criticism," I replied. And the truth was, I *did* have a theory as to why the cuts were so clean on the organs here in New Mexico and so messy on Tignon in Texas.

"Ross Tignon made messy cuts back in 2013 when he attacked the three women in Florida," I said. "But Fisher in the eighties was more precise."

"So our killer isn't just making some sick homage to old murders," Shooter said. "He's imitating them, down to the method and blade."

"Which means he has information about past crimes that few people know," Frank said. "Is anyone checking if this guy is law enforcement?"

"Cassie is." I turned to her. "You're liaising with Marly in HQ, right?"

"At this point, we're besties," she said.

I considered how our suspect was making his way around town. "I've been thinking about traffic cams," I said. "Rawlings is a town of only sixty-two hundred, but they must have two dozen reliable cameras. Banks. Post offices. Then there's neighborhood camera systems. Ring and Nest cams."

"You're thinking some camera captured a vehicle heading to Fisher's house?" Cassie said.

"Not just one camera." I held up my hand, moving a finger down, one at a time, as I spoke. "Monday morning when our killer arrived. Later when he left with the body intact. Then when he returned before noon on Tuesday with the organs in bags. And the last one when he left again after stocking the fridge."

"So four trips?" Richie said.

"Precisely."

"Richie and I can chase down those cameras," Shooter volunteered.

"After that, talk to this Maurice Merlin," I said. "Find out what connection the priest had to Fisher. What they talked about."

"Done," Shooter said.

"So we're assuming it's one killer?" Cassie asked.

"Male and under forty," I said. "He's driving, and he made the trek from Ashland, Texas, to here in Rawlings, New Mexico." I stood up. "He could still be here, even. But my assumption is that he's left already."

"He's prepping for another kill," Frank said.

I nodded. "It's too risky for him to fly around the country, and he's using a lot of equipment. I imagine he'd want his own transportation. A van or an SUV. Something easy for hauling bodies."

"Should we start looking into prospective targets?" Cassie asked.

"Meaning what?" Richie asked. "Other serials as possible victims?"

"I like that idea," I said. "Places nearby. Phoenix. Los Angeles."

Shooter made a noise with her nose, and we all looked over. "This is not me talking, guys." She put up both palms. "But there might be some people who think that maybe we let this guy get a couple more notches on his belt. The people he's clearing off this Earth . . . these are not good people."

Gallows humor was common in law enforcement, and I didn't fault Shooter for saying what everyone was probably thinking. Still, it had to be shut down.

"We don't have the luxury of choosing which murders don't count, Jo," I said. "Plus, we need to know how he's locating these victims. The all-mighty FBI didn't know where Ross Tignon was. I ruled him dead seven years ago."

"Like I said," Shooter said. "Not me talking."

But it *was* probably how the conversation had gone in the director's office in D.C. before PAR was put in charge. If we failed, what great loss was there?

I shifted the discussion. Told the team I wanted to focus on Ross Tignon. Apply our collective brainpower to seeing connections.

Frank moved over to the couch and sat down. "Seven years ago, did the Tignons have kids?"

"No," I said.

"Has anyone checked in with the wife?" Shooter asked. "The husband supposedly died in that fire in 2013."

"You're wondering if the wife knew what really happened?" Frank said.

Shooter shrugged. "If you loved your spouse and you weren't really dead, you might find her and tell her, once the coast was clear."

"Someone should take a run through her credit," Cassie said. "Her social security."

I looked to Frank. "Why don't you take that on?"

We circled around like this for another ten minutes, until I'd filled a page with questions.

"What makes us so sure that Tignon went inactive?" Richie asked. "Shouldn't we check unsolved cases in the Dallas area? Missing women? Anything that matches his old MO in Florida? In case he just moved locations."

"Rook's got a good idea," Shooter said.

I nodded, wondering why I'd not thought of this myself. "We left Texas pretty quick to come here. Someone should go back."

Everyone's head was down over their computers and notepads.

"Richie," I said. "You'll contribute the least to solving the case here. Why don't you go."

Frank and Cassie both looked up, their eyes huge. And the voice in my head made a *tsk* sound. My phrasing had been wrong.

"Whatever you need, Agent Camden," Richie said. "I'm here to help."

"Go tomorrow once you're finished with the organs," I said. "Check in with the Dallas office when you arrive."

I let everyone go then, knowing they still had to write up their reports and get them to me by morning.

Richie hung back. "I'll help you clean up."

I moved to the room next door and grabbed two trash cans, one from the bedroom and the other from the bath.

"Agent Camden," Richie said after a minute, "I can do more than administrative tasks, you know."

"I am aware of that."

"So the Texas comment . . . me heading there?"

"You wanted to look into other crimes Tignon may have committed, correct? The ones that match his MO in Florida?"

"I think it's worthwhile," he said.

"Then it makes sense for you to be in Texas. You can liaise with local police."

Richie nodded slowly, collecting the sides we hadn't eaten. "So that's why you said I should go?"

"Why else?" I asked.

Richie tossed the containers that held potato salad and baked beans into the trash and carried the can out to the hallway to get the smell out of the room. Piled the extra napkins and unused plastic silverware on the counter.

I watched him. I am not the kind to fill empty spaces, but earlier Richie had not satisfactorily answered the question of why he had chosen PAR.

"You were number one in your class," I said.

"Yeah," he replied.

"Statistically, nearly every top-five graduate either returns to their home state or selects New York, Miami, Chicago, or LA."

"Not me," he said. "I chose Jacksonville."

"You have relatives in the area?"

"Nope."

"You just . . . like northeast Florida?"

"Seventies and eighties in the spring and fall," he said. "Yeah."

I stared him down, never blinking. Richie had put his jacket back on. It was cut as well as Frank's.

"I guess I was curious," he said finally. "Puzzles. Stalled cases. The promise of solving something impossible." He glanced around the room, his face anxious. "I should go. Gotta write up my report still."

After he left, I closed the door to the adjoining room and put on CNN, mostly to get some imagery flowing in my periphery.

At some point, my eyes became heavy, my mind filled with images of bloody kitchens and bags filled with organs. And me, back in the field after four years in a cube.

And two before that in a windowless building in the El Paso office.

"Time is a strange mistress," my old partner Saul used to say. He was philosophical that way. Always saying things that meant something and nothing at the same time.

There was a point in my life where everything I cared about was connected by at least one point to Saul Moreno. I met his daughter Anna when Saul and I stopped one day at the bank where she worked. And for the first time in my life, I had other things on my mind than solving cases.

Anna brought out a lightness in me that was strange and pleasing, even while it was uncomfortable. She was a brunette with olive skin and hair the color of a chestnut in some places and dark chocolate in others. We moved in together; a year later, we found out she was pregnant. When she asked if I could imagine life without her, I answered honestly, and logic dictated I put on my best suit and walk with her to city hall.

We named our daughter Camila, and things became wonderfully settled. Delightfully predictable, the way I liked. I fell into a rhythm of getting up early and taking care of our baby, then running three miles along the Venetian Causeway before going in to work.

I have never considered myself lucky, because I do not believe in luck. But with Anna, I felt like I was the most fortunate person in the world.

Then, one night, I was up late with Camila and saw something. A piece of Anna's business paperwork I couldn't help but analyze.

It began with a state seal.

In every version of Florida's seal, there is steam coming off the boat. But in this one, there was no steam. To others, this might appear to be an inconsequential detail. To me, it was a reason to search through my wife's business documents.

I stayed up that whole night while Anna slept, at first moving through a series of spreadsheets that did not tally properly. From there, I found a locked hard drive. I tried Camila's birthdate, and it opened, revealing a bank account under Anna's name with which I was not familiar. Then images of counterfeit heavy-metal certificates bearing the names of defrauded senior citizens.

In my mind, three options appeared. Then two. Then only one.

In the morning, I went to my boxing gym and hit the bag until the skin on my knuckles was gone. But it brought me no peace. So I walked home, called the RICO task force, and explained what Anna and her boss had done. They arrested the pair at the bank where they worked at 3 p.m. that afternoon.

Two hours later, her father Saul had a heart attack.

The family was in shock, more over the stress I had caused Saul than anything illegal Anna had done.

But who had they thought I was?

The pursuit of the truth had become my life's singular goal. My comfort zone. And love? Love was a new emotion for me. That night it felt strange and illogical.

On the jet yesterday, I'd been contemplating that time period, from the Tignon case to when everything went sour with me and Anna and her family. The reemergence of Tignon had triggered something, had caused me to wonder: Could this new investigation be a chance to put my career back on track? My life?

Saul had been beloved in Miami. When the incident with Anna happened, he had recently retired. But now, seven years had passed. New personnel had joined the FBI. And no one at PAR knew me back then.

But one part of the equation had stayed the same.

Me.

Three years ago, at Thanksgiving, my uncle Gary had asked, "Would you do it again? Seeing what became of Anna? How you were forced to ask your mother-in-law to help raise your own daughter?"

Before I could answer, my mother interrupted. "Are you asking would Gardner still have the courage to do the right thing, Gary? To tell the truth and honor his commitment to the Bureau?"

Uncle Gary just smiled and asked me to pass the peas. Among Camdens, certain faults were understood, if not commended.

The truth, however, was more complex than my mother's answer.

There is an expression I use frequently in written reports at PAR: "judging by results." Meaning it is not relevant how the investigating officer thought at the time about a crime. Or even what he or she thought after. All we can do is judge the scenario by its results.

For what happened with Anna, the results were simple: my fifty-seven-year-old partner Saul had a heart attack. My daughter cried herself to sleep every night for two years after her mother went to prison. And I have not been in a relationship since Anna was arrested.

Judging by results, everyone lost.

CHAPTER TEN

A SOUND AWOKE ME.

My feet were propped up on the bed, but I was not in it. I had been sleeping in the hotel armchair in a T-shirt and boxers.

Though the window, the horizon was just turning orange—above it, a purplish gray. On the bedside table, my phone was blipping.

FaceTime. "Camila" the screen read. Below the words, a picture of my daughter from last year's birthday party.

I hit the button, and the screen flickered to life. My seven-year-old appeared, dressed in a purple short-sleeve shirt with a butterfly on the front.

"Morning, Daddy," she said. Camila was in her room, holding a clear plastic cup filled with Cheerios and milk.

"Good morning, Camila."

I hadn't told her that I wasn't in Florida, where it was almost 8 a.m.

"You look tired, Daddy," she said.

Camila's skin was a shade darker than olive, and black ringlets flowed around her oval face.

"You curled your hair again," I said.

Camila smiled, her brown eyes huge.

About six months ago, I'd bought my daughter a curling machine she'd seen in a video on her iPad. The machine sucked her hair in and held it inside while it heated and curled the strands into spirals.

"Nana helped me," she said. "You like it?"

"It's not getting caught in the machine anymore?"

"Only once," she said.

"Well, like I showed you, you have to be very cool when that happens and not yank at it. Are you being cool?"

"Like a cucumber," she said, repeating back what I'd told her the last time I was in Miami. "I listen for the click, and it lets go of the hair."

Camila had spoken early. Learned to read early.

I looked at the time. It was 7:44 a.m. in Miami.

"You ready for school?"

"Nana said to be *listo* in five minutes, but I'm dressed early," she said. "I was thinking about this weekend. My friend Sophie told me the carousel in the mall is working again."

I had requested Friday off, and I already had a flight booked from Jacksonville to Miami to see my daughter. But that was before the murders.

"I need to talk to your grandma about that," I said.

Camila powered ahead, playing with her spoon as she spoke. "Nana said she's getting up at four in the morning tomorrow to go see Mommy. Or she might leave tonight instead."

Her grandmother, Rosa, was visiting my ex, Anna, in the Florida Women's Reception Center in Ocala, a prison northwest of Orlando.

On the screen, Camila gave me her best stern look. "Are you not coming, Daddy? Because we were going to read the book about magic together."

"I realize that," I said. "But you know how my job gets."

"I know," she said. "I just miss you." She lifted her eyebrows, then squinted. "Daddy, that doesn't look like your bedroom behind you."

"You've got a sharp eye, honey," I said. "I'm in New Mexico right now."

I placed my phone against a pillow and stared at Camila. "I'm gonna try and find a way to get there this weekend," I said. "I promise."

I hesitated then. *Was this true?*

An indent formed between my daughter's eyebrows. "New Mexico? Daddy, did you make the big boys club?"

Camila had been asking over the past two years: *What would it take for me to move to Miami? For us to live together?* At one point I'd explained that I'd made mistakes at my job. That I was stuck in Jacksonville in the "little boys club," as I'd called it, while other agents in the "bigger boys club" got to travel around the country. Those agents could pick where they wanted to live. They could make the choice to live in Miami and work out of the local office. Use that as a hub from which to travel.

"Well, we don't call it that, Camila. That's something I said when you were six."

She scrunched up her forehead. "The large agents club?" she tried instead.

"Camila," I said.

"How long have you been in New Mexico?"

"A day," I replied.

"You were at home before that?"

"I was in Texas before that. But—"

"The gigantically important association of investigators!" Camila yelled.

I do not smile often, but my daughter has an infectious energy. She is also funny in ways that I could not dream of being.

"I'll talk to Nana," she said, her mood lifted.

"Camila," I said. "I will talk to your grandma, okay? In fact, why don't you put Nana on right now so I can—"

"Gotta go!"

"Camila," I said. "I have to solve the case before the big boys would even consider—"

The phone made a beeping noise. And she was gone.

I immediately rang up Rosa. But the call went to voicemail, so I wrote a text, letting her know I might not be able to fly in to get Camila. Then I showered and dressed. It was early, and I had to assemble everyone's reports into one consolidated summary for the director of the FBI. A report that covered any public safety or press concerns from the case.

By eight thirty, I had been typing for ninety minutes. I heard a knock and opened my door to find Frank outside.

"Good," he said. "You're up."

Frank wore a dark blue suit with a gray vest and a light blue tie. "I checked with a friend at Social Security on Beverly Tignon."

The wife of Ross.

"Her social security check gets mailed to an address north of Dallas," Frank continued. "All the information was under her maiden name, Beverly Polis."

Tignon's wife was still alive. This was likely how Ross Tignon had been located in Ashland. Our killer must have spoken with her. Gotten Tignon's address.

"I was thinking of flying there," Frank said.

"No," I replied. "I should be the one to interview her. Saul and I had time with the wife years ago."

Frank nodded slowly. A role reversal—me telling him the next steps.

The autopsy of Tignon would also be ready today in the Dallas field office, and I wanted to be there for it.

"Why don't you go to breakfast with Cassie?" I said. "Chat up Fisher's brother, see what he remembers about the visitor he toured through the house."

"You'll head to Texas, then?" Frank asked.

"With Shooter," I said.

He left, and I packed up my paperwork. Threw clothes into my carry-on. When I was ready, I saw a text had come in from Cassie, asking to see me before I left.

When she opened her hotel room door, she was dressed in a tan pantsuit with an aqua blouse.

"Thanks for coming," she said. "I tried on this bracelet." She held up her hand, "but now it's giving . . . frivolous vibes."

I examined her wrist. "I'm not the best person to offer advice on—"

Cassie laughed. "I'm not looking for an opinion, Gardner. I need help getting it off. Come in a sec, will ya?"

I followed her over to the kitchenette, and she sat down on one of the barstools, holding up her wrist. I studied the bracelet.

"When's your flight to Dallas?" she asked.

"In two hours," I said, carefully unclasping a piece of metal that was hooked around the edge of the adjoining piece. "But we have to drive to the El Paso airport first."

"Well, I wanted to tell you something," she said.

I stopped working and looked at her, our faces close.

"This is a good color on you, bee-tee-dubs," Cassie said. "This shirt."

I glanced down at it. I had four of these shirts, all identical.

"That's not what I wanted to tell you," she continued. "I haven't gotten through all those names yet. The agents who checked out both Tignon's and Fisher's files."

"I didn't expect you would," I said. "I imagine there are hundreds."

"There's a lot," she said. "But here's the thing."

She hesitated, and I waited. Behind Cassie, her suitcase was packed, her running shoes sitting atop it. Cassie was a marathoner, and she did five miles every morning.

"Someone we know?" I asked.

"Richie."

"Our Richie? He checked out both files?"

"I dunno if he's *our* Richie yet, but yeah. I'm not surprised about the file on Fisher. I told you, a lot of the NATs study it, and he did, two months ago at the Academy. But Tignon?"

"When?"

"Ten days ago."

I finished unhooking the bracelet, stood up, and handed it to her.

"Did he mention he was familiar with the file?" Cassie asked.

"No," I said.

"Well, you wanted to know," she said. "Now you do."

I nodded. "And you're doing more than a simple 'yes' or 'no' with who checked out the files?"

"Of course," Cassie said. "I've been looking at timing. What home office they're from. I've got eight parameters I'm considering."

In very difficult cases—the type PAR inherits—math is essential as a forensics tool, and Cassie is our expert. I have seen her re-create a scene, measure the distance to a victim, and use a tangent formula to determine the correct height of the shooter. All in her head.

My phone buzzed. Shooter was ready downstairs.

"I need to go," I said.

"Of course."

I rolled my bag out into the hallway and moved toward the elevator. As I took it down five floors, I considered the finding about Richie.

His research on the Tignon case could've been part of the personnel study he mentioned. Then again, he'd told us that he'd worked backward from *solved* cases. The three murders involving Tignon were closed, but technically unsolved.

And then there was Richie's tone last night as we cleaned up the food. His actions in picking PAR. Both were incongruous with my expectations of a rookie.

When I'd given Cassie the assignment, I'd estimated she would narrow her pool to two dozen hits. That, eventually, there would be three or four names of people we knew on it. But one on our own team?

I texted Cassie to keep an eye on the rookie as Shooter and I boarded the plane in El Paso. Keep him busy, I messaged. She wrote back a minute later.

> Donezo.

As I settled into my seat, I closed my eyes, thinking of other things. My life. My career. My daughter.

I had been with PAR for four years, and lately I wondered if my job was going anywhere. Last Friday, Shooter and I had been in the elevator when we overheard a guy talking on his cell. "Oh, those guys are getting shut down," he'd said. "You can pull their salaries from that worksheet."

The elevator door opened on 2, and he stepped off. The budgeting floor.

As the doors closed, Shooter flicked her eyebrows at me, waiting for possible gossip on which group was getting the axe. But as it closed, we heard three more words: *The Head Cases.*

We'd been called this moniker a lot, but rarely to our faces. Like most FBI nicknames, it was half insult, half compliment. After all, we did have good "heads for a case." We had the ability to synthesize.

To see things others couldn't. To connect disparate elements into one unified story.

But the name meant other things, too. That we were oddballs. Rejects. Nutsos. Not my words. But words I'd heard used to describe us.

I reclined my chair as the plane topped ten thousand feet.

If things were changing for PAR, did I care? I had been wondering how long I could keep this up, flying from Jacksonville to Miami to see Camila on weekends. My daughter's grandmother was fifty-nine and raising Camila largely without complaint, especially given everything that had happened.

The heart attack Saul had after Anna was arrested was the first of two. The second one, a week later, killed him.

And the family put the blame squarely on me.

CHAPTER ELEVEN

SHOOTER AND I PULLED OFF U.S. 35 IN OUR RENTED HYUNDAI Santa Fe, and my GPS told me I was 9.2 miles from the address Frank had supplied for Beverly Polis.

If our job today was going to be easy, it would start by speaking with Ms. Polis and having her admit that she knew where her husband had been for the last seven years. Then, if she could tell us about anyone else who had been asking this same question, we might have a good idea of what happened next. How something she said led a killer to her husband's door.

I made the turn and glanced over. Shooter had been organizing her notes on the plane, and we hadn't spoken much.

"So." I steered around a curve on State Highway 121. "You've got a new partner."

A mob of live oaks closed in around us, and the drive became more rural.

"Yeah," she said. "That's gotta mean something, right?"

I knew this was a reference to the conversation we'd overheard in the elevator. I also understood the normal response to this news was not as casual as mine. It was anxiety.

"Did you talk to Frank?" she asked.

"Not yet."

Shooter blew a gust of air toward her reddish-blond bangs. "They wouldn't add a new guy if they're shutting us down, right? It's not logical."

I considered whether half of the decisions the Bureau made could be called logical. Then I thought about my position on this case. Part of a lead's job was keeping agents on task.

"No one's shutting us down," I said. "They wouldn't have put us on this case if they were."

"Exactly," Shooter said, just as the GPS dinged.

I turned onto a gravel road and saw a series of bright orange strings, zigzagging their way north and south, each wrapped around the trunks of towering cedar elms. A sign read PRIVATE PROPERTY, but I kept going. After another minute, the road straightened, and we came to a clearing. I parked in front of a sprawling craftsman-style home.

A Black woman in her sixties had the door open to a screened-in porch. She was sweeping dust onto a set of steps that led down to the gravel.

As I put the car in park, I typed in the address of the house Ross Tignon had been found in two days ago. It was 3.2 miles from here.

"Good afternoon," the woman said as Shooter and I stepped out of the rental.

She was tall and slender and wore what my mother would call a housedress. A one-piece in pale blue that began with a scoop neck and ended below her knees. Her hair was covered in a white scarf, but a handful of gray strands hung down over her forehead.

"Good afternoon. We're looking for Beverly Polis," I said, using the maiden name that Frank had provided.

"And your names?" the woman asked, her voice ringing with a tone of deference.

"I'm Joanne Harris," Shooter said. "This is Gardner Camden."

"Well, Ms. Harris and Mr. Camden," the woman said, smiling gently, "Ms. Polis passed away a year ago. Is there something I can help you with?"

Dead?

I pulled out my badge. "We're with the FBI, ma'am. We're following up on an issue related to Ms. Polis's husband, Ross Tignon."

"I'm afraid he passed, too," she said. "Well before his wife."

"Do you mind if we come in and sit down?" Shooter asked. "We've been on our feet all morning."

This was a line a lot of agents used to get a look inside a house.

"Not at all," the woman said. Except she didn't invite us in. Instead, she motioned at a pair of wrought-iron chairs by a wagon-wheel table on the screened-in porch. "Take a load off."

"I don't think we caught your name," I said.

"Dolores Hadley," the woman replied. "Most people just call me Doll."

"Are you a family member, Ms. Hadley?" Shooter asked. "A relative of Beverly Polis?"

The woman blinked. Stared down at the dark skin of her arm. "Do I look like a relative of Beverly, Agent Harris?"

Shooter smiled, her hands palms out. "No ma'am," she chuckled. "No, you don't."

"I've worked for the Polis family for thirty-one years," Dolores said. "I raised Beverly's sister's and brother's kids."

I thought of how Frank had located Tignon's wife. "Ms. Polis's social security checks still come here," I said. "Are you aware of that?"

"I've got a stack of them in the house," she said. "I keep telling Mr. Alex to call the government and clear that up. He's her brother."

"Did Miss Polis live at this address before she died?" I asked.

"This was the Polis family summer home," she said. "They grew up in Dallas. Stayed July and August here. But Beverly *did* spend her last few days on the property."

Days? Was the old woman confused? I decided to back up, earlier in time. Much earlier.

"Mr. Tignon died in a fire in 2013," I said. "You are aware of that?"

"Yes sir."

"But that's not when Miss Beverly came here?"

"No sir," she said. "We didn't see anything of Beverly until October sixteenth. A little over a year ago."

Shooter glanced at me, then at Hadley. "You recall the specific date?" she asked.

"It was my seventy-fifth birthday, Agent Harris, and I'm an early riser. I received a call from a nurse. Beverly had a stroke, and the hospital listed Mr. Alex and this number as her emergency contact."

"You went to a local hospital and retrieved Beverly?" Shooter confirmed. "After years of not knowing where she had been?"

Hadley nodded. "This was her home. You can always come home."

Shooter shook her head just slightly, as if moved by the sentiment.

"Who checked her into the hospital?" I asked.

"A man, they said. He told them his name was Alex Polis. But it wasn't our Mr. Alex."

I sat back, feeling the warmth of the iron chair on my back. Ross Tignon had left his wife in a hospital in terminal condition, then had her family pick her up.

"You call the police?" I asked.

"We did," she said. "And Mr. Alex raised a fuss. But what were we asking them, exactly? She was a grown woman, and she was finally home. Unfortunately, she had speech and hearing issues. Couldn't walk."

"What kind of condition was she in?" Shooter asked.

"Poor," Ms. Hadley said. "Eight days later, Jesus took her."

I glanced through the screen door at the property, which appeared to go on for miles. And I thought of the ruse played in New Mexico, with our suspect posing as a real estate investor.

"Is this property for sale, Ms. Hadley?" I pointed up the road. "We saw orange strings between those cedars on the way in."

"Mr. Alex subdivided the land," she said. "Twenty-two lots."

"Do the interested parties drive up here to the house, or just look down the road?"

"Mr. Alex is looking for a developer, not individuals," she said. "But yes, men come down the road, just like you two did."

"Do you recall if any of these real estate men asked about Miss Polis?"

Ms. Hadley considered this. "There was one man," she said slowly. "This time last week. Said he knew Beverly from when she was younger."

"What did he look like?" Shooter asked.

Hadley shrugged. "White. Dark brown hair. Well-dressed."

"Age?" I asked.

"Forties, maybe. Sometimes I don't wear my glasses."

I wondered if anyone else had seen this man. "So it's just you that lives here now?"

"Mr. Alex asked me to stay. It keeps the property safe from vandalism."

"You're pretty deep in the woods," Shooter said. "You good with a shotgun?"

"Good enough to lift it to the sky and scare off kids," Hadley said. "Plus we got security cameras all over the place. Mr. Alex had 'em mounted up on the trees last year." She dropped her chin then, her eyes studying us. "Now, I am old, but I am not unsophisticated. You two are from the Federal Bureau of Investigation?"

"Yes ma'am," Shooter said.

"What exactly are you looking for?"

I wanted to reveal what we knew about Tignon and get her reaction. But one didn't usually trust civilians with too much information.

Still, I thought of Frank. How he'd told Fisher's brother elements of the case, but at the same time, used those aspects to convince him not to speak to the media.

"What if I told you Ross Tignon did not die in that fire, Miss Hadley?" I said. "What if I told you he'd been living under a false name three miles from here?"

"Then I would get that address from you and drive over there directly."

"He was murdered," Shooter said, her green eyes focused on the old lady. "Three days ago."

Hadley squinted at us, her forehead crisscrossed with lines.

"The family hired a private investigator," she said finally. "A week after we took Miss Beverly home from that hospital. He found prescriptions in her name in a Dallas pharmacy. The pharmacist said she'd come in with a man."

"Description?" Shooter asked.

"White and medium build."

"No one suspected it was Ross?" I asked.

"The man had been burned to death," Hadley said. "You hear of something like that . . ."

"Yeah," I said, understanding.

Shooter pointed back to the land. "I'd like to see what's on those cameras, ma'am. Can we get Mr. Alex's contact information?"

Ms. Hadley went inside and came out a moment later with a piece of paper. In the trees, I heard starlings chirp. My phone dinged. Ross Tignon's autopsy was ready at the Dallas office.

I stood up and thanked Ms. Hadley. Shooter advised her that it was safer if she did not repeat what we had told her about Tignon to anyone.

"Not to Mr. Alex either?"

"Well," Shooter said, "do you care about his safety?"

That was how Frank would do it. Through implication.

"Of course," Hadley said.

"Then I think you know the answer," Shooter replied.

"All right," Hadley said nervously. "I understand."

"There's something else," I said. "When I told you about Ross being alive—your instinct was to get in your car and drive over there. Give him a piece of your mind."

"I guess that wasn't very Christian of me."

"But you never suspected the fire was a fake? Even after you heard about the man in the pharmacy?"

"That's right." She nodded.

"The logic of that does not track, Dolores."

"Sometimes," she replied, "I observe things that don't track."

Her phrasing was odd.

"I am a young man," I said. "But I am not unsophisticated."

Dolores Hadley smiled. "The day after we took Beverly home, I came out onto the porch. We had her in a wheelchair right where you two were just sitting." She hesitated a moment. "I smelled a man's cologne in the air that day. A scent I recognized. Until now, I thought I was crazy . . . that I imagined it."

We thanked Dolores Hadley and turned toward the steps leading down to the rental car.

"You seem like a very straightforward person, Mr. Camden," she said.

Shooter chuckled, and we turned back.

"He can't help it," she said.

"I'm curious about one thing," Hadley said.

"What is it?" I asked.

"The accusations . . . what they said Mr. Tignon did. In Florida. Did he do those things?"

"Not alone," I said.

"He had a partner?"

"Mrs. Tignon," I said. "She lied. Covered for him. Then apparently found him again here in Texas. She lived with a serial killer most of her life."

A tear moved down Hadley's cheek, and I stopped talking. Shooter was glaring at me.

"I'm sorry," I said to the woman. But Tignon was a bad man, and now I was lying. I wasn't sorry.

I turned. There was an autopsy to get to.

CHAPTER TWELVE

WITHIN A HALF HOUR, I WAS TRANSITIONING OVER TO STATE Highway 12, heading east. I slowed onto the exit lane toward the Federal Building in Dallas, then glanced over at Shooter, who had her head down over her laptop.

"I'm out for the autopsy," she said.

I reminded myself that the members of PAR are not regularly in the field, and that this was the first time we'd be on the road as a team. Usually, we look at files after they've gone cold. "If you're not comfortable around a dead body . . ."

Shooter looked up, her nose pinched, her mouth a half grin. "I've been dressing animals in the field since I was six, Gardner. It's not that. You assigned me the cameras in New Mexico, the follow-up on the prison visitors, the priest. I've had Richie pulling stuff and emailing me, but I gotta review it."

"How's he working out?" I asked.

"So far, good," she said. "But he's just a rook, you know. I need a desk, a phone, and four hours of quiet to examine everything."

I nodded. "Stay for the initial look," I said. "I want a second set of eyes on Tignon. After that, I'm sure you can find an office upstairs."

Shooter agreed, and we parked in a visitor's lot. Inside, we showed our IDs and found our way to the ME's office in the basement.

Dr. Lourdes Abrieu was in her late forties with an athletic figure and olive skin. Her long hair was divided into four sections, two of which were colored red and braided together with her natural brown shades.

We introduced ourselves, and Abrieu got up from her desk and put on gloves. She headed to an adjoining room, where Ross Tignon's body was laid atop a gurney on a stainless steel tray. The initial incisions had been made on his body, and his skin was loose. The primary cut ran transversely across his thorax, from shoulder to shoulder, just above where the 5–0 had been carved. A second cut formed a T and ran south toward his stomach, where the hole had been cut open by his attacker. Both of these cuts indicated that the ME had done an initial inspection of the body, then waited for us.

"Thank you for holding the body," I said.

"Not a problem," Dr. Abrieu replied, wheeling the metal tray into the center of the room where the overhead light was brightest.

Taking her place on the side opposite us, she began by running down the basics of the victim.

"Mr. Tignon was a white male, sixty-four years of age, six foot one and two hundred and thirty-eight pounds," she said. "His BMI was thirty-two, and his time of death was measured by rigor and body temp as Sunday, January twelfth. Between twelve and four p.m."

Atop the sheet that covered his legs was a clear bag with Tignon's jeans and shirt. The Levi's tag listed a waist size of 36.

"The body was inspected from head to foot and in supine and prone positions," Abrieu continued. "I noted that an unknown subject had cut Mr. Tignon's abdomen open and severed multiple arteries. The abdominal aorta, renal artery, and the mesenteric artery."

"Tignon bled out from those three?" Shooter asked.

"Yes," Dr. Abrieu said.

Decomposition begins within four minutes of death. As blood stops pumping, the body becomes oxygen deprived, and its enzymes digest the outer membranes of their own cells. In Tignon's case, this was mid-day Sunday. Now by Thursday, there was a smell in the air that the fan overhead just couldn't clear.

I thought about the order of the attack. First, Tignon had to be subdued.

"We left a note with the agent who brought in the body," I said. "About a puncture wound in the neck."

"I received that," the doctor said. "And I collected two samples to test for drugs. One from the heart with a needleless syringe, and the other from the femoral vein."

Medical examiners took two samples, because while extracts from the heart were inaccurate for drug concentration, they did offer a quick yes or no on foreign substances in the blood.

"What did you find?" Shooter asked.

"He was injected with something, all right," Abrieu said. "In terms of what exactly, that's gonna take a few days."

The ME wore bright red lipstick, and when she wasn't speaking, she ran her tongue across the front of her teeth, dragging little bits of lipstick with it. Her teeth shimmered the slightest pink color.

"What about suspicions?" Shooter followed up. "Your gut?"

The doctor shrugged, looking from Shooter to me. "By your note, I'm guessing you thought it was a paralytic."

"I did."

"And what did you base that on?" Abrieu asked.

"The initial cuts," I said. "They appeared to be antemortem."

"Yes," she said, confirming that the cuts preceded Tignon's death.

"Our working theory," Shooter said, "was that the killer *wanted* Tignon to observe what was going on. To suffer."

"For what reason?" Abrieu asked.

"Pleasure," I theorized. "Or revenge?"

The doctor motioned to Tignon's stomach, where the hole had been carved. "That tracks," she said. "The initial cuts here are clean and smooth. The victim was not moving when they were made."

"That also confirms an element of torture," I said.

"Sure." Shooter nodded. "A paralytic doesn't alleviate pain."

"Was Mr. Tignon's liver missing?" I asked.

I hadn't noticed this on the first day of the investigation, but I wasn't officially assigned the case at that time.

"No," the doctor said. "But it *was* cut free of the body on one side. I'm curious—what made you ask that?"

I explained to the ME how Tignon had removed the livers of his own victims, back in 2013. If this new killer had cut only one side of the organ free, perhaps he had been interrupted.

"Maybe his intent was to take the liver with him," Shooter said, confirming my train of thought. "But he got spooked. A noise? A neighbor?"

"I suppose it's possible," Abrieu said. "That could explain why one side is so neat and the rest of the slices are rough."

My eyes moved up to Tignon's chest, where the numbers had been carved. "Based on these and other cuts, broadly speaking, what kind of training do you think the killer had?"

Abrieu flipped the red and brown braids off her neck. As she did, I noticed that they covered a string of eight or nine bumps, each pro-

truding approximately three centimeters off her skin. A line of harm-
less lipoma.

"It's not someone in the medical field, if that's what you're asking.
But I'd say they hunt."

"Based on what?" Shooter cocked her head.

"To remove a liver, you move it around. Laterally. Medially. Up and
down. But it's also covered by a peritoneum, which forms a thick layer.
Almost like ligaments, where it sits above the liver, but not true ligaments. You know what I'm getting at?"

"You're talking surface landmarks," Shooter said. "They guide you
on where you are in the body cavity."

"That's how the killer knew where to make the incision?" I asked.

"Perhaps," Abrieu said. "Your killer removed the peritoneum.
Carefully. Then, once he got part of the liver free, and only then, he
sliced the thing to all hell. Real messy."

Like in Daisy Carabelle's murder.

"What makes that the work of a hunter?" I asked.

Shooter jumped in. "If you hunt deer, Gardner, you want to remove
and store the meat. You need to be fast, which means messy. But you
need to be careful, too. Remove the hide and peritoneum. But gingerly.
Negligence pollutes the meat."

"But these cuts," I said, "they're not from some buck knife."

"Right, I see where you're going," Abrieu said. "But uh . . . I grew
up with four brothers who hunt. I was talking about the approach, not
the blade."

"So what *was* he cut with?" Shooter asked.

"This." Dr. Abrieu held up a surgical knife with a short, curved
blade. Its shape was similar to that of a paring knife.

"A surgical instrument?" I said.

"Specifically what we call a number twelve," Abrieu said. "So I think you're right about the paralytic. I think your killer injected Mr. Tignon. Bled him out fast."

I took two steps back, processing this. A number of things were still unclear. Tignon was found twenty feet inside his home, behind a kitchen island, with no visible signs that his body had been moved. There were also no signs of a break-in. Did he know his attacker?

Abrieu promised her report in two hours, and we thanked her, moving out into the hallway. There, Shooter and I stood near a work sink.

"I gotta go," she said. "A friend who works upstairs pinged me. They found me an office."

"Let me know what you find out after going through those camera feeds."

Shooter took off, and I used the hall bathroom. As I came out, Dr. Abrieu was waiting.

"You've got a call," she said. "You can take it over there if you like."

I made my way to her desk. "Camden," I said, wondering if Frank or Cassie had hit gold during their breakfast meeting with Fisher's brother.

But it was neither Frank nor Cassie on the line.

"Gardner Camden," an unfamiliar voice said calmly.

Immediately, I knew it was our killer.

CHAPTER THIRTEEN

I CANNOT SAY EXACTLY HOW I KNEW IT WAS HIM, BUT I DID.

"I see you made your way back to Texas from New Mexico," the male voice said.

I turned, the phone still to my ear. Dr. Abrieu had moved back to the gurney and was sewing up Tignon's body.

"For me, the west is too hot," the man continued. "The blood coagulates too quickly and, well. You saw how messy it got between the legs of that fat old angler."

"Who am I speaking with?" I asked.

"Think of me as a helper," he said.

The man had an accent, but one that shifted. In one word, southwest. In the next, a twang that rang of the south.

"I'm calling to offer you a courtesy," he continued. "'Cause I like you."

How did the killer know to call me here? Know my name?

And: *He liked me?*

"Skip this case," he said. "Let someone else take it on."

I hesitated. "I don't decide what cases to investigate. I serve at the pleasure of the director of the FBI."

A frustrated exhalation, followed by a beat of silence.

"Do you know chess, Agent Camden?"

"I have played."

"Then you're aware of the roles of pawns," he said. "To clog up the paddock."

His voice sounded young, but his language was odd. *Clogging the paddock?*

"Or they're marched into the field for slaughter," he continued. "You don't want to be slaughtered, do you?"

"These two men," I said. "Was it revenge you were after?"

"Revenge is for people with small brains," he hissed. "My acts are dictated by my own conscience."

"If I understood what's bothering you—"

"Who said something's bothering me?" His voice rang with annoyance now.

"I could help with—"

"I don't need *your* help," he interrupted. "If anything, you need mine."

I paused. In New Mexico, Frank had called the killer "a game player." Did that mean I could incite an emotional response?

"You may think you're smart," I said. "But you're leaving clues. Everywhere."

"Oh, you have no idea," he replied. "You haven't even found the good ones yet. I mean, you'll find 'em. I'm counting on it. But too late to do anything. It's a game, don't you know that?"

"Not to me."

He made a squeaking noise with his teeth before going silent. Then:

"I was assuming, perhaps wrongly, that with all the work you'd put in on Ross Tignon, there'd be some appreciation."

"For what?" I asked.

"Me. Officially closing your case. You know what they say about gratitude. A little goes a long way."

There was no way I was thanking this guy for killing Ross Tignon.

"We're not on the same side," I said.

He didn't speak for a long time, but I didn't hear a dial tone.

"I had a . . . mentor," he said finally. "He used to tell me that some people don't take things seriously until they have skin in the game. Maybe that's what you need, Agent Camden. Something personal, to get your blood pumping."

"What kind of mentor?" I asked, moving back to the word he'd used.

He made a noise with his nose. When he spoke again, he sounded weary. "You're not even listening, are you? But I warned you, little mouse."

I could sense he was about to hang up.

"What should I call you?" I asked. "Presuming we speak again."

"God," he said. "When we talk again, you can call me God. Who gives and takes all life."

"You're going to be caught, God," I said. "We always get our man. You know that, right?"

He made a huffing noise. "Tell that to the families of Ross Tignon's victims."

I went silent. He was right. I had failed the Tignon victims.

"Daisy Carabelle was a sweet girl. If only the dead could speak."

A dial tone rang out, and he was gone. I felt a pulse of something unfamiliar move through me. Irritation? Anger?

I hurried over to Dr. Abrieu, who was still sewing up Tignon. "Who transferred that line here?"

"I dunno." She shrugged. "The operator, I guess. Why?"

Without answering, I moved back to her desk and grabbed a glossy brochure for scalpels. Flipped it over and started jotting down every phrase from the phone call.

- *Do you know chess?*
- *Pawns clog up the paddock.*
- *Helper.*
- *My acts are dictated by my own conscience.*
- *Skin in the game . . . something to get your blood pumping.*
- *Call me God. Who gives and takes all life.*
- *If only the dead could speak.*

Then I called up Lanie Bernal, who runs a tech desk at Quantico. After I told her the details, she disappeared for three minutes before coming back on.

"We have four calls around that time, Agent Camden." Lanie's voice bore no accent, and she pronounced her words slowly, articulating every syllable. "All under one minute. Except one. Which was two minutes and five seconds."

Dr. Abrieu had been waiting for me in the hallway. The phone call had been longer than I'd thought.

"The two-minute one," I said. "I need a location on that."

I knew what would happen next. Lanie would identify the cell carrier, then reach out to her liaison at that company with a digital exigency report, so the phone could be pinged.

"Let me call you back," she said. "Give me ten minutes."

"On my cell," I said.

After hanging up, I looked again at the body of Ross Tignon.

Earlier I had noticed the slightest of bruising on his neck, but assumed it was related to the fall at the house, like the cuts on his face and temple.

"This mark on his neck," I said, approaching Dr. Abrieu. "If a victim was strangled, I'd expect petechia in his eyes, but there wasn't any."

"No," she said. "It's not strangulation. Hand marks would have appeared by now."

"So what would cause this?" I asked.

"I don't want to guess," she said. "What I'm thinking—it doesn't make any sense."

"Call it a hypothesis."

She flipped one of her braids off her neck. "A bruise like this happens during mastication, Agent Camden. The problem is, by definition, that stops when consciousness does."

"It happens during eating?"

"Yes."

"But it's a postmortem bruise?" I confirmed.

"Right. See how it doesn't make sense?"

I thought of the killer's words on the call.

If only the dead could speak.

"Cut his neck open."

"Agent Camden—"

"Now," I said.

Dr. Abrieu grabbed a two-inch block of wood and placed it under each of Tignon's shoulders. Then she propped up his head—any dissection of the musculocutaneous layers of the neck required elevation. Taking her blade, she made an incision upward, toward the flap of skin that hung below Tignon's jaw.

Removing the skin from its connection to the body involved not just the surgical knife, but the help of pliers. The doctor worked fast. In minutes, she opened up a two-by-two-inch square flap.

She placed her fingers into Tignon's neck and pulled the esophagus forward. She was hunched over his head, but I saw three lines form across her forehead.

"What is it?" I asked.

"There's something inside."

CHAPTER FOURTEEN

DR. ABRIEU USED HER FINGER TO DIG INTO THE TINY HOLE she'd created, pulled an object out, and walked it over to a tray.

The item looked like a bolus of something mashed and white. Taking two mini forceps, Abrieu teased it apart, until it was clear that it was a scrap of paper, no more than one inch by two.

"Is something written on it?" I asked.

"Yes," she said. "But I want to be careful that the paper doesn't tear or smear."

I took out my cell and snapped two good photos, each from a different angle. Then Abrieu used the forceps to pull the crumpled piece of paper even further apart.

"Part of a word," she said.

There was the loop of an *n*, then a left-to-right mark that looked like the edge of another letter. A lowercase *g*, maybe.

"N-g," I said aloud, then snapped a picture.

"Looks like it."

"Someone jammed that in his mouth after he was dead?"

"I'd guess while he was semiconscious," Abrieu said. "Then they manually stimulated his jaw."

"You're saying they forced him to eat this paper? That's what caused the bruising?"

Abrieu nodded, and my phone buzzed. I took two steps back from the body.

Lanie was calling from Quantico.

"The call originated from a disposable cell," she said. "The signal is moving north along Interstate 5 in Los Angeles."

"Now?"

"Yes sir."

I gazed down at the paper on Abrieu's metal tray. "California Highway Patrol needs to get that car to the side of the road," I said to Lanie. "Extreme precaution."

"That's gonna take a minute," she said, then told me she'd ring me back.

I hung up and turned to Abrieu. I needed to be on the road to the Dallas airport. From there, LA.

"I want no mention of this paper in your report," I said. "Anything else you come across, speak only to me."

She nodded, and I headed toward the door. Before walking out, I turned.

"Good work, Doc."

•   •   •

Ten minutes later, I was in my rental, on the way to DFW airport. I stared at the brochure with my handwritten notes.

Paddock, I thought.

Middle English. Germanic specifically. A field of grassland. A farm enclosure.

My cell rang, and I was patched through to our LA office. Assistant Chief Henry DeGallo told me that a patrol car had a family pulled over on the side of the 101 Freeway.

"The cell was hooked to a roof rack with a hiking carabiner, Agent Camden," DeGallo said. "Mom and Dad are in the back of a police cruiser, but they claim they don't know where the phone came from."

DeGallo spoke like a drill sergeant, even when he wasn't raising his voice.

"Can you patch me through to the officer on the scene?"

It took a minute, but soon I was speaking to a patrolman named Ruiz.

"Officer Ruiz," I said. "Describe these people for me."

"They're from Germany," Ruiz said. "Barely speak English. They were headed to Universal Studios Hollywood."

"And their car?"

"It's a rental," he said. "From Avis. They told me they got off the five about twenty minutes before I pulled them over. Got gas at a Mobil station in Downey. The driver still has the receipt."

I pictured the man who called himself "God" at the same gas station. Clipping the cell phone to the tourists' car. "They remember anyone from the station?"

"No one, Agent Camden. The kids were on their phones. Dad went inside and got some snacks for the family. A couple bags of gummy worms are up on the dash. Matches the receipt."

These people were clearly innocent, and I didn't want them in this killer's crosshairs.

"We can hold them," Ruiz said, "but you should advise on what to do with the kids. They're minors and not citizens."

"Bag the phone and the carabiner for the Westwood office and let the tourists go," I said. "Get me their info, please. Their hotel and itinerary."

"Will do."

"Can you go by and see if there are cameras at the gas station? You have a time stamp with the receipt, right?"

The cop agreed, and I hung up, glancing at the brochure on the passenger seat. I was moving along 183, ten minutes from DFW.

A gas station in LA? The killer had made another comment that I hadn't written down. *For me, the west is too hot.*

He'd been referring to Tignon's death in Ashland. But something about his tone didn't ring true. Like it was another misdirect.

At least I knew where the killer was right now: Los Angeles. One more crazy in a city filled with them. I didn't have a positive view of LA, thanks in large part to the man my mother had met in her fifties, an Angelino who'd moved her to Texas. He'd since passed away, leaving her in the Lone Star State largely for the continuity of her medical care.

As soon as I returned my rental car, I got Frank on the line.

"Who knew Shooter and I were coming here?" I asked.

"Me," Frank said. "Cassie. Richie."

Richie.

"Why?" Frank asked.

I explained about the call and the burner cell clipped to the tourists' roof rack.

"Jesus, Gardner," Frank said. "He called you guys at the FBI?"

As Frank said "guys," I realized I'd forgotten to tell Shooter that I'd left the building. "Me," I said. "Shooter had work to do. Grabbed a desk."

"So he asked for you by name?"

"Yes," I said, explaining to Frank that he wanted us to call him "God."

"The heck with that," he said. "What about 'dog' instead?"

God, backward.

"I presume you mean just among our team," I said. "Not to the press."

"Exactly," Frank said.

"Then I'd rather we call him Mad Dog. He's clearly a sociopath."

"What do you need from us, Gardner?" Frank asked.

"Get on with the LA office and brief them," I said. "Then get out there. Have Shooter get on a flight, too. We need to look at serials throughout Southern California. Start with men who made violent attacks on women. Convicted. Released. If his pace keeps up, murder number three happens after ten p.m. tonight."

"Did he have an accent?" Frank asked.

"Inconsistent," I said. "One moment, a touch of the southwest. Then immediately after, panhandly or southern. North Texas or Oklahoma. Arkansas, maybe."

"These expressions you wrote down—send them to us, will you?"

I agreed.

"He knows who you are, Gardner," Frank said. "You've thought this through, right? The director needs to be kept abreast."

"I'll send him a note."

Grabbing my bag, I headed toward the airport. Since leaving the Dallas office, my brain had been building up theories about the paper found in Tignon's mouth and the cuts, which resembled those a hunter might make. But as I entered Terminal C, I wasn't focused on any of that.

I had a mentor, the killer had said. *He used to tell me that some people don't take things seriously until they have skin in the game.*

I stood at the American Airlines counter while a clerk filled out the Armed Passenger Authorization form.

Maybe that's what you need, Agent Camden, he'd said. *Something personal, to get your blood pumping.*

"Can you hold on a second?" I told the woman.

She looked up. "You don't want the flight to LA?"

"Give me two minutes."

I stepped away from the desk and found the Favorites screen on my phone. Hit the button beside Camila's name, which rang to her iPad.

A blipping sound. 7:03 p.m. Florida time. Camila did not answer.

I called Rosa next. After five rings, I heard her voicemail.

I began backtracking over the last three hours. A green Toyota I'd seen on the way to the house near Ashland, then seemingly again on I-35. The security guard at the Dallas office who got up when I walked into the FBI.

He's in LA, the voice in my head said. The rational voice I hear every day.

But another voice was creeping in.

My mentor, he'd said.

Frank and I had wondered if the work was too much for one killer. Was it possible Mad Dog didn't work alone? He had referred to personal sacrifice. To getting my blood pumping. He'd called it a game.

I hit redial.

"Rosa," I said when Camila's grandmother finally picked up. "Where are you?"

"I'm on 95," she said.

"You got my text, right? About not being able to come?"

"I didn't get the impression it was negotiable," she said. "So I didn't call you back."

My relationship with Rosa was cordial, but complicated.

"Is Camila with you?" I asked. This would have been unusual, since my ex forbade Rosa from bringing her daughter to see her.

"Camila's with a friend of mine," Rosa said.

"I need to speak with her. Make sure she's safe."

Behind Rosa, I heard the sounds of the highway. "She's very safe, Gardner, you know that. She gets straight As. She lives in a good home."

"Rosa," I said. "Are they staying at your place? Your friend who's watching Camila?"

"No, but they may go back there. My friend has a one bedroom. Camila would have to sleep on the couch."

A single friend of Rosa's. My mother-in-law had gone through a revitalization after she hit fifty-five. With no husband around, Rosa took salsa classes and dated. She was part of a particular social scene in Miami, one that sometimes required babysitters and friends doing favors to watch Camila when Rosa went out.

I thought of the call coming into the ME's office.

Was it possible that Mad Dog was in Dallas and had seen me? Or his mentor had?

"Rosa," I said. "I want them to stay put. At your friend's place. Did you talk with anyone about where you were going?"

"I talk to lots of people," she said. "Gardner, you're scaring me."

I had not raised my voice with Rosa, but perhaps the nature of the questions had put her on alert. I attempted to flatten my speech. "Have any strangers engaged you in conversation recently? White men? Midthirties. Brown hair?"

I heard the noise of a trucker, laying on a horn. "I don't know," Rosa said. "What kind of question is that?"

I thought of who I knew in the Miami office. Agents from years ago. But if I called in a favor, asked someone to keep an eye on Camila, the conversation would be logged in our system. And if the killer had access to that, as we had speculated, *I* could be the one putting Camila in danger.

"Text me your friend's address," I told Rosa. "I promise to call in ten minutes and tell you more."

"Okay," Rosa said.

The line went dead, and I stood there.

He's in LA, I told myself.

Unless he was working with an accomplice, and one of them had been in Texas, following me. I estimated the odds on this at 37 percent and walked back to the woman at the American Airlines counter. "What if I wanted to go to Miami instead?" I asked.

She looked at her computer screen. "Tonight? You're gonna get in after midnight. Or there's a red-eye with a stop."

Mad Dog knew my name. Where I'd traveled from. If he or his accomplice was in Dallas, one of them could've easily beaten me to the airport. They could be on their way to Miami right now.

"Let me ask you a question," I said. "Other Miami flights from here that might've left before the one you're looking at . . . flights in the last hour. What time would they get in?"

"I'm not following."

"If someone got here an hour before me, how much earlier would they get to Miami?" I asked. "I'm trying to make up time. To see how far behind I am."

She paged through several screens on her terminal, then looked back up. "An hour and ten minutes maybe, if they got lucky. More likely forty minutes."

"You can see all the airlines in there?"

She nodded, and my phone buzzed. A text from Rosa.

I cannot reach my friend. Should I be worried?

I pulled my work bag onto the counter and rummaged through it until I found a business card. The one Travis had left after the private jet trip the other night. I computed the difference in travel times: commercial airliner versus Gulfstream. A faster flight by one hour and thirty-eight minutes.

Travis answered on the first ring, and I reminded him who I was.

"If I needed to get to Miami," I said, "in a rush, what are the chances of there being a plane today? Something private out of Dallas?"

"My colleague is fueling up right now," he said. "Leaves in twenty. But I haven't seen a request from the agency."

"This is personal," I said. "A personal emergency."

Was it?

These were not things I said or did. I am not a person who acts rashly.

But Camila . . .

Travis checked on the details, and I waited on hold.

"It's a private charter," he said when he came back. "Three guys going sport-fishing. I told them how low maintenance you are, and the guy hosting agreed to share the plane if you kicked in thirty-five hundred bucks."

I considered my savings. What I sent to my mother's nursing home each month. To Rosa for Camila. And what was left.

"I'll be there in ten minutes," I said.

CHAPTER FIFTEEN

THE CORNER OF EIGHTEENTH STREET AND THIRTY-FOURTH Avenue was in the Grapeland Heights area, the northwest edge of Rosa's neighborhood. An Uber dropped me off within a block of the apartment where Rosa's friend Beatriz was watching Camila, a fact I'd learned via text exchange before the Gulfstream left Dallas.

The night was quiet as I moved down an alley and across an intersecting street.

The address Rosa had given me was for a duplex, and the TV was on in the downstairs room. But after watching from the street, I saw no Beatriz. No Camila.

Doubling back down the alley, I came up behind the apartment. The back of Beatriz's place had a screen door with slotted glass windows. The rectangular panes of glass were levered open, almost horizontally. A woman's purse sat on the kitchen counter, a cell phone beside it.

Rosa had contacted Beatriz and told her I was coming, but no one was home.

I stood quietly at the back door, but the only sound was from the TV.

I tried the knob and found it locked.

Was someone inside? Hurt? Or worse?

I had seen a set of garden shears atop a brick planter by the next apartment. I found my way back to them. Returning quietly in the dark, I sliced along the side of the screen, right where it met the rubber edging. I slid my hand past the screen material and through the open glass levers. Unlocked the door without a sound.

Pulling my Glock, I stepped into the tiny galley kitchen. Past the purse and keys and into the adjoining living room.

SpongeBob SquarePants was playing on a forty-two-inch TV mounted on the far wall. I saw Camila's backpack. It was unzipped and laid out on an oak coffee table beside a set of candles. A pile of empty Starburst wrappers was crumpled beside it.

My foot pushed open the bedroom door, and my free hand switched on the light. No one in the bedroom. No one in the adjoining bathroom.

"Camila?" I said. "Beatriz?"

The place was empty.

CHAPTER SIXTEEN

I HUSTLED BACK THE WAY I CAME, PHONING ROSA FROM THE alley, but getting her voicemail.

As I hung up, my phone buzzed, and I looked down. It was Cassie, texting me.

> What's up, partner? Did you head to LA?

> Frank said you never called with your flight info.

I ignored the text and put my phone away.

I had nowhere else to go, except to find my way to Rosa's, two blocks away, so I hustled toward where the Uber had dropped me. It was a Thursday night, but the neighborhood was far from the busy nightlife of South Beach.

As I approached Rosa's house, I heard the sound of someone scraping a trash can in from the curb.

I called Rosa again.

Again, voicemail.

I kept to the left side of the alley, my body hidden under the palm trees that lined the cracked asphalt. Behind the twelve-hundred-square-foot home, I saw the space where Rosa's 2012 Chevy Equinox normally parked. It was empty, but a light was on inside her house.

I flipped the safety off my Glock and edged toward the back door. Tried the knob and felt it turn.

I swung open the door against the stucco wall and entered quietly. Switched on the light and cleared the kitchen. "Camila?"

I turned the corner, my Glock held out in a shooting stance.

"Daddy?" A voice rang out.

My seven-year-old stood there, a woman in her forties behind her.

"Are you two alone?" I asked.

The woman who stood behind Camila nodded, and I secured my weapon. Rosa's friend Beatriz wore bright orange lipstick. Her reddish hair was black at the roots.

"Rosa didn't tell you to stay put?" I asked.

Beatriz looked down sheepishly. "She said we could come back if we wanted. Just to be careful. Camila needed her giraffe."

Through the kitchen window, something white flashed across the alley. The shape moved again, heading toward the back door.

I put a finger to my lips and motioned them into the bedroom. *What if this was Mad Dog? And they had come back for a stuffed animal?*

I pushed my back against the kitchen wall and slid along it until I found a position beside the door. I saw the white of a man's shirt. Turned the knob slowly. Then bullied the door open with all my weight, smacking the man who was behind it and knocking him to the ground.

In five seconds, I had him on his stomach, his chin pinned to the concrete and his arm bent behind him.

"Let's start with your name," I said. I pushed my gun into his space below his rib cage.

"I was just looking for Beatriz," he mumbled, and I smelled rum on his breath. "We had a fight, and I knew she was watching the kid."

I stepped off the man, my gun still trained on him. Called to Beatriz.

"Oh my God," she said. "Reynaldo, are you okay?"

My heart rate was slowing, and I thought of what Saul would say if he saw this. His expressions were colorful and voluminous, and this scenario would have been labeled "a fucking goat rodeo." It was a term he used in situations where others often say the word "clusterfuck."

"I could have shot you," I said to the man.

I turned to Camila, who was standing by the door. "Get packed," I said. "Four outfits for you. Four for your Nana. I don't care if they match. Two minutes."

"Daddy, are we—"

"No questions," I said, my voice urgent.

Beatriz glared at me, and I turned to the drunken man. "Get lost."

I walked inside. Helped Camila fill a large purple duffel bag with four of everything: underwear, shoes, sweaters, and hats. As we packed, I requested an Uber.

A few minutes later, we locked up and walked outside. Beatriz's friend Reynaldo was nursing a cut on his face and mumbling something about police brutality. I saw the car pull up and didn't even turn to them. I needed to be heading west by 7 a.m. to meet the team in LA.

I had done some prep work from the air about where I could hide Camila and Rosa. And while I didn't have family in the area, I was not without help.

As I'd traveled to the private terminal in Dallas three hours ago, I'd called Mitchell Hannick. Back in 2012, I'd saved his son from a horrible man, hell-bent on abusing and killing the boy, just like he had done to three others in the family's neighborhood.

There is a permanent bond you make with someone whose life you save. That bond is even stronger when you save the life of their child. For years, Hannick's family had invited me to bring Camila up to their ostrich farm, which was located west of Lorida. I'd never taken them up on the invite, but had shown Camila pictures of the place on her iPad.

Inside the Uber, I placed the duffel across our laps.

"Miami International?" the driver confirmed.

Camila's eyes went wide. She leaned into me, the fluff of her Hello Kitty sweater soft against my neck. "Are we going on a plane?"

"Yes," I said to the driver.

Twenty minutes later, he left us at Concourse D, and we walked into the airport. We took the elevator to level 3 and boarded the people mover over to the rental car center.

"We're not going on a plane?" Camila asked as we walked out to a car I'd reserved.

"Why don't you take a rest, honey?" I said. "No more questions tonight."

"Are we safe?" Camila asked.

I propped her up on a booster in the back seat. "We are," I said. "Because we were smart. But we have to continue to be smart. Your dad is chasing a bad man. Until I catch him, I want you to be somewhere where he can't find you. Where no one can."

"I have school tomorrow," she said.

Camila had entered preschool a year early and was now in third grade. "This will be a vacation from school," I said. I got in the front and started the car.

"Are we going to a beach?"

"You live near a beach." I headed out of the lot. "That wouldn't be a vacation."

"Is it a farm?"

"Yes."

Her eyes got big. "The farm on the internet? With the ponies and ostriches and emus?"

I glanced through the rearview mirror at Camila. "Do you know where your grandma is staying tonight?"

"She had me take a picture," Camila said. "To give to Miss Beatriz."

Camila handed me her iPad, and I saw a photo of a Hotels.com reservation. Rosa was staying at a Motel 8 south of Lake Apopka, in a suburb called Winter Garden.

I explained to my daughter that I was not going to be there when she woke up on the farm tomorrow. That her grandmother would arrive by late afternoon. Until then, she had to listen to Mr. Hannick, who was a friend of her dad's.

"Okay," she said, her voice quiet.

I got on 95, and Camila started to fade. Before she fell asleep, she began to speak more slowly, the fatigue coming.

"Daddy," she said. "We were going to read the book about magic. But now you're gonna be gone."

"I realize that," I said, eyeing her through the rearview mirror. "I'm sorry."

She nodded in acceptance, and something inside me stirred. The fact that Camila gave in so easily. What that implied about me as a father.

"Did you bring the magic book with you?" I asked, thinking about my own youth. The absence of a father in my life.

"Uh-huh," she nodded.

I slowed the car and pulled over, off the state highway and onto a side road.

"Let me have it," I said, and she grabbed the book from her bag.

"There was once a magical girl," I said, opening the inside page. "But not any ordinary magician. This girl was special. She had a gift that no one else had."

Camila's eyes fluttered. She yawned and stretched her socked feet.

"It wasn't a gift you could see with your eyes, like magical vision. She wasn't born with the knowledge of certain spells."

After another two minutes, I glanced up and saw that Camila was asleep. I placed the book back in her duffel and glanced at my phone, studying the directions to Hannick's farm—and from there to Rosa's hotel. After committing every detail to memory, I removed the SIM card from my phone and turned Camila's iPad off.

Was I being paranoid? Overly cautious? I was a professional, tasked with profiling crimes that others could not solve. Yes, it was unlikely this killer had the eyes and manpower to cross the country. But I couldn't take any chances with my daughter.

As I drove, I thought of a different road trip and another time.

When my mom relocated west, Anna and I agreed to drive the remains of her stuff out from South Carolina. Mom flew east to meet us, and the four of us, including an eighteen-month-old Camila, hit the road.

Along the way, Anna insisted on buying a onesie at every stop, and my mom took pictures with Camila in each one. In Atlanta, the onesie read "I drool red and black," along with a Georgia Bulldogs logo; in Jackson, Mississippi, it was, "Jackson is calling and I must go."

When we arrived in Texas, Anna found the last one, a pink number that read "Sorry about the spit-up. Thought I saw an Aggies fan."

There were good times between me and Anna, right up until everything went south, and some of the best parts were watching her and my mother together. They were from different worlds, but they somehow connected, the same way Anna and I had. When the fraud occurred, my mother was in disbelief.

Time had slid by while I was reminiscing. I looked up and saw the exit for Hannick's farm. I pulled off, moving along a dirt road until I got to the gate, where he buzzed me in.

The ranch was open to the public on weekends, and the four large animal pens had colorful painted signs with instructions explaining the behavior of the Italian emu and the American quarter horse. Two other signs were for wayfinding and directed patrons to an area with brush-tongued parrots and restrooms.

At the main house, Hannick stood out front, a series of security lights on the porch turning the night to dusk. Hannick was white, in his late forties and fit, with small gray eyes and a goatee.

"Agent Camden," he said as I got out of the car. Still addressing me as he did during his case.

"Mr. Hannick." I put out my hand. "I appreciate you taking Camila on such short notice."

Hannick waved me off. He wore blue wind pants and a green John Deere T-shirt. "I told you on the phone. You have unlimited credit with us."

I grabbed a sleeping Camila from the back seat of the car and lifted her petite frame over my shoulder. Her body was warm as I followed Hannick inside and laid her down on a bed in his spare room.

"You're sure this is okay?" he asked. His accent rang of central Oklahoma, where he'd grown up. "Her waking up, I mean, and you being gone?"

"No," I said. "I'm not sure."

Hannick stared at me, waiting for more.

It was an open question when Anna first got pregnant—whether I was capable of an emotional relationship with a child. But as Camila began to speak, I noticed something odd. She inherited many of my personality traits. But she was a better person by those traits being weakened and mixed with those of my wife's family. She was funny like Anna. Thoughtful like Saul and Rosa. Clever like my mother.

"I've evaluated other options," I said, "and being here is the best one. Her grandmother will arrive by afternoon."

I kissed my daughter on the head and turned to Hannick. "Camila's favorite stuffed animal is a giraffe called Manny. It's in her bag. She'll eat Cheerios all morning, and she's going to ask a lot of questions. About the farm. The animals. Rosa will know the rest when she gets here."

"All right," he said.

"Keep her from calling anyone. Same with Rosa."

Hannick nodded, but I needed to be clear with him.

"The whole idea of her being here is to keep her safe." I looked around. "You guys, too. If Camila and Rosa don't call anyone, no one will know they're here. I'll be back in a couple days."

Hannick nodded. He understood the kind of monsters I hunted. I thanked him and turned without thinking for another moment. Got on the road.

Rosa's hotel was ninety-two miles south of Ocala, where Anna was housed. After the prison visit, Rosa would have to stay at the ranch, too. I drove back toward the highway, but before I got on, I knew I needed to check in with PAR.

I headed ten miles east of the ranch to a nearby police station. Pulled into the parking lot and put the SIM card back in my phone. On the chance anyone was tracking my signal, this would offer no connection to Hannick's ranch.

I called up Cassie.

"Hey," I said.

"Hey yourself. Where *are* you?"

I glanced around the parking lot. "Florida."

"You went home?" she asked. "What for?"

A patrol car pulled into the lot, and the officer eyed me. I hesitated before answering.

"I need to trust someone, Cassie," I said.

"I know," she replied. She paused before going on. "I can tell you're trying. And that's what matters."

"I'm with Camila," I said. "I didn't want anyone to know where we were. Just in case . . ."

Cassie was silent for a moment. But she knew me well enough to follow my logic. "Gardner," she said finally. "Who in PAR would put Camila in jeopardy? Me? Frank? Jo? C'mon. I mean, Richie's new. We don't know him. But the rest of us are fam."

"I see that logic," I said. "But—my mind doesn't work that way. And I screwed up, years ago."

"Well, is Camila safe? You stash her somewhere?"

"I did."

"So when are you coming back?"

"The morning," I said. "I'll be on the first flight to LA."

"Okay," she replied. "Then I'll say something to the group. But I won't say Florida. I'll make something up."

"Thank you."

I put the rental in reverse. I had to get back on the road.

"Gardner," Cassie said. "We all care about you. You know that, right?"

"I'm aware of this."

"*I* care about you," she said.

"I know you do."

"Be safe."

I didn't answer. And after a moment, I heard a dial tone.

I removed the SIM card again and got on the highway, headed to Rosa's hotel.

At the Motel 8's front desk, I badged the night manager and received Rosa's room number. I knocked firmly until she came to the door in a satin robe with purple flowers on the side. The same one I'd seen her wear at her home.

"Gardner," she said, surprised. Rosa had pronounced cheekbones and wavy hair that flowed past her shoulders. She'd lost twenty-five pounds in the last two years. The effect enhanced the curves of her hips, which were evident in the thin robe.

"Camila is fine," I said.

"I know. Beatriz called me after you left. She told me you punched out her friend."

I held out a paper with written directions from the Motel 8 to the prison. And from the prison to Mitchell Hannick's ranch.

"Camila is already at this . . . farm?" Rosa asked, not taking the paper from me.

"She is," I said. "And I need your cell phone. To make sure no one can track you."

Rosa's face was uncertain. "I always treat you like family, Gardner, because my Saul is looking down on me. He would want that, especially for Camila."

"I know you do," I said. "I wouldn't ask you this if I didn't think your safety and Camila's was in question."

Rosa's gaze moved past me, toward the highway. In the dim light outside the hotel room, her cheeks were shiny from some skin product.

But the shift was purposeful. She couldn't look me in the eye.

"Do you remember a case Saul and I worked?" I asked. "A man who was killing women in south Florida? This particular man was using women's body parts to fish with."

Her dark brown eyes returned to mine. "Yes."

"Saul and I thought the guy burned alive. But we were wrong. He was killed four days ago by a man who is hunting serial killers. The same man threatened my family. Which means he threatened you and Camila."

Rosa's squint turned to a scowl, and now she made full eye contact. "My Saul worked in the Bureau for twenty-five years," she said. "You know this, right, Mr. Big Brain?"

This was my nickname when Rosa was not happy.

"Yes."

"Do you know how many times he had a conversation like this with me? About my own safety? About him putting the family in jeopardy?"

I shook my head.

"Never." She tapped her index finger on my chest. "Never, Gardner."

I went quiet.

"Say something." She poked me again. "Feel something."

I swallowed. Looked up. "Saul was my friend, too. I only want—"

"No," Rosa interrupted. "Not about him. Don't talk about him."

I looked down. What could I say?

"You make it so hard for me to forgive you," she said. "But I keep praying." She reached into the pocket of her robe. Handed me her phone and ripped the paper with the directions from my hand.

"Thank you," I said.

She turned and slammed the door.

CHAPTER SEVENTEEN

I ARRIVED AT THE ORLANDO INTERNATIONAL AIRPORT AT 7:09 a.m. and filled out the Armed Passenger Authorization form outside of Terminal 2. Received my paperwork and headed toward Gate 73.

At the gate, I presented the same form to the agent, alerting him that I was carrying a firearm. The flight was half empty, and the agent put me in first class.

I reclined my seat and took out my laptop. Began constructing a timeline of the events I'd pinned down in the murders of Tignon and Fisher. A timeline that extended back before we'd been pulled onto the case.

WEDNESDAY, NOVEMBER 18

Kenny Smith visits his brother Barry Fisher in Otero Prison. Smith offers his brother a year of free housing, which Fisher accepts.

WEDNESDAY, JANUARY 1

Smith gets a call from a real estate investor using the name Creighton Emwon. Emwon is interested in buying the rental home for cash. Smith is intrigued and sets up an appointment for the next day.

THURSDAY, JANUARY 2

Smith tours Emwon through the rental home. He informs the investor that if he's interested in purchasing, he needs to make an offer quick as his brother is moving in soon. Smith never hears back from Emwon.

FRIDAY, JANUARY 3

Barry Fisher receives a visitor in Otero Prison named Maurice Merlin. A priest.

THURSDAY, JANUARY 9

A man visits the home of Beverly Polis-Tignon, only to discover that Beverly has already passed. It is not clear if this is our killer.

MONDAY, JANUARY 13

The body of a man known as Bob Breckinridge is found dead in a home in Ashland, Texas, killed the previous day. Locals print the man and discover he is Ross Tignon.

MONDAY, JANUARY 13—SAME DAY

Barry Fisher walks out of Otero Prison in New Mexico a free man, after serving thirty-one years. The same afternoon, Fisher is most likely abducted from his brother's rental home.

TUESDAY, JANUARY 14

I arrive in Ashland, Texas. An hour after I leave Jacksonville, Frank also leaves. He heads to New Mexico, where the body of another serial killer has been found, this time Barry Fisher, cut up and bagged. Frank arrives in the evening and locks up after sending the index finger to Albuquerque for an ID. The time between kill and discovery is speeding up.

•   •   •

I sat back from my laptop. The flight attendant had left a bottled water for me, along with a packet of miniature Oreos, covered in chocolate.

Eating the cookies, I divided my thoughts into two parts: *curiosities* and *to-dos*.

Under the heading *curiosities*, I contemplated the killer's movements from New Mexico to Texas. There was a gap in time between his presence in Texas on the ninth, when he possibly visited the Polis home, and his reappearance in Ashland, Texas, on the twelfth, when he killed Tignon.

A similar gap existed in New Mexico. A tour of the home on January third. Then nothing for six days.

Did Mad Dog commit other murders in between, which have not yet been reported? If not, what did he do in the intervening time?

Or was he a local to one of these areas—Texas or New Mexico— and had simply gone home?

An image flashed in my head. Something I had noted the first day of the investigation but had not seen as relevant.

Tignon had a small bar cart off of his kitchen, with four bottles of liquor and ten highball glasses. Two of the ten glasses were turned face up, and each had a half inch of water in the bottom.

I took a mental note of this, then moved on to the to-dos.

The first related to how Mad Dog had located Tignon. My original theory was that he had received some information from Beverly Polis-Tignon. But now that I knew Beverly had passed a year earlier, this was impossible. So how did the killer find Ross Tignon in Ashland, Texas?

Shooter would be following up with Alex Polis, Beverly's brother, about the cameras mounted on trees near the family's summer home. If we found a suspicious man on camera, it might officially connect the two cases.

I closed my eyes for a moment. Felt a bump and opened them. The LAX tarmac appeared out the window. Twice in two days I had cat-napped on a plane.

Passengers were getting up from their seats and gathering their belongings. I inserted the SIM card back into my phone and turned it on. Before I could stow it in my pocket, Frank was calling.

"Where are you?" he asked.

"LAX," I said. "Do I need a car?"

"No."

"Westwood?" I said, referring to the location of the main federal office in Los Angeles.

"No," he said. "But not far from there. I'll text you an address."

Murder number 3.

"Who is it?" I asked.

There were nerves in Frank's voice. "Maybe you want to look at the scene first."

"Enough with the bias avoidance," I said. "I'm the lead. Let's hear a name."

"Ronald Lazarian," he said.

Ronald Lazarian *wasn't* a convicted killer; he was on trial for a series of murders. But it was a foregone conclusion that he was guilty. He'd admitted as much himself.

"Gardner," Frank said. "The murder happened in a federal safe house. With two of our own on the job watching him."

The side door of the plane had opened, and passengers were muscling each other for access to the aisle.

PAR had been called in to consult on the Lazarian case last year. Specifically, Cassie and I. Which now connected one of the three murders to our unit. Two of the murders to me personally.

"Text me the address," I said to Frank.

A third murder didn't surprise me. That's why I'd sent Shooter, Cassie, and Frank to LA. But a specific image was forming in my head.

"Lazarian," I said to Frank. "Is his head cut off?"

Frank let out a deep breath. "Yeah," he said. "Most of it."

CHAPTER EIGHTEEN

THE TAXI LEFT LAX, HEADING TOWARD THE CITY'S WEST side, and I texted Cassie to see how far along she was with her study of which agents had checked out the old case files. Now that we had a third dead serial killer, it would make things both simpler and more complex. Cassie had to see who had checked out this third case, which would limit the field. But if agents had been watching Lazarian and somehow missed a killer entering a safe house, it also meant there was more information to take into account.

A message came back from Cassie.

> On the phone. Send you a note in twenty.

As the taxi wound its way through side streets, I mentally reviewed every detail of the Lazarian case.

Over a period of seven years, four women from Southern California had been brutally murdered by Ronald Lazarian. The victims were blond and young: twenty-six, twenty-nine, thirty, and thirty-three. Each had been stabbed at least thirteen times.

Cassie and I had received the Lazarian file on a Monday morning last February. We'd pored over the police data, but LAPD had done an exhaustive job already, and we uncovered nothing on the first day.

On our second day, though, I woke with an idea. By lunch, I had found Cassie and Frank in the small kitchen near the PAR cubes.

"HVAC repair," I said.

I remember them staring at me. Then I explained that each of the buildings our victims lived in had been built between 1961 and 1968. "The heat pumps from that era," I said, "their fail rate has been phenomenal in the last eighteen months."

"Heat pumps?" Frank repeated.

"Fail rate?" Cassie said.

"Each attack came one week after a cold spell," I explained. At least, "cold spell" as defined by LA locals, where fifty-eight-degree daytime weather demanded a heavy jacket.

"An HVAC workman is the most likely person to intercept all four women," I said. "He wears coveralls, gloves, and disposable booties. This is also how he leaves no evidence. No prints."

When we passed on these details, local police balked at the specificity of the occupation and the examples of the failed heat pumps, which I listed by brand. But two of the jurisdictions compared notes anyway and landed on a name: Ronald Lazarian.

Lazarian was thirty-one and owned a heating and cooling business, one that specialized in historic buildings and retrofits. The other two cities discovered that Lazarian was also the vendor in *their* victim's buildings. They put him under surveillance and followed Lazarian into the unit of a woman who scraped his face—just as police rammed down her door.

The taxi slowed on Goshen Avenue in an area of LA that backed up to retail on one side of Wilshire Boulevard and, a block later, morphed into the beginnings of the suburb of Brentwood.

"There's a bunch of cops up here," the taxi driver said. "Not sure if I can get you any closer."

I paid him and got out. My phone buzzed. A text from Cassie.

> Need another few hours on agents. As for our team, Jo and Frank are clean. Still looking into Richie. Lil sus though. His personnel file is encrypted.

"Sus" was a big thing with Cassie. Anything out of place was sus. Someone weird was sus. I'm sure before she met me, *I* was sus. Suspicious behavior was everywhere.

Still, she was using Marly's access to do this study, and there was no reason Richie's file would be encrypted to Marly Dureaux.

Moving under the outermost piece of yellow tape, I badged an LAPD cop. He examined my ID and pointed. A quarter block had been closed off, and I walked down the center of the road. Up ahead, I saw the apartment complex where the murder must have occurred. It was the one building where the yellow tape turned inward and blocked sidewalk access.

As I arrived, I saw the place was in the shape of a U with a central pathway and units spread left and right over two stories. At the back of the property, two metal gates led out to an alley. I counted sixteen doors total.

The what and why of this being a safe house was immediately clear to me. Apartment 211 was at the back, second floor. Its position allowed a quick look down at the other units. A smart federal unit would sit an agent outside as observation.

I also noted that the back left second-floor unit had its own stair-well, which led to what was probably a gated garage out back. If I was correct about that, it meant the garage was below the unit, meaning no one could hear when someone was in the safe house unless you were inside the locked garage that came with it. And, from my initial glances left and right, apartment 211 appeared to share just one common wall with any other unit.

As I got to the bottom of the stairwell, cops were clearing a path. At the top of the stairs, Shooter and Cassie stood beside Frank. Richie had been left in New Mexico.

"Looks busy," I said.

I'd counted twenty-two uniforms so far, and I recalled a statistical analysis of crimes where over eighteen cops signed in at a scene. Those cases resulted in a twenty-nine percent decrease in conviction.

Shooter eyed me. No smile. No smart-ass comment. Sometimes what's missing is more conspicuous than what's not.

"Welcome to LA," Frank said, his voice flat.

They led me into the apartment, and from there, into a hall bath.

Inside, the body of Ronald Lazarian hung from the showerhead. A six-millimeter metal wire wrapped around the fixture before coming around the front of his neck, cutting into his throat, and holding his body suspended.

Lazarian was fully dressed in jeans and a black T-shirt, but his neck had been sliced 60 percent through.

I walked closer to the tub, visually inspecting the wire, which was slung over the fixture and came down along the underside of Lazari-an's jaw, cutting into his throat four inches below his chin. The wire had severed his omohyoid and sternocleidomastoid muscles and was buried deep in a mess of mangled skin.

The bathtub itself was striped with arterial blood spray, but no one was looking at that. Shooter's, Cassie's, and Frank's eyes were on the wall outside the shower.

The killer had used bright red spray paint.

Two phrases. One stacked atop the other.

Too slow, Gardner.

But don't worry. I got this one, partner.

CHAPTER NINETEEN

"DO WE HAVE A TIME OF DEATH?" I ASKED, LOOKING AWAY from the wall.

"TOD is between midnight and one a.m. this morning," Shooter said.

The call from Mad Dog had come in at 3:43 p.m. in Dallas, 1:43 p.m. here. Our killer had waited more than eleven hours between when he'd spoken to me—and when he'd entered the safe house.

"A local team started compiling a list of former killers who'd be likely victims," Frank said. "Lazarian wasn't even on the list. Agents were looking at parolees, mostly."

"Not anyone on trial," Shooter clarified.

"And here we have someone who wasn't yet convicted," I replied.

"A variation on the pattern," Cassie said.

Shooter squinted. "Is it?" she asked. "I mean, technically Tignon was never convicted, either."

"True," I said. "But in Lazarian's case, justice was expected to prevail."

The evidence to convict Lazarian was, in fact, overwhelming. Yet Mad Dog had not waited for the jury.

I turned and faced the body. Beside the cuts in his neck, I noticed a bloodstain in the center of Lazarian's chest. My mind shuttled through each of his victims, connecting pieces of their injuries to what I was seeing. The cut in the neck was similar to Nicole Conkert, his third victim. The wound in the chest recalled Katrina Bremer, victim number 2. I looked for some detail that could be an homage to victim number 1, but did not see any.

"What was he doing in federal custody?" I asked.

"There'd been threats against his life," Frank said from behind me. "Lazarian was in solitary at County. On a ten-minute break to the infirmary, he was stabbed."

"His attorney insisted that it wasn't safe for him in jail," Shooter said. "The county asked for assistance, and our LA office put him up here during the trial."

I gloved up and leaned my body over the tub. Someone had stuck a stopper in the drain, and two inches of reddish-black blood had collected in the basin.

"How did he get past our people?"

"The agents got a text," Frank said. "Federal agent down one block over and in need of assistance."

I turned to face Frank. "That text went out to all LA agents?"

Cassie shook her head, answering before Frank could. "Just the two junior guys on duty here. It directed them to cuff Lazarian to the radiator and lock up all the doors to the safe house."

More evidence that our killer was in or had been law enforcement. Only a Bureau insider would know which agents were on duty and how to get them to panic and ignore protocol. Only a cop would have a key to unlock those cuffs.

I turned back to the body. Ronald Lazarian's trial had gotten head-lines. His attorney had moved past the question of his guilt early on. He was getting press coverage because of a defense strategy. Specif-ically, the argument that his crimes were so heinous they could not have conceivably been committed by a sane person. It was a new ap-proach to the insanity defense, one that could pave the way for use by other wildly violent criminals.

I thought about the value system our killer was using to select his targets. The word *helper* he'd used on the phone with me.

"The phone number the agents got the text from—" Shooter said.

"It was a burner," I finished her sentence.

"Yeah."

"And where is the medical examiner?" I asked.

"I'll grab her," Frank said.

A minute later, he returned with a Korean American woman in her thirties. She wore a blue FBI windbreaker over a crime scene coverall and glasses with purple frames.

"Wendy, this is Gardner Camden," Frank said. He mentioned that he and Dr. Song had collaborated on a case six years ago.

"So *you're* Gardner?" she said, her eyes flitting from the wall to me.

She moved closer then, beside Lazarian's body. The victim's frame was primarily suspended from the showerhead by the three inches of his neck that were not yet sliced through. I pointed toward the omo-hyoid muscle. "The inside cut there is sharper than the outside. What kind of instrument would produce that?"

"A surgeon's blade," Dr. Song said. "A number twelve or four-teen."

The ME in Texas had mentioned this type of tool.

Dr. Song motioned to a particular area. "A twelve has a smaller, crescent-shaped curve. It can produce an indent like that."

"Presuming you were keeping the body suspended until I arrived," I said, "have you looked at the rest of him?"

"Quick visual only," Dr. Song said.

"You find burn marks?"

She cocked her head at me, curious. "Yeah, there's one on his buttocks."

"Like from a cattle prod?"

"Certainly could be," the doctor said.

"He's combining elements of the murders," I told my team. "Allison Fadden was Lazarian's first victim. She was subdued with a stun gun. It's probably how Mad Dog incapacitated Lazarian while the agents were gone."

"The amount of risk-taking," Shooter said, shaking her head. "He's inside an FBI safe house. He had to be aware we'd trace the call and know he was in LA."

I turned to face the ME. "Thank you," I said.

"You're very welcome," the doctor replied, staying close by my side.

I was trying to get her to leave but wanted to be careful about how I phrased things. Not like I had with Richie in New Mexico.

"We appreciate your hard work," I said, and Frank picked up what I was doing.

"We need to huddle as a team, Wendy," he said. "We'll bring you back in here in a smidge."

Song left, and I pushed the door shut behind her.

"There's a traitor among us," I said, leaning against the sink. "The size of 'among us' is the only question. I had Cassie start with PAR."

"With us?" Frank cocked his head.

"I'm pleased to report that everyone in this room has been cleared."

Shooter squinted at me. "Thanks?"

"In Texas, I theorized that our killer might've been an angry fed, based on details from Tignon's case," I said. "So when he called himself a helper, I was thinking—"

"Vigilante," Shooter interrupted.

I nodded. "Except now he's actively interfering. Sending agents one way while he goes the other. There's something larger here that we're not seeing."

I turned to Frank. I had been leaning on everyone's strengths in a way that I had seen him do. But I hadn't applied the same calculus to the boss himself. He had trained with the best profilers in the country. Given Richie's interest in unsolved cases, I wondered whether this was also part of his request to be at PAR. A chance to work with Frank, as much as me.

"Do you have a profile?" I asked. "I presume that's what you were working on in the diner?"

"Yeah, of course," he said.

He stared from Shooter to Cassie to me.

"Should I do a drumroll?" I asked, recalling Frank's question from two days ago.

"The guy's actively looking for recognition," Frank said. "He exploits others without shame or guilt. He didn't like it when you corrected him on the phone, so we know he demands deference. Feels entitled. He wanted us to call him God; he looked down on the role of a pawn. I presume he's probably felt that way his whole life. Like a pawn, that is." Frank took a breath. "He wants to be chased, Gardner. But he views it the way a parent looks at a child chasing them."

"As someone who can never catch up?" Shooter asked.

"Exactly." Frank nodded.

I knew all of this already.

"What else?" I asked.

"I imagine he was expecting to rattle you," Frank said. "In Dallas on the phone. He wasn't expecting you to be so . . . unshaken."

I'd been called worse. Unconcerned. A weirdo.

"That's why he wrote your name on the wall," Frank continued. "To get us focusing on you, as much as him. Maybe a picture of the wall leaks to the press. Right now, we're controlling the media, and I'm guessing he didn't expect that. None of his work is out there. The public can't cheer about someone killing these awful men. Someone doing what the justice system couldn't. Or talk about how we're too slow to stop him. Specifically, how you're too slow."

The information was helpful, but it didn't answer my question. How was Mad Dog getting his intel?

I needed to huddle privately with Cassie. See how far she had gotten into the list of agents who'd checked out Tignon and Fisher's files. Now Lazarian's, too.

"We need to keep this quiet," I said. "No one can find out—"

Frank held up his hand. "That brings me to the last part of the profile. Mad Dog picked Lazarian because we *can't* keep it quiet." He pointed in the direction of the street. "See those two news vans? Lazarian's attorney already put it out there that something bad happened. He's gonna hold a press conference, and a firestorm will follow. The FBI will look foolish. PAR will be called incompetent. You'll be called—"

"Then we muzzle the lawyer," Cassie said. "Put him under protective custody."

"It won't matter," Frank said. "Mad Dog will make sure it goes public."

There was a knock at the bathroom door. When I opened it, a man in his thirties stood there. He was short and balding and wore a dark blue suit that was one size too big.

"Art." Frank shook his hand. He explained that Art Koenig was the press information officer for the LA office.

"We're not making a statement," I said.

"That's not why I'm here," Koenig replied. "The media has connected the three victims."

I swallowed. I couldn't control this case. It was evolving in ways that were unpredictable and didn't follow logic.

"How?" Frank asked.

"I don't know all the details yet," Koenig said. "But a reporter from *USA Today* just asked me if a vigilante is murdering serial killers. She mentioned Ross Tignon by name, and she knows about Lazarian. Said she has another name, too."

Frank's profile was right. Mad Dog had contacted the press.

"Did she provide any other details?" I asked.

"Yeah." Koenig studied his notes. "Today wasn't her first tip. The guy reached out to her forty-eight hours ago. She thought it was a prank."

"A prank how?" Cassie asked.

"Well, Ross Tignon had burned to death seven years ago, so when she was first told that name—"

"What exactly did he say?" I asked.

"In his first contact," Koenig said, "he told the reporter it's lucky that regular people like him are standing for justice, since the FBI isn't. She researched Tignon's name. Saw he was dead. Thought the call was from a whacko."

"And the next two murders?" I asked. "What'd he say about them?"

"Oh, you're gonna love her answer there." Koenig flicked his eyes. "If we want that information, she advises us to buy a *USA Today.* The only other thing she told me is the name of the person who leaked her the info."

"Let me guess," Shooter said. "His name is God."

"No," Koenig said. "The person who called her identified himself as Frank Roberts."

Frank's jaw tightened.

I wasn't the only one the killer was playing with.

CHAPTER TWENTY

BY EVENING, TEN NEWS VANS HAD SET UP SHOP NEAR THE mouth of Goshen Avenue.

Shooter walked down to a taco truck near Wilshire Boulevard for food. As I moved out to our van on the street, I saw her returning, a cardboard box under one arm and a six-pack of Coke under the other.

I opened the door to the van, and Shooter got in first. Cassie was there, along with Frank.

Shooter flipped the top off the box, and I counted eight tacos, each covered in lettuce and cheese. Grease marks marred the cardboard, and tortilla chips were crammed all around the food.

I looked for somewhere to sit, and Shooter smiled at me. "I'll go over here," she said. "You can sit next to your partner."

Cassie rolled her eyes. "Sit wherever you want, Gardner."

"All right." I plopped down. "We got a lot of media out there. Let's talk through this. Did anyone go door-to-door yet, canvas to check what neighbors saw?"

Shooter grabbed a taco and held it over a napkin. "Two guys from the LA office did," she said, a piece of pork falling onto the floor. "Nothing from the neighbors. The attack was late, Gardner. One a.m.–ish."

"They found something, though," Frank said. "The clasp on the back gate was sheared clean off."

"So the door to the back parking," I said, pointing in that direction. "It closes, but doesn't lock?"

"Presumably Mad Dog got into the garage that way," Frank said. "From there, he's down the steps from the apartment and doesn't pass any other neighbors' units."

I nodded. The van we'd borrowed was a surveillance unit, and it had a small counter for a laptop and other equipment. I pulled my chair closer to the counter and grabbed a taco.

"Wait, can we back up?" Cassie said. "I'm still on questions from New Mexico and Dallas."

"Of course," I said. It was a good point, especially considering we hadn't met as a group since Rawlings.

"Should I get Richie on the phone?" Shooter asked.

I eyed Cassie. We'd left the rookie in New Mexico. "No, let's have him keep working," I said. "Can you speak for him?"

"Sure, no problem." Shooter took a bite of her taco and pointed in my direction. "Richie did great work on the cameras in Rawlings. There were only five or ten professional cams. So he went door-to-door. Got footage from about fifty neighbors' cameras. Rings. Nest cams. It's a lot to go through and nothing conclusive yet, but we'll get there."

"Good," I said. I turned to Cassie and Frank. "You never told me about the breakfast with Fisher's brother. What happened?"

Frank undid the third button down on his dress shirt and tucked his tie into the space. "A whole lot of nothin'," he said, getting ready to eat without spilling on himself. "The brother told us how he toured some fella around his rental house, just like he said to Cassie."

"Description?" I asked.

"Generic," Cassie said. "White guy, brown hair, twenties or thirties."

I turned to Shooter. "And Merlin? What did we learn from the priest?"

"Apparently some guy came into his church a month ago. Donated some money. Said he was friends with a prisoner in Otero. His friend was sick, and he asked the priest to see him."

"Fisher was this imprisoned friend of the guy who donated?" I asked.

"Or so he claimed." Shooter nodded. "This mystery donor told Reverend Merlin that his buddy in Otero was ready to make amends. Apologize for what he'd done."

"And the description of the guy who donated?" I asked.

"White, Merlin said. Brown or black hair."

I looked around the van. "Really?" I said. "Everyone is white with brown hair?"

"I pushed him." Shooter put up her hands. "That's all he remembers."

"So what happened?" I asked. "When the priest went to the prison?"

"Well, at first Merlin didn't want to give anything up," Shooter said. "Confidentiality and all. Eventually Merlin tells me how he took a bus to the prison. Went through all of Otero's check-in procedures, only to come up with nothing. He met with Fisher. And Fisher told him to buzz off."

"And that's the end of it?"

"Not exactly," Shooter said. "Merlin got a phone call two days later. Same guy who donated. Says he's gonna give more money. But he wants to know if Merlin was able to make it out to the prison and meet with his buddy. Merlin tells the guy he did, but sorry, your friend wasn't ready to talk."

Frank crossed his legs, and I noticed how shiny his Italian loafers were. I glanced at my own dress shoes. I had bought the first ones in the store that fit, a process that seemed efficient at the time.

"I hunted down the number that called into the church to follow up," Shooter said. "Burner. No other calls from it."

Fascinating, I thought. Mad Dog had anticipated us tracing the call and covered his tracks.

Frank popped open a can of Coke and drank. He eyed the food, but took just a single chip. Dipped it in green salsa and ate it.

I grabbed my second beef taco. Wrapped it in two napkins and laid it in front of me.

"What about the cameras on the property in Texas?" I asked Shooter, wondering if Mad Dog had covered his tracks there, too. "The ones the old lady, Dolores, told us about. Did we catch any images on them?"

"An agent from the Dallas office scrubbed that video, Gardner," she said, pulling back her hair and tying it out of the way. "The guy who talked to Dolores was a bona fide real estate investor. Went to grammar school with Beverly Polis, just like he told the old lady."

So Mad Dog hadn't gone to the Polis summer home. Which meant he'd already known where Tignon was. He'd found him some other way.

Cassie laid a soft taco out flat on a napkin and used a plastic fork to pick at the pork pieces. "You think Mad Dog was looking for an apology?" she asked. "Via the priest?"

"An apology?" I shook my head. "No, you send a priest, you're looking for a confession."

I thought of the calls the journalist at USA Today had received. The call I'd received. Mad Dog was careful in covering his tracks, but he was also being provocative. Taking chances.

"Odd A-F, if you ask me," Cassie said. "Someone expecting a serial killer to say sorry. After thirty years."

Frank nodded. "Makes you think this guy who donated money—he wanted to be absolutely sure of something."

"Yeah," Cassie said. "Like Fisher's lack of remorse."

We talked for twenty minutes more, covering the HBO writer and the daughter of the old victim, both of whom had visited Barry Fisher. I'd followed up on the CHP officer who'd found the cell phone Mad Dog had called me from. None of the three panned out with new information.

Frank stepped out for a call, and we took the opportunity to polish off the remaining food in the cardboard box. But all I could think about was how careful Mad Dog was.

When the boss came back, his tie was untucked and his jacket back on. "The press have a picture," he said.

"Of Lazarian?" I asked.

"Strung up in the bathtub," Frank said.

My mind ran through a half dozen possibilities. Had a cop leaked it? Someone from the medical examiner's office? Or had it come from the killer?

"We've been called for in person, Gardner," he said to me.

"D.C.?"

"Quantico," he said, and added that we'd make a report first thing in the morning to the director of the FBI.

An hour later, Frank and I settled into two big seats in the back of a Gulfstream at Van Nuys airport northwest of LA. I'd put Shooter in charge of LA and asked Cassie to keep after the crimes in Texas and New Mexico.

Frank took out his yellow pad, and I flipped open my laptop. I waited until we were in the air and the cabin steward had left us before speaking.

"I don't believe Richie is involved," I said. "But he checked out both files. Tignon and Fisher."

"*That's* why Cassie was buzzing him with questions in New Mexico," Frank said. He squinted at me. "Gardner, Richie was in Fisher's brother's house when the suspect called you. He was in New Mexico during the LA murder."

"True," I said. "But he had to be checked."

"And you're satisfied?" Frank asked.

I hesitated. "His files are sealed, Frank. Even Marly can't see his background prior to the Bureau. And he's got no social media."

Frank's brow wrinkled. "Has Cassie made it through every other agent?"

"No," I said. "She estimates she'll have a name in the next one hundred and twenty minutes."

"Good," Frank said. "So what can *I* help with?"

I kept an open items list. Normally I made this in my head. But since I was the lead, I had memorialized the list on my laptop.

"There are two things," I said. "First, Tignon's autopsy."

I showed Frank pictures of what looked like an *n* and a *g* on the scrap of paper that Dr. Abrieu had pulled from Tignon's throat.

"What do you make of those?" he asked.

"Well, letter and word frequency is a science, but two letters doesn't give us much to go on," I said. "Samuel Morse, when developing Morse Code, had to figure out the most commonly used letters so he could assign the simplest codes to them. He used printer's type."

"If I'm supposed to be following you—"

"The letter *n* appears in 6.6544 percent of words," I said. "The letter *g* in 2.4705 percent. You can use simple math to combine those, but what you're going to arrive at is a percentage and no information. And that's before you include proper nouns, abbreviations, acronyms—"

"So you have nothing?"

"If we had a list of suspects," I said. "I could perform analysis. Work backwards from the names. Make educated guesses at what is being spelled. Or where the paper might have come from. Right now all I have is that a killer is hiding clues on a body. Which is different than *leaving* a clue on a body. The five to zero on Tignon's chest, for instance, was not hidden."

Frank took off his gray jacket, patting down the wrinkles in the pink long-sleeve shirt he wore underneath. "You're making that distinction why?" he asked.

"Because it's possible we haven't found other clues."

"What else did you get from the autopsy?"

"The doctor thought the cuts were the work of a hunter."

"A game hunter?"

"The same," I said.

"So what's your biggest question on Tignon? You know that case better than anyone."

"Tignon got away clean seven years ago, Frank. Saul and I—we were sure he was dead. And no one fooled us."

"Except him."

"Except him," I repeated. "So that's what confounds me about Tignon. If we concede that somehow Mad Dog has access to the FBI servers . . . or is an employee in the Bureau . . . *the Bureau* didn't know that Tignon was alive."

Frank sat back and loosened his tie. "Every case has mysteries."

"To some people, maybe," I said.

Frank shook his head at me. At my arrogance.

"You mentioned two things," he said. "On your open items list."

"The other one," I said. "It's a word from the killer's call to me. *Paddock*."

"He said that referring to a game of chess, right?"

I nodded. "The word means an enclosure or a small field. So maybe the latter could refer metaphorically to a chess board."

"Like the field of play," Frank said.

"But etymologically speaking, there's no precedent for it in the English language."

The plane hit a pocket of rough air, and a memory came to mind. Shooter and I on the plane to Dallas. *Are you going to ask Frank?* she'd said. About the rumor that PAR was closing.

"What is it?" Frank said.

I was a straightforward person by nature. Unable to be any other way. But for some reason, I was avoiding speaking to Frank about this topic.

"How are we doing, incidentally?" I asked.

"Who?"

"PAR," I said. "We're heading to see the director of the FBI. Is he . . . happy with us?"

"PAR has done nothing but fulfill its mission, Gardner. Don't worry about that."

I took this in, nodding.

"You got a specific idea on *paddock*?" Frank asked. "You said etymologically speaking—"

"I do." I nodded. "In certain Middle Scots, *paddock* doesn't mean field. It means *frog*. The most famous use that survives is in the story 'The Paddock and the Mouse.' And Mad Dog called me 'little mouse.'"

"Like Aesop's," Frank said. "'The Frog and the Mouse'?"

"Similar," I said. "But Aesop was all action and no philosophy. A mouse wanted to cross a river. A frog obliged by offering a ride on his back, all the while knowing he was going to drown the mouse once he got him out in the open water. But when they're in the river, a hawk sees them fighting, comes down, and kills them both. The lesson is simple. Those who try to harm others get harmed themselves."

"Like our serial killers," Frank said.

"Yes," I said. "Except it's not that way in 'The Paddock and the

Mouse.' In the Scots poem, the two animals discuss in advance that the drowning may occur. How the frog looks deceptive. The discussion is about the difference between *appearing* virtuous and *being* virtuous. Then the two animals cross the river tied together, but the paddock betrays the mouse and in comes the bird. Same ending."

"I hope we're the bird," Frank said.

"This story may have been formative to him, Frank. He could have heard it as a child and be using it to communicate a message."

"Okay, I'll bite," Frank said. "The FBI appears virtuous to him, but in fact we're not?"

"Meanwhile," I said, "Mad Dog exercises *real* vengeance for victims. He *is* virtuous."

"So what's the message?"

"I don't know," I said. "But there's something more complex we're not seeing."

"You said that before. Some endgame he's got in mind?"

"Likely. What I know for sure is that Mad Dog is not your garden variety sociopath, and this is not Killer 101. Anyone who thinks so is not reading these details right."

Frank nodded. "I guess that's irrelevant if we can't find him."

"Exactly," I said. "And we can't find him until we figure out how he's accessing our information."

"Well, hopefully in the next one hundred and twenty minutes, Cassie'll—"

"Eighty-six now," I corrected him.

Frank shook his head and smiled. "In the next eighty-six minutes, Cassie will tell us."

"When we land," I asked, "do we go directly to the meeting with Director Banning?"

"When the big man wants to talk, yeah. Why?"

"I was thinking: what if we ignore what the director wants? If Cassie can't tell us who logged in, we go to the EAD for Tech. Stay there until Marly or Cassie lets us know who checked out Tignon, Lazarian, and Fisher's files."

Frank looked at me like I was crazy. "You know who we're meeting with, right?"

"William Banning, director of the FBI," I said. "And Craig Poulton, deputy director."

"Sure," Frank said. "But do you know anything *about* them?"

"Poulton is fifty-three. A UVA grad. He originally worked in—"

"Stop," Frank said. "There's the facts, Gardner. And then there's the color."

I used the controls to push my seat back. "So what's the color?"

"Director Banning retired. Out of the Bureau. Then the president of the United States personally plucked him to come back in."

"So he's well connected."

"'Well connected' is a guy who gets you in the back door of a great club. The president has to go through the DOJ to have a two-minute chat with a fed. Any fed, even the top one. The president flew to Banning's ranch outside of Houston. They did it with a handshake."

"Okay," I said. "And Poulton?"

The plane shimmied for a moment. "He's more of a mystery to most people."

"You don't know him?"

"Oh, I know him well," Frank said. "I'm talking about his rise to power. No 'wow' moments. No splashy cases. I worked in the same building years ago in D.C. He had this reputation for working late. Word was, the man didn't sleep. Went eighteen hours a day."

"Okay."

"Except Layla stayed in Texas my first year in D.C.," Frank continued, referring to his wife. "So I'd burn the midnight oil myself, you know? Nowhere to go except back to the rental apartment to watch TV. And you know what?"

"What?"

"My office was near Poulton's, and I'll tell ya, he didn't work late more than once a week. But he'd send emails at eleven p.m. Two a.m. Four."

"So he was scheduling his emails?" I said. "Automatically?"

"This was years ago. Back then, you couldn't do that with emails. I think he was waking up and hitting SEND. You know what they say—'perception is reality.'"

I took this in. Frank's familiarity with both men was an advantage in the conversation we were about to have.

The flight steward came over and told us she would be serving a meal of steak or salmon.

"What would you gentlemen like to drink with dinner?" she asked.

"No food for me," I said. "Just two bottled waters. The caps still on and sealed."

The woman offered an odd smile at this detail.

"You gotta eat, Gardner." Frank turned to the woman. "Salmon for him. Salmon for me. And two Cokes."

She left then. Five minutes later, she returned with our food.

I devoured the salmon and rice, thinking of my family. Of Camila on the farm with the emus and ponies. Of Rosa, arriving yesterday afternoon after visiting Anna in prison. Would she be able to tolerate a stay at a dusty ranch, far from her busy Miami life?

I felt fatigue coming and closed my eyes.

You need rest, Gardy. My mother's voice sounded in my mind. *You cannot function without rest.*

A black fuzziness shrouded my vision, and I inhaled. Exhaled. Faded into sleep.

The blackness faded, and a bright patio came into view. I stood at a hostess station, carrying a baby carrier. I looked down. Saw a six-month-old Camila.

"Can I help you?" a woman asked.

I glanced up. Behind me, I could hear the sounds of the boardwalk. A place called Muffin that Anna and I used to walk to.

"We've been waiting forty-two minutes and sixteen seconds for a table," I said.

The woman smiled at me. "Yeah, it's busy right now."

My voice remained calm, as always. "In the last nine minutes, five groups have been seated that arrived after us."

"Well, we only have so many tables and servers. It may not appear complicated, but—"

"You have six open four-tops," I said. "Three two-tops. Four tables of six. Five booths that can fit three to four people, depending on their size and weight."

"Hey," a voice said.

I looked to my right. Anna stood there, back from the bathroom. "What are you doing, handsome?" she asked.

Anna had this ability to break my focus. Sometimes she would run a finger along my face, and I could not concentrate for minutes.

Me, distracted. A strange power.

"There is a question of fairness," I said, directing my comment at the hostess.

Anna turned to the woman. "We'll be over here, and we appreciate anything you can do. C'mon, family," she added in a singsong voice to me and Camila.

She steered us away from the hostess, and Camila made a farting noise. Anna took the baby carrier and placed it on a seat. Then she moved her face close to mine, our noses touching. "Your mind is wonderful and precise, my love."

Over Anna's shoulder, I could see the hostess motioning at us. Talking with her boss.

"Look at me," Anna said. "You say that crazy detailed stuff to me next time, okay? Your ability to be perfect. Your need for details. That's not for others. I claim it all for myself. It's mine to explore. *Entiendes*?"

"*Sí*," I said. Yes. I understood.

"Gardner?" the hostess announced. The name I'd put in for our table.

"Gardner," I heard again.

It was Frank. I opened my eyes. The sun was cresting the horizon, and the Gulfstream was touching down on a private airstrip in Stafford, Virginia.

I thought of Anna. Of how she'd made me feel right with myself. With my quirks. And what I'd done to her in return.

"It was like rigor mortis set in," Frank was saying. "You were out cold. I thought Mad Dog got you in your sleep."

He stood up, steadying himself by holding on to the seatback in front of him. "This case is getting press, Gardner. Lotta media trucks in LA. Not sure if you noticed."

"There were ten," I said. "The local channels, plus two foreign language media and two nationals."

He smiled at me. "After a case goes high-profile like this, a task force is typically assigned."

Frank was talking about handing off our work to another team. To someone more polished.

"It's not that leadership at the Bureau cares any more about Fisher or Tignon or Lazarian," he said. "As far as they're concerned, good riddance to bad rubbish."

I wondered if they'd used this expression to Frank before they let PAR have the case three days ago.

"But they do care if a vigilante is doing our job," he continued. "They'll care if someone's got access to our servers. And they care *a lot* about bad press. They don't want some crime junkie podcaster solving this before we can."

"What are you saying?" I asked.

"If we're getting moved off the case," he said, "remember to keep it classy. Yes sir. No sir. Goes a long way."

I put on my blazer. "Yes sir."

CHAPTER TWENTY-ONE

A BLACK SUBURBAN WAS WAITING TWENTY YARDS FROM the Gulfstream. A driver in marine TDUs sat up front, and he hustled us onto nearby I-95. The camo'd soldier informed us that we'd be at Quantico in twenty minutes.

The director of the FBI doesn't regularly work at the training campus, which is located in northwest Virginia. His office, as well as that of the deputy director, is at FBI headquarters in D.C., on Pennsylvania Avenue, between Ninth and Tenth. The fact that Banning and Poulton were in Virginia might be a sign that a media firestorm was underway in D.C., making Quantico a more productive place to regroup. It could also mean a task force was forming, like Frank suggested.

Frank was scanning his phone for news.

"Last night's story was about how Ross Tignon escaped us seven years ago, only to get caught by this guy," he said. "This morning, it's Fisher in bags. How he got his due after being paroled five years early."

I noted the themes. Punishment. Retribution.

"The press have a picture of Fisher in bags?" I asked.

"One bag," he said. "The heart."

The Suburban exited at Russell Road, and the driver showed our IDs at the guard gate. We took the winding road onto campus, over to J. Edgar Hoover Road, and from there to the main building at 57 Bureau Parkway.

I followed Frank out of the Suburban and into the structure ahead of us. I had spent my rookie year at this location, but Frank had worked in this building for four years and knew it better.

As we crossed the lobby, I counted six black scuff marks on the floor. We got into the elevator, and I hit the button.

But as we started up, Frank hit the emergency stop, and the elevator bumped to a halt.

"What's wrong?" I asked.

Frank faced the line of buttons but didn't immediately speak.

"I need to explain something," he said. Again, hesitating. "It's, uh—"

"Frank," I said, knowing where this was going. "I'm not going to say something stupid that jeopardizes your career or—"

"It's not that," he said.

The elevator chirped a warning sound, and he turned to face me. "I don't know how this will go with Poulton."

"He doesn't like you?" I said. "Us?"

Frank was normally so smooth, but he was struggling.

"There was this conference in D.C. The last spring I was stationed here. A party at the end of the week. Layla was at her mom's, so I went alone."

The right side of Frank's mouth turned up. "Poulton's wife was there, and he was off schmoozing. Working the room. The wife and I got a shot together. Then another."

"You slept with his wife?"

"Of course not," Frank said. "But there was a moment." He hesitated. "Poulton had told her he was headed back to the office. He came to say goodbye, and we were at the bar again. I walked away, to give them some space. His wife had slid her hotel room key under my cell phone. I picked it up, thinking it was my own. Then checked my pocket."

"Poulton put two and two together?"

"And thought I initiated it. Said as much before he dragged her out of there. A month later, my boss retired, and they re-org'd the profiling group. My career stalled until I came up with the concept for PAR."

So Frank was damaged goods, just like the rest of us.

A voice came through the elevator's speaker. "Is everything all right?"

Frank pulled at the emergency button, and the elevator lurched upward. "Sorry," he said into the speaker. "I hit that button by accident."

"Ten-four," the voice said back.

"So would you have?" I asked.

"Would I have what?"

"Gone with her if Poulton hadn't come over?"

"Nothing happened."

Frank tightened his tie, and I knew I was not going to get an answer. But it addressed a question that I had been curious about.

Two things united all of us at PAR. One was Frank's pitch for a unit comprised of agents with an intellectual bent toward solving puzzles. The second was the political mistakes we'd made. Me with Saul. Shooter and that target range. Cassie and some incident with a superior in Denver.

At lunches when Frank was not around, Shooter and Cassie had speculated about the boss's misstep. Now I knew.

The doors to the elevator opened, and we got out. As we did, a vibration buzzed in my pocket. I grabbed my phone and stared at a message from Cassie.

"You got an answer for us?" Frank asked.

"What?"

"A name?" he said.

I clicked the phone off and shook my head.

In an outer office, Frank introduced me to a woman named Olivia, who told us Banning and Poulton were finishing up another meeting. She buzzed us into a room that overlooked Administration Way.

A wooden coffee table sat in the center. It was made from a thick slab of Texas black gum tree, the side of the wood three inches thick and etched with a series of shapes. Circles mostly, with crosshairs atop them, followed by a series of consonants. Atop the table were three neat stacks of paper, facing down.

The balance of the room was a seating area. I counted three parallel lines made by a vacuum cleaner and stepped carefully between the nearest two.

From a door at the far side, two men came in, neither of whom I had met. They were midconversation, and I could tell the subject was a school shooting that had occurred three days ago.

"Frank." The older man put out his hand. "It's been a minute."

Director Banning was white and stocky, in his late sixties. He was muscular with a thick head of nuclear white hair. He sported a blue suit with an American flag pinned to the coat lapel.

"This is Gardner Camden." Frank motioned at me.

"Your work precedes you, Camden," he said, shaking my hand.

He dropped into the nicest chair in the room. His chair, you could tell.

"Craig," Frank said to the man behind Banning. This was Deputy Director Poulton, the man who would soon take over the agency. The one whose wife apparently had a penchant for shots.

Poulton was younger than Banning by fifteen years, with a tall frame and dark hair spiked slightly with gel. He had sharp, craggy features and wore a charcoal suit with a burgundy tie.

"Gardner Camden." I put out my hand.

"We know some of the same people," Poulton said. "I came up in the Miami office. A few years before you."

Miami. So he knew my story.

The four of us took our places in the seating area, and I began walking through the highlights of the Tignon, Fisher, and Lazarian murders. The men listened, neither of them saying a word about a task force. Or whether PAR would be pulled from the case.

"How certain are you that the threat's from within, Agent Camden?" Poulton asked when I finished.

Was he looking for a percentage?

"I don't pursue low probability outcomes," I said.

Poulton smiled at Frank, then glanced back at me.

"The only way the perp could have known to call me at the Dallas office is if he was law enforcement," I said.

"So he's a cop?" Poulton said.

"He also had access to our victim's FBI files," Frank added. "Knew the movements of our agents in LA."

"You're saying he's a fed?" Poulton said. "Anyone? Me? You?" He fixed me with his gaze. Was he trying to inflame the situation? "Is your list *anyone* on our payroll, Agent Camden?"

"My list narrowed to two names this morning," I said. "One is a rookie in our group, Richie Brancato. Who is the newest member of PAR. But he did not check out Lazarian's files or know about—"

"No way," Banning said. "I've met that kid. The Academy. When he asked to go to PAR."

The director remembered meeting Richie? I had been number 2 in my class and never met the director. But perhaps times had changed.

"That just leaves one other name," I said. "One I found out five minutes ago."

Frank swiveled his head in my direction.

"This individual accessed FBI records on Tignon, Lazarian, and Fisher," I continued.

"Gardner?" Frank said.

"This person also knew the whereabouts of Agents O'Riley and Nguyen at the safe house in LA where Ronald Lazarian was held."

"Well, out with it, son," Banning said. "Who is it already?"

I turned to face Director Banning. "It's you," I said.

CHAPTER TWENTY-TWO

BANNING STARED AT ME, HIS FACE CONTORTED.

"Jesus H. Christ, Camden," Poulton said. "What kind of stunt is this?"

"I'm not sure how you prefer to handle this, Deputy Director," I said. "But protocol would be to remove Director Banning from office, at least temporarily while I question him."

"The hell you will," Poulton said.

I looked to Frank, but his mouth was agape.

"You're relieved of your command in this investigation," Poulton said to me.

"I would ask that you let Agent Camden explain himself," Frank said.

"Why doesn't he start by explaining himself to *you*, Roberts? You're his boss, and you obviously had no idea what he was about to say." Poulton looked to Frank, his lip twisted in a sneer. "Isn't that your job, Roberts? To control these . . . brilliant freaks who report to you?"

I was listening to their face-off, but my eyes had remained on

Banning. He had crossed the room to the desk. Flipped open his laptop. Now he was examining something on the screen.

"He's right, Craig," the director said, his mouth a wide circle.

Poulton looked over, and the room went quiet.

"Of course I've never checked out those cases." Banning pointed at his screen, exasperated. "But I'm on the screen with my case search history. And here I am, checking them out."

My eyes were on the director. "Does your secretary know your password?"

"No," Banning said.

"Your wife or children?"

"Of course not." The director shook his head.

"Jesus," Poulton said. "This is the sort of issue you bring up to your superior, Camden. You get that information five minutes ago? You bring it up five minutes ago."

"On Tuesday, I was assigned as senior lead on this case," I said to Poulton. "I received an email at 7:39 p.m. eastern standard—"

"Roberts, what's he talking about?" Poulton cut in.

"His direct report changed," Frank mumbled. "To William Banning, the director of the FBI. The same person who checked out the files."

I turned to them. "You see, then? My conflict?"

"Craig," Banning said, spinning his laptop so it faced us. "Look at these time stamps. We were in a Senate intelligence meeting for six hours on Thursday." He looked at me. "You see this, right, Camden? Even if I got a hankering to cut up some shit-bird and put him in Ziplocs, I couldn't have logged in at two twenty-one."

"You have an assistant?" I asked. "Someone who knows your schedule?"

"Olivia does. But I already told you. She doesn't know my—"

"We need to cross-reference where you were physically," I said, "with the location of every IP address that logged into your account."

"You think someone spoofed the director's account?" Frank asked. "That they're logging in from somewhere else?"

"Presuming Director Banning is innocent," I said, "it's the only possibility."

Banning let me behind his computer, and I examined the two dates when Tignon's and Fisher's files had been accessed.

January 14 was the first.

"This is the day I arrived in Texas," I said to Frank. "Mad Dog was logging in to see who was assigned the case."

Frank shook his head, almost surprised we were right. "You see any other times when he could've—"

"Two days ago," I said. "The sixteenth."

"It's how he knew you were at the Dallas office," Frank said, bouncing on his heels.

"I'm getting on the horn with Tech." Poulton stood up. "I'll get the director's password changed out, stat."

I turned to Poulton. "Operationally," I said, "that's unintelligent."

The deputy director blinked, his voice spiking. "What did you just say?"

Frank flicked his eyebrows at me. *Careful.*

"Our killer is using Director Banning's credentials," I clarified. "The worst thing we could do right now is change them."

Poulton's voice rose again. "And continue to let a madman inside our system?"

"No." I shook my head. "Tech should assign Director Banning a new ID but leave his old one active. We can wall off appropriate areas. National security."

"Easy enough," Banning said.

"You're gonna allow some nut—"

"Gentlemen," I said. "We don't have a solid lead on this guy. So Mad Dog logging in again—that's the best pipeline to him. Understand? Operationally, it's . . ."

Poulton's face was red. "Yeah, I got it, Camden," he said. "Unintelligent."

"What do you recommend, Gardner?" Frank asked.

"Have every field office ready to roll on a location," I said. "The next time Mad Dog logs in as Banning, we track his IP. Pick him up."

An IP, or internet protocol address, doesn't necessarily reveal a location. Still, it can provide a geolocation: a city or zip code from which someone was accessing the internet. It would also provide the internet service provider, who would work with the FBI to pinpoint an exact location.

The director stood up, seemingly as an indication for us to get going. "This investigation has leveled up, gentleman. If someone has gotten to my clearance level, I have serious concerns about FBI security."

"I'll put a task force together," Poulton said.

"Good," Banning replied. "Have Camden lead it. Frank, play support."

"Bill?" Poulton's face was scrunched up, his mouth almost in a smirk. "I understand we have different management styles, but I don't think anyone wants *PAR* leading this . . ."

Banning turned to Poulton. "Management style's got nothin' to do with it, Craig. You still don't understand why I put Camden on this, do you?"

"Honestly," Poulton said. "No."

"It's called vision. First, mine in picking him. Then his, in coming here and showing us some psycho's gotten into our system. *Posing as me*. When I leave this office, Craig—if I leave—you can start *your* management style. Until I retire, we do it my way."

Banning surveyed the three of us, a stoic look on his face. The FBI's recruitment numbers had run low, and Banning had put himself in an advertisement for the Bureau, one that touted his history and acumen as a profiler.

"I got a breakfast meeting to get to. This Mad Dog fella may think he's smart, but we're smarter. Am I correct?"

"Yes sir," I said.

"So let's get hands on this guy and toss the key."

Banning turned and left the room via the side door he'd come in from. When he was gone, Poulton lifted his eyes from the floor. His ears were a shade of crimson.

"Craig," Frank started to say.

But Poulton cut him off. "Sooner or later, the old man's gonna be gone," he said. "If you two fuck this up, just know that I'll set up an office on the moon so I can send you both there."

CHAPTER TWENTY-THREE

AT THIRTY-FOUR YEARS OLD, MARLY DUREAUX IS THE youngest executive assistant director of Tech in FBI history, something the Bureau desperately needed at a time when disrupting ransomware, digitally countering domestic terrorism, and breaking down online networks run by child predators were top goals.

Craig Poulton walked us over to Tech and let Marly know that the case had bumped to the top of her priority list.

"Can we set up shop here?" Frank asked. "Camp out in your conference room?"

"Like you own it," Marly said. She threw her long black hair over her right shoulder and led the way.

I didn't follow. Instead, I walked over to Lanie Bernal, the tech who had helped me track the call from Mad Dog to the burner phone in LA.

"Thanks for keeping us so busy," she said. Lanie had a dry delivery, but I suspected her comment was sarcastic.

"You're welcome," I said. "What's the latest?"

"Your guy Mad Dog didn't just access case files. He looked at personnel records, too."

"Of whom?" I asked.

"Director Banning," Lanie said.

I contemplated the contents of those records. Retirement documents. Time-off requests. Health and medical information. Write-ups of employees.

Frank and Marly walked over with Poulton, and I shared this new intel with them.

"When we were in New Mexico," I said to Frank, "you told me the director was forgetful. What was that based on?"

Frank's eyes got huge.

"I'm sorry, Frank." I glanced at Poulton. "I don't have time to wait until the deputy director is not present or in some other room."

Frank exhaled, exasperated. "A retired colleague," he said. "He went to Banning's book tour stop in Houston."

In the nine months that Banning was gone from the Bureau, the director had written a book about his time at the FBI.

"There was a Q and A," Frank explained. "My buddy told me Banning struggled to answer questions about book details, but was informative about case details. It was a subtle difference, but he thought it was odd."

"Have you noticed a similar issue?" I asked Poulton.

"Not at all," he said. "Bill's as sharp as ever. I'm working overtime to keep up with him."

I turned to Lanie, holding up Banning's schedule for the past two months, which we'd just procured from his assistant Olivia.

"How fast can your team go through IP addresses for every time the director logged in?" I asked. "Correspond with the local provider and get us a physical location for where each login occurred?"

Lanie stared at the paperwork. "Director Banning moves around the country, from office to office. Each ISP is going to require a formal request. Some a subpoena." She looked to Marly.

"Tell us what you need," the EAD said.

"Two days," Lanie said. "And four additional bodies." She flicked her eyebrows. "And Gardner Camden not standing behind me. Why don't you leave me the schedule and go find another piece of paper in some dead guy's mouth?"

Marly chuckled, but I cocked my head, thinking about Lanie's comment.

"What is it?" Frank asked.

"We have a video conference in an hour with the ME in LA," I said. "Lazarian's autopsy."

"You think there's some clue on that body?" Poulton asked. "Like in Texas?"

I stared across the row of twenty-two cubes that filled the workspace, picturing the strip of paper in Tignon's mouth.

"The five to zero was carved onto Tignon's skin," I said. "The paper was hidden inside."

Could that be part of the killer's game? One clue on the body. Another one in it? In New Mexico, Mad Dog had left us a finger to print, neatly bagged and left atop the other organs. That could be the outside detail.

"Where is Richie Brancato right now?" I asked.

"Still in New Mexico," Frank said. "Cassie had him set up in the Albuquerque office. Fisher's body parts are there, and she knew a guy who could keep an eye on him."

I rang Richie's cell. "Find me an ME," I said when he picked up. "Tell them to drop what they're doing."

"Okay," Richie said. "What am I looking for?"

The photo that Mad Dog had leaked out.

"Find the bag with Fisher's heart in it," I said.

This was the organ that Fisher himself had left in bags on the counters of his victim's houses in the 1980s.

"Okay," Richie said. "Then what?"

"Cut it open and call me back when you're looking inside. There's something in there."

CHAPTER TWENTY-FOUR

IT TOOK TWENTY-ONE MINUTES FOR RICHIE TO CALL ME back. When he did, it was on a video call.

I hit the button to accept, and the familiar look of a cadaver lab flickered across the screen. "You're on with me, Frank, and Deputy Director Poulton," I said. We were standing in the conference room near Marly's office. "What have you found?"

Richie's phone moved across the room, and our view settled on a square pewter tub, in which Fisher's heart lay.

The organ we had found in the refrigerator in New Mexico had been kept fresh by being frozen. Now, days later, it had lost its reddish luster and turned a brownish color. The arteries protruding from it looked like saggy orange rubber tubing.

"Okay," Richie said. "So Dr. Monsher here laterally sliced open each of the major arteries feeding the heart." ·

"He found something," I said.

The phone flipped, and we saw a microscope set up on a table. The side of Richie's face. He swiveled the camera just slightly. "It was inside the left anterior descending artery. A piece of vegetation, one centimeter square."

"One centimeter?" Poulton said.

We saw a petri dish. Something tiny and green in the center.

"Can you see that?" Richie asked.

"No," Frank said.

Richie adjusted the focus. "It's a piece of evergreen," he said. "Except half the size of a peanut—and paper thin."

"You're saying that was inside Fisher's heart?" Poulton said.

Richie nodded. "All the doc can say for sure is that there's no way it got pumped in there. Someone *placed* it inside the artery after the heart was cut from the body."

"Evergreen as in the tree?" Frank asked.

"Yeah," Richie said. "And there's something else . . . bugs."

"Something other than Calliphoridae?" I asked.

Calliphoridae, or blowflies, arrive on a dead body within minutes and begin laying eggs.

"Different insect," Richie said. His phone zoomed in on a second petri dish, and we saw what looked like a fly. Except the markings on the petri dish indicated the insect was miniscule. Two to three millimeters at most. Too small to be a blowfly.

"We don't know what kind of insects these are," Richie said. "But Doc Monsher thinks that they came in with the plant."

For decades, scientists have studied how insects are carried long distances, sometimes inside the husks of plants. Other times they are eaten by birds and their eggs survive undigested, spawning in the birds' own excrement.

"Pack the leaf and bugs up," I told him. "Head to the airport."

"Where am I going?" Richie asked.

"When I know, you'll know," I said. "Wherever it is, I'm meeting you there."

Richie hung up, and I turned to Poulton.

"You need an expert," he said.

"I do. But there are dozens of types of evergreens. Until we know more, I need the preeminent expert on all of them. Conifers, pine, hemlock, live oak, angiosperms, club mosses."

The deputy director glanced out at the hallway, flipping his key card in his hand. "Text me that list," he said.

He took two steps away, then turned back to face us. "You're smart, Camden," he said. "Bet if I give you forty-eight hours, you'll prove how valuable this group of yours is. And we'll have this guy in cuffs."

Was this a challenge to show what PAR could do—directly from the top?

"Absolutely," I said.

Poulton turned to Frank, who had a smirk on his face.

"It's hard to say, isn't it, Craig?" he said. "The word 'sorry'?"

The deputy director's forehead creased into lines. "How 'bout we hold apologies until we actually catch this guy."

Poulton turned and left.

CHAPTER TWENTY-FIVE

FRANK AND I SPENT ANOTHER HALF HOUR IN TECH, BUT DIS-
covered nothing more of value.

At some point we got a call from Olivia, Banning's assistant. "There's a car waiting for Agent Camden downstairs," she said.

I hung up and took the elevator down.

A kid in his twenties met me in the lobby. He was there to bring me back to the airstrip in Stafford, Virginia. To get on a plane heading west.

"Montana?" I asked as we walked out to his car, guessing where I was headed.

I recalled an article in *Botany Magazine* by a Montana State professor who studied the connection between CO_2 levels and the amount of water needed to sustain deciduous plants, specifically evergreens.

The kid nodded. "Deputy Director Poulton said he'd send you an email with a bio."

I got in the SUV.

Montana State University has an extensive agronomy farm and horticultural department. The bulk of their facilities are focused on animals, feeding, and cattle, but a small group of specialists study plant science and pathology.

Ten minutes later we were back in Stafford, and a flight engineer was refilling the same small plane that Frank and I had come in on.

"It'll be ten minutes," he said. "Why don't you wait inside. I'll come get you."

I walked into the one-story box of a structure that overlooked the private runway. Took out my cell phone to make a call.

My mother's number rang twice, and then I heard her voice.

"Hey," I said, "it's me."

"I know it's you," she replied. "The phone's got a picture of you on it."

I'd set up my mother's cell phone with a photo of me and Camila, standing together outside her nursing home.

"I'm just calling to check in," I said. "How are you, Mom?"

"I'm perfect," she said. "I was just giving advice to my nurse Flavia, who had an issue with her estranged husband. I can't discuss the details, of course. Privacy issues and such."

When she was lucid, my mother still acted like she was practicing.

"I was bragging to her about my son. Showed her pictures of Camila. When are you bringing my gorgeous granddaughter by again?"

"Well, she's in Florida, Mom. You're in Texas."

"So get on a plane," my mother replied.

"Spring break," I said. "She'll be out of school, and we'll come for a weekend."

"Then it's settled. What else is going on?"

"Just work. Do you remember the case we talked about?"

"Of course."

I paused. *Did she?*

"Well, it's mine to lead," I said. "This particular serial killer . . . I think he grew up playing puzzles, like me. He leaves odd clues. A paper in a mouth. Insects inside a heart."

"Serial killer?" she repeated, and I wondered if I'd lost her.

"Mom?" I said.

"The expression 'serial killer' is just a convention of man, Gardy. Of cops and journalists. You know that, right? At the end of the day, every killer is just a human, searching for something. Validation. Understanding."

This was the woman who raised me. Always unraveling the complexities of human behavior. Even abnormal behavior.

"It's your job to dig deep inside for that kernel, Gardy. The meaning behind the maniac."

I stared out at the airstrip. "I know," I said.

"When you do, son, be careful with it. It's a privilege to understand another person. Even an evil one."

My mother was always teaching. Always trying to instill some lesson.

And then she said something I'd heard a hundred times.

"Gardy, never use your intellect as a weapon."

The pilot waved that he was ready, and I put a hand up.

"Okay," I said. "I gotta go, Mom. I love you."

She replied with the same, and I boarded the plane. By 2 p.m. local time, I had touched down in Bozeman and found Richie in the lobby of the corporate airport, finishing up a corned beef sandwich.

"Ready?" I asked.

He dumped the remains in a nearby trash can and stood up.

A half hour later, we were escorted toward a nondescript brick building and the lab of Dr. Brent Volus on the MSU campus. A light snow covered the ground, and the weather felt like it was high thirties.

Inside the building, a short woman led us down a hallway, where multiple doors opened onto lean-to–style greenhouses. She brought us to the last one on the left and pointed inside.

The temperature here couldn't have been more different than outside. Four raised boxes of soil sat in pine containers, and the air was humid.

At the back of the space, hunched over one of the beds, was a man in his fifties. The doctor. He wore a long-sleeve denim shirt and tan slacks under a lab coat. His long, wavy gray hair flowed loosely past his shoulders.

When he saw us, his blue eyes, adorned with horn-rimmed glasses, lit up.

"Ah, the boys from D.C. Thank you, Tonya."

The woman turned and left. Volus's wild eyes and unkempt hair gave off the impression that he didn't get a lot of visitors.

"Dr. Volus." Richie pulled out his badge. "This is Agent Camden. I'm Agent Brancato. You received the pictures I sent."

"I certainly did." He pulled up two stools, and we sat around a raised pine box whose contents looked and smelled like manure.

"By the reference markers in the photo, you've got a small piece of evergreen," Volus said. "I'd bet my salary it's a *Hellebores*."

I flipped open my pad.

"Two *l*'s?" Richie confirmed, taking notes on his phone.

Volus nodded, his hair shaking as he did. He looked similar to a neighbor that my college roommate had called "that crazy hippie down the hall."

"Are you familiar with a Christmas rose, Agent Camden?" he asked.

I was seated across the box of dirt from him, and I met his eyes. "I am," I said, remembering one my mother had once brought home. The plant had green leaves and white flowers with yellow and green interiors.

"Well, your sample is part of the same family."

"So it's domestic?" I said, knowing our next step would be to trace the origin of the evergreen. Where it could be purchased or grown. This could indicate where our killer lived or worked.

"They're grown domestically," Volus said. "Everywhere. But to be clear, they're not native to this country. Hellebores grow wild in Greece and Eastern Europe."

So the plant was ubiquitous. Unhelpful.

"Richie," I said. "Could you show the doctor our sample?"

Richie took a petri dish from his bag and handed it to Volus. The glass was five inches round, and the top was sealed. The piece of greenery was a tiny spot in the center.

Volus tapped at the glass. "Now aren't you the prettiest little *Helleborus foetidus* at the dance?"

I translated the scientific name. "A stinking *Helleborus*?"

Volus flicked his eyebrows and smiled. "Someone paid attention in Latin class."

His eyes were on the second petri dish, which Richie had taken out, but not handed to him. The one with the tiny bug in it.

"And you," he said, grabbing the dish. His voice changed, as if he were scolding a dog. "You are a nasty little bugger," he said to the insect. "And we know what you eat, don't we?"

Richie side-eyed me.

"Dr. Volus," I said, focusing him.

Volus looked up, returning to his natural voice. "A smart gardener might call this guy a hellebore leaf miner." He lifted the second petri dish. "But in the scientific community, we know him as *Phytomyza hellebori*."

"This insect feeds on the leaf in the first dish?" I confirmed.

"Not just feeds on it. He digs little tunnels into the leaves of *foetidus*.

Lays larvae in there." Volus shook his head, as if describing some-thing criminal. "The larvae eat the plant from the inside out, Agent Camden."

"What's their purpose?" Richie asked. "Do they do anything . . . valuable?"

"The plant or the insect?" Volus asked.

"Let's start with the insect," Richie said.

"Well," Volus glanced around, his blue eyes glistening as if he was about to say something treasonous. "I could give you a speech about the circle of life, Agent Brancato. Tell you that all life has value. But be-tween us girls." He paused and smiled. "These little guys are just pests."

"You're an expert on *Phytomyza*?" I asked.

"When you study evergreens like I do, you have to know their pred-ators. These bugs feed on developing seeds. They produce galls, which are like warts for plants. They destroy bark, attack plants of agricultural or ornamental value. The only thing they're good for is target practice." He made his finger into a gun and pointed at the dish. "Pikow. Pikow."

And people said I was odd.

"The strip of evergreen," I said. "This is the primary plant that *Phy-tomyza hellebori* eat?"

"That's how I figured out what the plant was from your pictures."

"And the plant's use," I asked him. "Agriculturally?"

"Nothing critical."

"Why are they called stinking?" Richie asked. "Do they smell?"

"Not unless you crush them," Volus said. "They're also called dung-wort and bear's foot, depending on the area of the world you live in."

"And why *would* you crush them?" Richie asked.

"You wouldn't," I answered, "Because if you do, you'd release gly-cosides that are poisonous."

Volus turned to me. "Ding ding ding. Winner winner, chicken dinner."

While Richie was peppering the doctor with questions, I had been mentally reviewing plants used for poison. The oleander. The vinca. The periwinkle. *The hellebore.* After all, we were chasing a killer, not getting a BA in botany. Was something about the poisonous nature of this plant a clue that I was not seeing?

"Wait," Richie said. "Poison?"

"Goes back to ancient times," Volus said. "Your Latin was good, Agent Camden. How's your Homer?"

"Above average." I didn't mention that I'd memorized the *Odyssey* and the *Iliad.*

"Then you know that Odysseus poisons an arrow. He taints that arrow with hellebore."

My mind sorted this fact alongside the others. The paper found in Tignon's mouth. A poisonous plant in Fisher's heart. What did they have in common?

Volus was rattling off information. "Symptoms of the poison include vomiting. Delirium. With enough quantity, death."

Except no one had been poisoned in any of our cases. In fact, the piece of evergreen was placed in the artery *after* death, which meant the poison had no bearing on Fisher's death. Were we even supposed to find it?

"The bug," I clarified. "Poisonous or not poisonous?"

"Unrelated to the poison," Volus said. "Just a predator."

Mad Dog had told me this was a game to him. I thought about where the plant had been placed. It had to mean something.

"Dr. Volus," I said. "If we told you we found this inside a human body, what would you make of that?"

Volus cocked his head. "Like in a nose? Someone inadvertently in-haled a piece while trimming a bush?"

"In an artery in the heart."

Volus picked up the petri dishes again, one at time. "Impossible."

Richie glanced at me, his face screwed up. I understood his confu-sion. The evergreen was a strange detail. It was a connection, but on its own, it didn't seem to lead anywhere.

"How many experts on this bug and leaf are there?" I asked. "In the United States?"

"Like me? Two maybe. Three?"

"So someone would come to you or these other two," I said, "for expertise."

"Oh sure. A colleague of yours was here last year. Asking about the delivery of *Helleborus* as a poison. How it would react in the blood-stream."

Richie and I exchanged a look.

"Someone asked about the *Helleborus foetidus* specifically?" Richie said.

"Guy like you." Volus pointed at me. "Thirties. White. Brown hair."

Exactly like the man we were chasing.

"He was a cop?" Richie asked.

"Oh yeah," Volus said. "I can't remember what branch. But you guys all talk to each other, right? After 9/11, you have databases and share files?"

We heard this a lot.

"If we bring in a sketch artist," I said, "do you think you could—"

"No. Plants, I remember. People—not so much."

Volus glanced at his desk twenty feet away, and I followed his eyes. The big wooden rolltop looked out of place, set down in between two rows of soil beds.

"What is it?" I asked.

"I might have gotten his card." He moved around me, toward the desk. "This guy didn't have a piece of a plant like you two, though. He also wasn't asking your kind of questions."

"What *was* he asking about?" Richie said.

"A bow and arrow," Volus replied. "If *Helleborus* could be delivered that way."

Volus opened a drawer and dumped scraps of paper onto his desk blotter. As he did, I contemplated this new detail. No victims of ours had been shot with an arrow. And in none of the original crimes of Fisher, Tignon, or Lazarian had an arrow been used.

Dr. Volus fished through the papers before stopping a minute later. He walked a few steps away and grabbed a textbook sitting on the corner of one of the planter boxes.

He came toward us, shaking the book upside down. As he got close, a piece of card stock fell from it.

It landed on the manure, face up.

And Richie and I saw the familiar crest of the Federal Bureau of Investigation.

Not just some cop.

An FBI agent.

CHAPTER TWENTY-SIX

"BURKE KAGAN," RICHIE READ FROM THE BUSINESS CARD.

Below the special agent's name was the address of the Oklahoma City field office.

I took out my phone and shot a picture of the card. I texted it to Frank and excused myself, leaving Richie with Volus.

"Who's Burke Kagan?" Frank grunted when he answered.

I explained to him the nature of Agent Kagan's questions to Dr. Volus. And suggested that Kagan could be Mad Dog.

I heard Frank typing. "Okay," he said. "Here he is."

My phone dinged, and I glanced down at it. An official FBI photo showed a white man with brown hair and a face the shape of an egg.

"He's retired," Frank said.

Kagan looked young. Too young to be retired.

"Cassie needs to go through every case Kagan investigated," I said. "Find some connection to Tignon, Fisher, or Lazarian."

"I'll get her on it. What can I do?"

"She takes the cases. You take the man. Where he came from.

Where he is now. Why he left the Bureau. And Frank," I said, "let's keep this quiet. No one outside of PAR."

"Ten-four," he said.

When I returned to the greenhouse, Volus was talking with Richie about seasonality and the *Helleborus*. I held up my phone, showing him the picture of Burke Kagan.

"That's the guy," Volus said. "So it's cool, then? That I talked to him?"

"Agent Kagan's questions about the plant," I said, motioning at the first petri dish. "Were they focused more on its toxicity to humans? Or the bow and arrow as a delivery vehicle?"

"The bow and arrow," Volus said. "He asked about the *Odyssey*. Whether it was factually accurate."

Was it possible Mad Dog had been homeschooled? Fiction as textbook? In that case, "The Paddock and the Mouse" could have been an intro course. The *Odyssey*, the advanced class.

"So this poison that Odysseus got from the *Helleborus*," Richie said.

"It was used by the Gauls," Volus replied. "Put in arrows."

"Not just that." I pointed out. "Toxins like *Helleborus* had other uses. For instance, to poison the well water of cities under siege."

I stopped, processing what I'd just said.

If Mad Dog's goal was to punish criminals more harshly than the justice system had, he could poison the water of a prison. Take out many at once, versus one killer at a time. Perhaps *this* was Mad Dog's connection to the poison. It was not something in the past. It was a future plan.

"Is the poison difficult to extract?" Richie was asking Volus.

"Not if you know how to recognize the plant and its seeds," the doctor said. "And not if you know how to grind them up. I mean, I'm not vouching for everything in Homer. One-eyed giants and all. But poison is poison. A mortar, pestle, and some hard work—you're ready to kill."

CHAPTER TWENTY-SEVEN

BY 4 P.M., RICHIE AND I HAD ARRIVED BACK AT THE PRIVATE airfield northwest of the university where we'd flown in. A Beechjet 400A was fueling up. I stood inside a glass building fifty feet away, talking to Frank and Cassie.

"So Kagan's in Georgia?" I said. "That's where we're headed?"

"You're putting down in a place called Elliot Field in Dawsonville," Frank replied. "It's four miles from the cabin where he lives."

"What do we know about him?" I asked.

"He left the Bureau this past December," Frank said. "Retired at thirty-eight. How much time do you have to talk?"

A flight steward was motioning a pilot aboard the plane. Turning my head, I saw Richie emerge from a building where he'd been using the restroom.

"Minutes," I said. "Give me a topline on his CV."

"Burke Kagan grew up in Atlanta," Frank said. "Went to Georgia Tech. Got a master's at UGA and was in the Bureau by twenty-six."

Cassie explained that Kagan had worked for five years on a team in St. Louis that investigated bank fraud and identity theft. In 2014, he transferred to the Oklahoma City office.

"So fraud was his specialty?" I asked.

"'Was,' as in past tense," she said. "In OKC, he worked in Crimes against Children."

This was a group tasked with providing a rapid response to abuse and exploitation. They recovered underage victims of trafficking and broke down networks that promoted the production of child sex abuse material.

"Bee-tee-dubs, Gardner," Cassie said. "I applied to that same division years ago. Hella hard to break into. No one ever leaves."

"So why did he?"

"If you trust what's in his file, he got burnt out," Frank said.

His file? I considered my own. It showed no reason why I was exiled to El Paso in the summer of 2013.

The plane started up, and Richie and I began walking toward it. "Any ties to our vics?"

"None," Cassie said.

I held the phone close to my ear as I crossed the small tarmac.

"And Gardner," Cassie added. "We found no connection to Montana State, either. Frank even checked Kagan's travel requisitions. No reimbursements from the Bureau for trips to MSU."

So Kagan had traveled on his own dime to speak to a botanist about how to deliver a poison. This felt like the most damning evidence so far.

"We've got locals coming in to assist with the takedown in Georgia," Frank said. "They'll meet you at a staging area. What else do you need?"

I walked up the steps to the jet. Richie was already settling in and blowing on his hands. "Nothing," I said. "Just keep digging."

"With a few calls to OKC," Cassie said, "we could find out the tea on this guy real fast."

I laid down my bag at the rear of the plane. "First we get eyes on him," I said. "The last thing we need is someone tipping him off."

I thanked them and hung up. The jet was an eight-seater, twenty years old, with cream-colored bucket seats. While the Beechjet had a solid safety record, I recalled reading about one that had overrun a landing strip at Cleveland-Burke Lakefront Airport. That ended in an ice accident.

I put on my seat belt and watched as Richie did the same.

"I did good, right?" he said. "Getting the bug here in the petri dish? The interview with Volus?"

I nodded, reminded that Richie was a rookie, still in his first week on the job. And that he was a member of PAR, not a suspect in this case.

"You performed acceptably, Agent Brancato," I said, and Richie beamed.

I sat back and heard the Beechjet's engine roar. The killer we were searching for had a high IQ. And so far, he'd anticipated every move we'd made. Could we surprise him this time?

I texted Frank before I lost signal.

Tell the locals—nobody near that cabin until we get there.

CHAPTER TWENTY-EIGHT

FORMER AGENT BURKE KAGAN WAS EITHER A DERANGED serial killer or his accomplice, hiding in plain sight.

On the flight to Dawsonville, Richie and I reviewed a PDF that Cassie had emailed. It detailed a series of high-profile cases that Kagan had led at the FBI between 2015 and 2019.

Two abductions involved girls under the age of twelve, and both ended with rescues. A separate investigation brought down a network of operatives selling CSAM, or child sexual abuse material. And Kagan had resolved two international child kidnappings with lives intact.

"Pretty impressive," Richie said.

I nodded. Was Kagan living a double life: a savior at the Bureau—yet, in private, a dangerous killer? Or had some incident set him off, launched him on a retaliation binge against his employer?

Richie paged back through the document on his laptop. "Who is this son of a bitch?"

"Keep an open mind," I said.

An hour later we landed and were greeted by a slender white deputy named Odin Filky who drove us to a forested area five minutes away. Filky pulled his squad car off a state highway and slowed under the bough of a large pine tree.

"Assuming you two don't want anyone seeing my vehicle," he said, "we gotta hoof it the rest of the way."

We got out. The gravel road became dirt, and we followed Filky for two hundred yards to a house he described as the staging area. A pale blue Tudor set among the trees.

Inside, Filky introduced us to two cops, a bald white guy and an athletic Black woman. "Zimmer is with SWAT," Filky said, motioning at the man. "And Suco's a local lent to us from Merchant Falls, a half hour away. Apparently she's a helluva shot."

The two locals wore dark SWAT gear with their last names on patches. Filky pointed to a pile, and Richie and I began strapping on Kevlar.

Suco handed me a pair of Bushnells with night vision and pointed out the window. "To the south," she said.

A log cabin sat in a clearing. The structure was made of white pine with rustic interlocking corners. The evening air was cold, and a plume of smoke drifted up from the chimney.

"He's home?"

"Oh yeah," Zimmer said, lifting a piece of plywood atop the kitchen counter. On the board, he had drawn a diagram of the interior of Kagan's house with a red Sharpie.

"Burke Kagan's home is fourteen hundred square feet," Zimmer said, pointing at the rudimentary sketch. "From what I could see during a quick scout, it's a one bedroom, one bath."

Detective Suco leaned in. "Two points of entrance here and here," she said. "Back door leads to a porch with a pile of firewood, an array of six solar panels laid out aboveground, and two acres of woods. Behind that, it's county parkland all the way back to the interstate."

I glanced out the window at the cabin. Then back at the diagram. "Two teams of two," I said. "Zimmer and Brancato at the back. Suco and I at the front. Mr. Kagan is connected to a series of murders, and the Bureau is feeling some heat on them."

"You want this by the book," Suco said.

"To the letter." I glanced from the locals to Richie. "If anyone has an itchy trigger finger, tell me now and stay here."

Zimmer looked to Suco and Richie, then back at his floor plan. "The last bit of light dropped over Pine Mountain before you got here," he said, "so we're good to go at any time."

"What about hazards?" I asked, moving through my mental checklist on raids. "Dogs? Family members? Booby traps?"

"Full preraid reconnaissance was not practical," Zimmer said. "But I got close enough for a dog to start yapping, and none did. From what we understand, Kagan lives alone."

"Communications?" I asked.

"We have four walkies," Suco said. "We can use hand signals to get over to the cabin before turning those on."

"Good." I turned to Zimmer. "I'll give one tap on the mic before I knock. You hear me say 'go' or tap a second time—you break down the rear."

This was a particular strategy in disorienting a suspect, especially in a small space. As a perp opens the front door, a rear entrance is kicked in. The suspect turns, hearing the noise. The team at the front takes him down.

When everyone was clear on our approach, Richie found the PDF of the warrant Frank had emailed over. He took out his phone and began a recording app to read aloud the details written on the affidavit. This was a new policy that many branches of law enforcement had adopted, mostly to avoid raiding the wrong home, which happened more times than we liked.

We strapped up. When everyone was ready, I headed north with Detective Suco. Richie turned toward the south with Sergeant Zimmer.

I moved slowly around a hedge of ironwood, weaving west and east of the tree trunks. When we reached a clearing, Suco and I sprinted across an open stretch of twenty yards before coming to a dense grove of pine trees.

We slowed along the side of the cabin, our bodies hidden in the dark.

"Ready?" I mouthed to Suco.

She gave an okay signal with her hand, and I turned on my walkie, tapping once on the mic.

Then I stepped onto the porch and banged on the oak door. Per procedure, I shifted my body to the left of the molding. Behind me, I could hear Suco breathing.

The door swung open. The man standing in front of me was 5'11" and white.

"FBI," I said, my hand on my Glock. "Please step outside, sir."

The man's eyes moved past me and landed on Suco. He wore a flannel and jeans and had two days' growth of beard on his face, in a mix of brown and red shades. In his right hand was a Sweetwater 420 beer bottle.

"Are you Burke Kagan?" I hollered.

My right hand was at my waist, equally ready to pull my Glock as to signal the walkie for Zimmer and Richie to bust down the back.

But Kagan just smiled.

"The good ol' FBI." He took a swig of his beer. "This isn't about those office supplies I took with me when I left the Bureau, is it?"

CHAPTER TWENTY-NINE

BURKE KAGAN SURRENDERED TO US AND WAS SEATED, cuffed in front, at a three-by-six pine table in his dining area. Behind him was a wood-burning stove, alive with a fire.

I'd made the decision to tell Kagan nothing until a preliminary search of the cabin was complete.

"You wanna give me an idea of what you're looking for?" he asked.

I glanced over from where I stood in the kitchen. "You read the search warrant?"

"I've seen a million search warrants, bud." Kagan tapped his fingers nervously against each other, and the cuffs clinked on the table. He had a hyper demeanor and spoke in quick bursts. "Any of them worth their salt are over-reaching, purposely vague, and say nothing about your investigation. Am I gonna find something different if I read this one?"

I didn't answer him, my eyes scanning the kitchen. Four empty bottles of Thirteenth Colony sour mash bourbon whiskey lined the molding below the window.

I'd assigned Richie and Suco the task of searching the place, using a methodology where each one inspected a specific area while I remained in a central zone, acting as what's called "the finder." As Suco and Richie located anything relevant, I made a record of it, thereby centralizing all evidence discovered to one person, who can testify in court.

Zimmer, meanwhile, stood sentinel three feet to my left, by Kagan.

I turned to the ex-agent. "You didn't seem surprised to find armed officers at your door, Mr. Kagan. Were you expecting us?"

Kagan's eyes shifted from the bedroom to me. "It's a dangerous country, I guess. Armed people are everywhere."

My brain was recording the number of times Kagan's foot tapped the ground. I passed two hundred and sixty and kept counting.

He turned sideways on the bench and faced me. "If there's something specific you're looking for, I'd appreciate the courtesy. I think I've earned it."

"Found something," Suco hollered.

I walked into the bedroom. There, laid atop a wooden bench, was a seventeen-inch crossbow.

"You said to look for weapons of any kind," Suco said. "I assume this counts."

I examined a quiver full of arrows beside the bow. Neither Richie nor I had told Suco or Zimmer about the *Helleborus*. Or the questions Dr. Volus had fielded about an arrowhead as a delivery vehicle for poison.

I turned to Suco. "I need you to bag that quiver. And do so without touching any of the individual arrows. You understand?"

"Copy on that," Suco said.

I gloved up and brought the bow out to the main area. Laid it on the dining table.

"Are you a hunter, Mr. Kagan?"

"Sometimes."

His voice was not the same as the man who had called me at the FBI two days ago, but that was not unexpected. I had arrived in Georgia assuming the chances were fifty-fifty that Kagan was either Mad Dog or his helper.

"Do you own a mortar and pestle?" I asked.

Kagan squinted. "A mortar and pestle?" He cocked his head at me. "That's what you want to know?"

"If there's any ground-up poison in this cabin," I said, "I'm giving you a chance to tell us, before anyone else gets hurt."

"This has gone far enough," Kagan said. He stepped toward me, and Zimmer took him by the wrist. Spun his body against the wall of the house.

"Another one," Suco hollered.

She came out with a black case in hand. Flipping it open, I inspected a second bow. This one had a custom paint job, with camo covering everything but the bowstring.

"A Scorpyd Aculeus," I said. "Four hundred and sixty feet per second with a draw weight of a hundred and eight pounds. The fastest crossbow on earth."

"Lawyer!" Kagan's voice was muffled against the white pine of the cabin's wall. "Put me in a squad car. Lawyer. Now."

Richie came in from the back door of the cabin, where I'd sent him to search the grounds. He glanced at the two bows, and our eyes met.

I nodded, and the detective steered Burke Kagan toward the door of the cabin, to get him into a black-and-white car. My mind ran through three scenarios. Then narrowed to two. But Richie's eyes stayed on me.

"What is it?" he asked.

Normally, I would've been happy with what we'd found, but Kagan's demeanor was off. The sarcasm when we first pounded on the door. His silence a minute earlier. And now this, him requesting to be placed in a squad car?

"Innocent people," I said to Richie, "when accused, become defensive and angry."

"The guilty ask incriminating questions," Richie said in response.

Which Kagan had not done.

"Agent Camden?" Suco said.

"Let's say you were chasing a case off the clock," I said to the rookie. "You bring it to me, but I don't believe in it. What do you do?"

"If I thought I was right?" Richie shrugged. "Probably keep looking into it on my own time. Until I could convince you otherwise."

I mentally flipped through the highlights of Kagan's employment. Six commendations in 2018. Then retired in 2019.

"Kagan's exit interview was conducted in D.C.," I said. "Not with his unit sup in Oklahoma City."

"Does that mean something?"

"The job of a unit sup is kind of like a handler in the spy business," I told him.

"Trust goes both ways." Richie responded. "You don't let me look into that case after hours—it means you don't think much of my judgment on other cases during the day."

I nodded at Richie. "Kagan was a smart-ass when we got here. Then jittery. Then misunderstood. Now he's silent?"

Richie waited but said nothing.

"Have you ever read a transcript of a disgruntled employee?" I asked.

"No," Richie said.

"Well, they're disgruntled because they're still emotionally invested. The two things are necessarily tied together."

I thought of my transfer to El Paso. Of what didn't show up in my own personnel file.

I walked out to the porch. Kagan stood with Detective Suco. Zimmer was moving his squad car over from the staging area.

"Change of plans," I said. "Detective Suco, please bring Mr. Kagan back inside."

Suco nodded, steering Kagan back toward the cabin.

"You didn't give me my phone call yet, pal," Kagan said. "Everyone heard me ask for a lawyer. This could shoot any case you got to shit."

Curious.

Kagan couldn't turn it off. Thinking like an agent.

"You haven't been arrested yet, Mr. Kagan," I said. "That's when your right to a phone call begins. You know that."

He flicked his eyebrows at me. "And the handcuffs?"

"Take them off," I said to Suco. "Mr. Kagan and I need to have a chat."

She uncuffed him, and Kagan massaged his wrists. Richie passed me and made eye contact. *I hope you're right*, he mouthed.

I closed the door behind him, leaving me alone with the suspect in his own cabin.

Was he a disgruntled fed? Or Mad Dog's helper?

"Have you ever heard of the Kalahari San people?" I asked.

Kagan shook his head, sitting down at his dining table.

"They collect the entrails of an African beetle called *Diamphidia nigroornata*. The larvae contain a toxin that's poisonous. The tribe uses bone-tipped arrows coated in that poison to hunt."

"Is that what you think I'm doing? Hunting someone with beetle larva?"

I shook my head. "The San tribe is twenty thousand years old, Mr. Kagan. As anthropologists studied them, they speculated that they didn't just hunt animals that way. Humans were killed, too. This means that poisoning by arrow is one of the oldest forms of murder by weapon.

Much older, incidentally, than the *Odyssey*, whose author we assume died in 701 BC."

Kagan's eyes got large as I referenced Homer.

"You found something," I said. "And no one would listen."

Kagan shifted in his chair. "And you're what?" he asked. "My pal? You're gonna make everything okay?"

"You worked in the Bureau long enough to know that's not going to happen," I said. "But you also worked there long enough to know that you can get pulled into something. And you are definitely getting pulled into something."

Kagan blew air out through his nose. He moved over to the sink and poured himself a cup of water.

"You found a pattern," I said.

"One no one cared about. I'm guessing someone important has been shot with an arrow? *Helleborus foetidus* on the tip? Some congressman?" He hesitated. "Hell, the president maybe?"

I evaluated how odd his statement was, relative to the crimes at hand.

"Several men are dead," I said. "But none by arrow." I focused on the phrasing that followed, knowing I had not yet cleared Kagan. "Three men of *disrepute*."

"Disrepute?" Again he snorted, turning. But something about the word caught his attention.

"If you want me to trust you, you need to show me the file," I said.

"What file?"

I stared at Burke Kagan without flinching. He knew Mad Dog. But not in the way I'd assumed two hours ago. Not as a partner.

"The one you keep here somewhere. You open it up at night and wonder."

Kagan glared at me, but there was pain under that look.

He glanced out the window at the flashing lights from the squad car. And I knew I was right. He had some lead on our killer. Something he'd investigated. Some file no one knew about.

Mad Dog had been feeding us evidence. Paper in a victim's mouth. A bug in a heart valve. It was a game to him, and the details meant something we hadn't yet figured out.

But Burke Kagan existed on his own track. Cassie and Frank hadn't found any files he worked on that connected to our case. So if Kagan was investigating something off the clock that was tied to these murders, it was new evidence that no one knew about.

Including Mad Dog. Especially Mad Dog.

If the evidence had to do with a *Helleborus*, it might be the first slipup that Mad Dog had made, feeding us this bug and leaf, not knowing another agent had been looking into it already.

Which could crack our case wide open.

"Please," I said to Kagan.

He glanced out the window at the squad cars, then back at me. "I want this place cleaned up and my bows put back. No bullshit about them being evidence in some crime when they're not."

"Done," I said.

"And when you catch this son of a bitch, I want to be credited in the win."

"You'll be on the podium," I said. "Right next to me."

"Okay," he said. And he began to tell me a story.

CHAPTER THIRTY

THE STORY BEGAN WITH A FAVOR KAGAN HAD DONE FOR AN ex-girlfriend.

"This was back in 2017," he said. "Her cousin's body was found in his truck on the side of Interstate Sixty, north of Tulsa. Do you know where that is?"

"Osage County," I said.

"That's right, just east of there. A town called Clarence."

"What was her cousin's name?" I asked, taking out my notebook.

"Dorian Pickins," Kagan said. "The cousin was a piece of crap with a sheet two pages long, but he was family to her, and you know how that goes. She's dating an FBI agent. Thinks we can pull any file. Get any cop to talk."

"You coordinated with local police?"

"There were three of them," Kagan said, the cadence of his speech as fast as Cassie's. "Clarence is about eight hundred souls."

"And?"

"They said Pickens ran out of gas. While he waited for a tow, he sat on the back of his truck's open bed. Had himself a heart attack or a stroke."

"Well, which was it?"

"In that town, there's no autopsies going on for three-hundred-pound white dudes who eat barbecue every day."

I nodded. "So you believed the story?"

Kagan put up his hands. "It seemed plausible enough. I did some due diligence and talked to Pickens's friends. When I did, I found out that his dog Rufus was missing. His buddies said he always had Rufus with him, so I drove back out to where his car had died."

"You found the dog?"

"Dead in the forest, twenty yards from the interstate. He might've been bit by a wild animal. Maybe ate some berries. His nostrils had dried foam in them."

"This was when in 2017?"

"Last week of June," he said. "And that was the end of Pickens. A year goes by. I stop dating that girl, and I forget about it. I'm doing a takedown on this smut peddler in a place called Hackell, right over the Arkansas border, and I'm in a diner after the bust. That's when I overhear two cops talking about a guy whose car died on the side of Ten. His front hood was open, and he had a coronary."

"When?" I asked.

"Mid-May 2018," Kagan said. "These two cops are talking about how the world is a better place without him. I think—here's another dead guy on the roadside. And he's an asshole, just like Pickens. Assault charges left and right. But he had family in the mayor's office. Every time he got arrested, the family got him kicked."

"You drive out there?"

"And I found nothing," he said. "Just a random arrowhead by the roadside."

"An arrowhead?" I blinked. "Why would that even feel relevant?"

"It didn't. Honestly, I thought it was cool looking. Tossed it in a bag in my glove box. A week or two later, I'm bored on a job, and I start a search on the computer. All I have is two guys who are shitheads, both found with heart attacks on the roadside."

The slight similarity to how Mad Dog had targeted serial killers struck me. Could this be the place from which our killer had escalated? Had he seen himself as judge, jury, and executioner from the beginning? Did he just begin with lesser offenses than serial murder?

"How did you approximate the . . . shithead factor?" I asked. "When you did the search?"

"Past criminal records," he said. "And I got two hits."

"In addition to Pickens and the guy in Arkansas?"

"Exactly."

"Any arrowheads?"

"None."

"So what made the two records come up in your search?"

"Roadside heart attacks," Kagan said. "I looked further. Both coroners noted that the men had defecated upon death."

"That's not uncommon in coronary infarctions."

"Which I know," Kagan said. "Except one of the coroners had this fit of sneezing. Then she vomited. Same thing happened to her in medical school, and she knew what it was."

"She tested the body for poison?"

"*Helleborus* is violently narcotic," Kagan said. "The dried powder has nasty purgative powers. Botanists have used as little as two grains as an enema. Or to induce vomiting. I go out to my car, grab the arrowhead, and have our lab test it. Not officially. Just a favor from a buddy."

"It's positive for the plant's poison?"

Kagan nodded and leaned back. His dining area was lit with a series of light bulbs that hung down on black wires from the log ceiling. A metal wagon wheel was affixed to the wall above the couch.

"These cases," I said. "You inspect the bodies?"

"Long gone by the time I got there," Kagan said.

"There must've been photographs in the case files."

"These are three- and four-person police departments," Kagan said. "Not small towns, Camden. *Tiny towns.* No medical examiner. Mortuary employees who double as the county coroner. And guys no one cared about. In one case, there were two photos of the body. In the next, one."

I took this in, my mind running through the data.

"If you're wondering if the bodies had arrow holes in them, the answer is that one of them might have," Kagan said. "The ME in Hackell described a puncture wound in the thigh that was smaller on the anterior side, with a similar wound on the posterior."

"An entry and exit wound," I said.

Kagan nodded. "I went to our local ME in OKC and asked her about arrow wounds. She said that if an arrow misses a bone or artery, the hole can close in on itself in as little as two days. Leaving almost no trace if you weren't looking for it. Apparently happened in battlefields all the time in the eighteen and nineteen hundreds."

I remembered Shooter telling me that the arrow had killed more individuals than any other weapon in history.

"But if it's tainted with hellebore," I said, "it doesn't matter if it's a through and through. The poison is in the system."

"Bingo," he said.

"And the other cases where there were no pictures? What about case notes?"

"In one other file," Kagan said, "a guy had a wound, but they didn't think much of it. He lived off the grid and worked outside. Hunted.

His arms and legs were apparently all scraped up, like he'd been in the bramble."

"So you have four roadside deaths that you suspect are tied to this plant. What do you do?"

"I go to Gene Bercini, my unit sup, and lay it out. He says to me: 'What you got are four deaths in three jurisdictions. One in Texas. Two in Oklahoma. One in Arkansas. But you have no weapons. You have no suspects. And other than one clear poisoning, the others have natural CODs.'"

"And this isn't your job," I said.

"Oh, that was a whole separate conversation," Kagan replied. "How if I had extra time to work, there were always more pedophiles to chase."

"What about your sick coroner?"

"Yeah, Gene thought that was hilarious. A sneezing fit by a doctor in one state and a piece of stone I found a month after a natural death in another."

"You figure out what the victims had in common?"

"The answer was nothing," Kagan said. "Except they were all shit-heads. So I reverse engineered it. If this killer is motivated to take out shitheads—how does he learn these people are, in fact, shitheads?"

"Smart," I said.

"I looked at newspaper articles they were in, stupid things they wrote online. Crimes they got charged for. One guy stole five hundred bucks from his church. The other crimes were violent, but not prose-cuted. There's some record of their misdeeds, in newspapers and the like. But nothing to tie to a killer . . . I ran dry."

"No leads?"

"None. Until one night I noticed something," Kagan said. "The cities the deaths happen in and what's going on at the time. There's a seasonality. Artisan craft fairs, gun shows, hunting shows. Kind of a circuit in that area."

"The arrowhead," I said.

He nodded. "Survivalists make them from anything. Cans, glass, old spoons. But old-school arrowhead design . . . it's a real specific process."

"Flint knapping," I said, referring to the classic trade of shaping a piece of flint, obsidian, or quartzite into an arrowhead.

Kagan's eyes widened. "Exactly. So I'm bringing this piece around to these fairs. And a couple guys tell me—they know of this hunter. He travels in a white RV and sits outside half the night, chipping away with a two-inch piece of PVC filled with copper. Apparently he could make what's called a perfect hundred-degree hertzian cone."

"And that's what yours is?" I asked. "The one from the roadside?"

Kagan nodded.

"They give you an ID on this guy?"

"Brown hair. Midtwenties. They told me he was from Texas."

"Based on what?"

"He wore a blue and red striped hat with a pump jack on it. Reddish outline."

Houston had lost their football team in 1996. "A throwback Houston Oilers hat?"

"From what they say, more like an actual vintage one."

"You go back to your boss with all this?"

"Don't even get me started," he said. "It was a waste of time."

"So what then?"

"I bought some bows. Went to each roadside location and started testing."

"You mean testing where a shot could've been taken from?"

"Oh yeah," he said.

"And you think what? That this arrowhead guy is disabling their cars so they go dead or run out of gas, then shooting his victims in a leg or an arm? They seize up, and he comes down from the hill, collects the arrows?"

"That was my working theory."

It seemed like a lot of work for one man.

"Maybe the arrowhead I found," Kagan said, "fell out of his pocket. Or it came loose from the arrow's shaft and he couldn't find it. Anyway, at this point, the season was starting back up. The craft circuit. I was excited."

He got up and refilled his water. "I got to two fairs," he continued. "One in Fawn City and the other in Deggville. No flint knapper. No white RV. No roadside deaths."

He finished the water in one gulp, his back to me.

"What happened?" I asked.

As he turned, his demeanor changed. The hyperactivity was gone. For some reason, the shift made me think of my mother. Her lessons about empathy. About noticing suffering.

"Mr. Kagan," I said. "If there's anything I can help with, I will try."

His eyes moved down to the table, and he spoke at a slower pace. "I'm focused on this arrowhead case at night," he said softly. "Traveling weekends. I missed something."

"Missed something how?"

"A case I was on for the Bureau." He looked past me. "We were chasing a guy, but I was focused on this damn fair in Tulsa." His voice shook. "This monster abducted twin eight-year-olds. He gave them Borax mixed with grape juice."

It made sense now, why Kagan's exit interview was done by corporate, instead of his own unit. His own colleagues didn't want anything to do with him.

He returned his gaze to me. "Bercini let me leave quietly. But my time with the FBI was over. I moved back in with my mom for a while. Then came here."

I eyed the line of sour mash bottles along the kitchen window. Thirteenth Colony was a boutique distillery south of Atlanta. That bourbon was 105 proof and smooth.

He came here . . . and drank.

Kagan pursed his lips and turned away from me, holding back tears. "The Bureau was my whole life," he said. "I never got married. No kids."

He turned back to face me. "I could've arrested this son of a bitch pedophile if I was focused on my job. But I was off in Tulsa chasing a ghost. A ghost no one gave a shit about. Who was killing a bunch of people who were horrible anyway."

He walked over to a cabinet. Opened it. Inside was a manila file three inches thick. He laid it down in front of me.

His white whale, hidden away still, just like I thought.

Kagan wiped at his eyes. "Find Arrowhead," he said. "Prove I'm not crazy."

On the front of the folder, Kagan had hand-drawn a *Helleborus* plant, carefully shaded its leaves with marker. Was it possible that he'd been chasing the same suspect as us, back in Mad Dog's warm-up years, before he took on serial killers?

And if so, why had Mad Dog fed us this plant and bug? Was it arrogance? Or did it mean something?

Standing up, I opened the door, wanting to get some fresh air inside the room. Richie and Suco were standing ten feet from the porch, talking in the dark.

I considered Shooter and her knowledge of weaponry. Under that smart-ass veneer was an expert in traditional firearms, even recreational gear, like bows. She would know how someone could taint an arrow, what distance they would have to shoot it from, the ways it could pierce the skin and become toxic.

I turned back to Kagan. "You know we have to hold you until we confirm this?"

He nodded, but didn't speak. Richie and Suco made their way inside.

"Detective," I said to Suco. "Can someone stay here? Consider it a temporary house arrest while agents in Quantico make some calls?"

"Of course," she said.

Kagan remained seated. Since he'd brought up the dead children, his entire posture had changed. His shoulders slumped like a man who'd been beaten.

CHAPTER THIRTY-ONE

WHEN RICHIE AND I ARRIVED AN HOUR LATE FOR OUR flight to D.C. from the Atlanta airport, we learned that it had been delayed by two hours. Fortunate, I thought.

After we made it through security, we split up. Richie went looking for food; I headed toward the gates. Getting off the train at A, I stopped in a store to buy a neck pillow. My head was pounding.

When I pulled out my wallet to pay, something by the register caught my attention.

My Life at the Bureau, the front of the book read. Below the title was a picture of a much younger William T. Banning in a dark FBI windbreaker.

A salesman rang me up, and I headed out, just in time to see Richie get in line at Starbucks.

"No food?" I asked.

"Nothing good open," he said. "You want anything here?"

"Two waters," I said. "I'll be at the gate."

I put down my bag at a seat near A-31 and opened Banning's book. In fifteen minutes, I had speed-read the first nine chapters, which detailed the director's rise through the FBI.

A shadow passed over me, and I looked up to see Richie, who handed me the two bottles.

As I grabbed them, one of the waters slipped into my lap, knocking the book to the ground. It fell open to an inside page, three or four sheets in.

My Life at the Bureau, the type read in two-inch-tall Times New Roman. Below that was five inches of blank space, then Banning's name and the publisher's logo.

I stared at the page.

The probability was 6.6544 percent. But higher than that. Since it was a two-letter sequence.

"Agent Camden?" Richie squinted. "You okay?"

"Director Banning went on a book tour in December," I said. "Frank had a buddy who used to work at the Bureau and saw him speak in Houston."

"Yeah, we know that."

I grabbed the book. Turned to that inside page—three or four sheets in—where an author puts his autograph.

I scribbled the signature 'William Banning' on the paper.

Then I ripped the page out of the book. Strategically tore a scrap of it out and handed it to Richie. "The paper in Tignon's mouth," I said.

Richie unfolded the tiny piece, staring at the *n* and *g.*

"The word was Banning?"

"There was only one tour stop," I said. "The Bureau asked Banning to hold off on pushing the book until he retired again. But this bookstore had already presold copies."

Richie was squinting at me. Holding on to the strip of paper. "How the hell did you figure that out?"

"You helped," I said. "You knocked the book out of my lap. With the waters. I saw the signature page and . . ."

Richie shook his head, incredulous.

"The director signed a book for him, Richie," I said. "You see what that means, right? Mad Dog *met* Director Banning. At the bookstore in Houston."

I picked up my bag and glanced at the Delta Airlines desk nearby. A uniformed woman stood behind it.

"I'm going to Houston," I said.

"Okay. What about me?" Richie asked.

"Head back to Jacksonville. Fill in Frank. Volus and the plant. Kagan and Arrowhead."

I grabbed my bag and started walking. But I saw something in Richie's eyes as I turned. The excitement of a discovery. And my response—to send the rookie home.

A rich life is full of people, Gardy. Not facts.

I flashed to my final year with Saul. Promise seemed endless. Success for me came fast.

But then Tignon. Anna. Saul.

I turned back to Richie, grabbing Kagan's file from my satchel.

"You joined the least admired and least respected team in the Bureau," I said.

Richie's eyes pinched together, a confused look.

"But the most talented," I continued. I tossed the Arrowhead file to him. "*You* start in on this. Not me. Get PAR together and dissect this thing. Everyone in the same place. Jacksonville, tomorrow."

"So we're gonna rehabilitate PAR's image?" he asked.

I smiled just slightly.

Youth.

"I'll be back by tomorrow afternoon," I said. "Get going now. Find something."

CHAPTER THIRTY-TWO

I FOUND MURDER BY THE BOOK ON THE CORNER OF BISSON-net and Morningside in Houston, just southwest of the city center. The mystery bookstore's signage was in the shape of a novel, opened up and turned sideways, running the length of the storefront.

Inside, a register sat behind a curved wooden counter eight feet from the front door. An attractive woman with shoulder-length red hair asked if I was looking for something in particular.

"The owner," I said, glancing around the store before settling on her again. I had perused the staff photos on the website. "Are you Mc-Kenna Jordan?"

"In the flesh." She smiled.

I showed her my badge. "Is there a place we can speak privately?"

Jordan led me toward the back of the store, and we stepped behind a curtained area. The same hardcover filled two library-style rolling book racks. Little slips of paper protruded from the inside covers of each book; the front featured a silhouette of a man, set against a fiery sunset. The book's title, *The Evil Men Do*, was designed into the silhouette.

I fished out my copy of Banning's book. "This is about William Banning," I said. "The director of the FBI."

"Sure." She smiled. "We had a great event here with Bill."

"A suspect in a case attended the director's event at your store," I said. "Received a signed book from him."

"Oh my God," she said. "Is Bill all right?"

From somewhere in the back of the store, a dog barked.

"He's fine," I said. "Do you oversee these events?"

"John and I were traveling for business that day. One of our sales associates, Freddie, covered Bill's night. I can find him if you'd like?"

I nodded, and she moved into the stockroom.

While she was gone, I wandered over to the far side of the store. An open space held thirty chairs, set up in six neat rows. To the left was a card table covered in black fabric.

"You the feeb?" a voice asked.

I spun around to see a short white man in his forties with curly brown hair and a green cardigan. Under it, he wore a denim shirt and an olive clip-on tie.

"Gardner Camden," I said.

The man seemed to be waiting for more, so I badged him. "Special Agent. FBI."

"Freddie Fanda." He put out his hand. "Specialist. Crime fiction."

"Director William Banning held a book event here on December seventeenth," I said. "I understand you oversaw it."

"Yeah, good guy, Bill." Freddie nodded. His right hand drifted down and adjusted his tie. "Personally, I'm not opposed to a domestic spy organization." His blue eyes glistened. "Just wanna throw that out there."

His delivery was odd, the words coming out in seemingly unplanned spurts.

"The FBI is not a domestic spy organization," I said.

"Of course not." He winked at me.

"Can you walk me through the night Director Banning was here?"

"It was pretty straightforward," Freddie said. "Bill got here at around half past six. Our usual event coordinator, John, was gone, so this was my time to shine." He touched his face nervously. "You know—press the flesh with the big names." He put out his hand again. "Freddie Fanda. Murder is my specialty."

I didn't shake it.

"Do authors come alone?" I asked. "Or does someone from the publisher accompany them?"

"Coupla the older successful ladies come with an escort," he said. "Your Patricia Cornwell types."

"And Banning?"

"He flew solo." Freddie shrugged, then added, like a humblebrag, "Guess technically I was his wingman."

I waited for more, and Freddie moved out of his daydream. "I got him a water," he said. "Then he signed about a hundred preorders. Fifteen minutes later, the event started."

I pointed at the table with the black cloth. "The authors sit there?"

Freddie nodded. "Bill read two or three pages. Then the audience asked questions."

"How big was the crowd that night?" I asked, getting to the crux of why I was there. "Were these chairs all full?"

Freddie grunted, smiling. "Well, it wasn't like Michael Connelly Day when they're shoulder to shoulder, you know?"

"Banning's crowd was much smaller?"

"Everything on this side of the store is on wheels, Agent Camden. So if it's Daniel Silva or MC, it's like 'everything must go!'" Freddie made a noise as if pushing furniture across the store. "Like a Black Friday Sale, you know?"

"And Banning?"

"Bill was from Houston and was the head of the FBI, so . . . it was a draw. Maybe fifty in attendance. McKenna said you think one of them is your suspect?"

"It's possible," I said.

"How about you feed me some deets." Freddie leaned in, using his hands as he spoke. "You help me. I help you. A little collab, like the kids say?"

I squinted at him. "Is there something you know, Freddie, that you're not sharing with me?"

"No no no." He shook his head, a nervous smile forming. "You're not following me. All we do here is read . . ."

I squinted, and he enunciated his words. "*About. Murder.*" He flicked his eyebrows. "Savvy now? We're kinda murder experts . . . like you."

"Right," I said, my eyes scanning the balance of the place. "There are no cameras in the store?"

"We record the back entrance. Store exterior. Mostly for car theft."

I wondered about receipts from that night. "The people who get books signed," I said. "Are they required to buy the book here?"

"They're supposed to," Freddie said. "Once in a while a guest sneaks into line with a book they got off Amazon."

If I was right about Mad Dog, he would pay in cash. Still, to be safe, I could have Richie go through the receipts from December seventeenth.

"What about pictures?" I asked. "Publicity? Social media?"

"Oh yeah," Freddie said. "I mean, I took some, but it's kind of John's thing and he was gone, so I didn't post. I didn't want to step on his toes. He can be particular."

I waited, but Freddie just stared at me.

"Freddie," I said. "Can I look at the pictures?"

"Oh. Yeah. Sure." He pulled a phone from his pocket. Began paging backward. "Did you wanna see Michael Connelly Day?"

"No," I said. "I do not."

Freddie kept paging along, stopping and smiling. "This is a good one." He showed me a selfie of him in a pink shirt. Atop it, he wore a black apron with the words "the husband did it."

Before I could complain, he paged one more over, and I saw Banning. He wore a collared blue shirt and a sport coat. The shot was taken over someone's shoulder in a crowd. Like Freddie had mentioned, all the chairs were full.

I considered fidelity. Of testing one fact I already knew.

Frank's buddy had told him that Banning had struggled to answer questions about the book, but had talked at length about specific cases.

"Mr. Banning," I said to Freddie. "Was he able to answer all the questions asked of him?"

"Oh yeah, he did great," Freddie said. "I mean, there was a guy kinda monopolizing the Q and A. We get that sometimes. He kept circling back to the same question. Like, 'Why did *these* cases make it into the book and not others?' The author's friend finally jumped in. Answered a few of those."

The author's friend. That had to be the retired Bureau guy Frank knew. Banning must've known him, too.

"This friend was an older man," I confirmed. "A retired agent?"

"It was an agent all right, but not old," Freddie said. "And not a he."

I blinked.

"A woman?"

"Yeah. I spoke with her after," Freddie said. "She mentioned she was staying at the same hotel as Banning. I assumed they had business in town."

I described Olivia, his assistant, but Freddie told me the woman was younger and Asian American. "Can I take a look?" I said, pointing at Freddie's phone.

He handed it over, and I swiped right. On the screen, I saw Banning motioning at the crowd, as if calling on someone.

"The man asking those questions," I said. "Can you recognize him in any of the audience pictures?"

Freddie looked over my shoulder, using his finger to move back and forth while I held the phone. He made a ticking noise as he worked, t-t-t-t-t, like a processor cranking through data.

"Him," he said finally.

The man stood in the autograph line, his head turned away from the camera. From his jaw and neckline, I estimated that he was in his twenties. He had freckled skin and brown wavy hair. The rest of the crowd looked older, fifties and sixties.

"In the Q and A, he was asking about Sam Little," Freddie said. "Do you know who that is?"

Samuel Little was one of the most notorious serial killers in American history. Also one of the least celebrated, in terms of publicity.

"Of course."

"There was a back-and-forth about interstate killers," Freddie said. "Their absence in Bill's book."

Banning's book covered the early history of the FBI. The big cases. Samuel Little had evaded capture by crossing nineteen state lines. Which Kagan's arrowhead killer had done as well.

"The FBI agent," I said to Freddie. "Is she in any of these photos?"

Freddie found her, and I stared at the picture. It was no one I knew. I paged to the next photo and saw the brown-haired man talking to this female agent. Again, the camera angle was from behind them. The next picture showed her grabbing a laptop.

"You think this man is your suspect?" he asked.

"I'm not ruling it out. Did you post these photos anywhere, Freddie?"

"Not really," he said.

I glanced up. "Freddie?"

"*I* didn't post anything, but this woman who was here . . ."

"The agent?"

"Different woman," he said. "She comes to the big author visits and puts up videos online. Has a fancy thing for her iPhone with a gyroscope. I didn't realize I was supposed to tell her to buzz off. We don't allow people to record in the store."

"But she recorded?" I confirmed.

"Yeah," Freddie said. "I screwed up."

Freddie pulled up the woman's website on my phone, and I watched her video. It was set to a piece of music, but amateurish and unedited. There were no good shots of the brown-haired man, but the 360-degree spin-around included the moment when the female agent took out her laptop. The agent punched in a code, and a program opened.

Was this how Mad Dog had gained access to the FBI servers? By playing back a fan's video in slow motion?

I remembered a seminar I'd attended in Miami. The topic was human intelligence, and the keynote speaker had recounted fourteen incidents in which companies spent in excess of ten million dollars on security, only to be penetrated by a human talking too much. Telling secrets in public. Or leaving their password on a Post-it.

But the possibility opened up more questions than answers. One, wouldn't Mad Dog have gotten into this other agent's account, not Banning's? Two, his first kill had been Tignon. There was no information on the FBI server on Tignon, anyway. We'd thought he was dead.

Freddie's voice broke into my thoughts. When I looked up, he was paging through his photos again. He zoomed in on one of them.

"You know how I told you I could help?" he said. "Collaborate? And you gave me that look? Same one as you're giving me now."

Freddie pointed across the store to a shelf marked AMERICAN AU-THORS. Above it was a framed painting of a woman, draped in a red sheet and holding a revolver. "That shelf is exactly six feet tall. And here's your guy standing by it." Freddie motioned at the picture on his phone. "He's turned away, but I'd say he's five foot ten and a half."

Walking over to the shelf, I lined it up with my own height. Freddie was right.

"Thanks, Freddie," I said, my voice tepid.

"You're not seeing it all." Freddie pointed toward the ceiling. A tiny round mirror, five inches in diameter, was clipped to the top of a bookcase. "I said we didn't have cameras, but we use other measures to prevent shoplifting."

I glanced at Freddie's phone again. In the upper corner of the photo, a visible slice of the store mirror contained part of a face.

"Don't you have software that can take a piece of that picture?" Freddie asked. "Fill in the rest?"

"Yes," I said. We had tools at Quantico to extrapolate a composite of Mad Dog's face from the features visible in the reflected mirror.

I turned to Freddie.

Just because you have all the information, Gardy, doesn't mean you have all the answers.

"Freddie Fanda," I said, putting out my hand to shake. "Murder expert."

He adjusted his cardigan and blushed. "Just don't tell everyone I did it for the man. I have a reputation to uphold."

I gave Freddie my email address and watched as he sent me each photograph in the highest resolution possible.

After three sequential serial killer murders, it had been sixty hours with no new crimes. Mad Dog was out there, waiting.

But he didn't know what we'd learned from Burke Kagan and Freddie Fanda.

He didn't know that in a few hours, we'd have a picture of him.

CHAPTER THIRTY-THREE

IN A TAXI ON THE WAY FROM THE AIRFIELD TO THE JACK-sonville office, I rang up Deputy Director Poulton.

"Banning was in Houston with another agent," I said, and described the woman in the bookstore.

"Well, he rarely does one thing at a time," Poulton said. "He was probably handling some agency business while pressing the book. Send me what you have on the agent."

"Will do."

"Is that all you've found, Camden?" Poulton asked.

I considered the pictures from the bookstore, which I'd sent to Marly an hour ago. If Frank was in charge, he'd wait until he had a digital composite of the suspect. Deliver his superiors all the information, rather than let it come in pieces.

"That's all for now," I said.

At the office in Jacksonville, I put my carry-on in my cube. But before I sat down, I saw an orange Post-it, stuck to my desk.

Hawks. 12 p.m.

Hawks was an indoor gun range two miles from the office. The owner, Andy, lived in the condo next door to me, and I'd brought Frank by to shoot one day.

The range had been converted from an old motel, and Andy had added a training classroom at one end to attract new customers interested in learning to shoot. When the whole team at PAR came back a month later, Andy set up a pizza oven outside the door to the classroom. That sealed the deal. The team adopted Hawks as our home away from home. A place we could eat. Shoot. Spread our case files out and brainstorm as a group. When the classroom wasn't in use, it was PAR West. And in exchange, Frank recommended the place to local cops.

Grabbing my bag, I drove to the range and found the team in the training room, our case folders laid out among platters of meatball and pepperoni pizza. I smelled gunpowder solvent, mixed in with basil and marinara.

"*There* he is," Frank announced, closing the door between the classroom and the adjoining range.

I grabbed a chair, filling in the team on what I'd learned in Houston.

"So we'll have a picture of this guy?" Cassie said. My partner was dressed down in a V-neck T-shirt and jeans. Her hair lay around her shoulders in dark, messy curls that contrasted with her olive skin.

"One or two hours," I said. "In the meantime, what've you guys got?"

Shooter sat up, pushing aside her plate. "I was just about to run through what Richie and I found on those cameras in Rawlings."

"Great," I said.

Our working theory on Barry Fisher's death was that the old man had been abducted from his brother's home, his body brought elsewhere to be cut up. Then he was transported back in the sealed bags we'd found in the refrigerator. The cameras Shooter referred to were the ones that might have caught our killer going to and from Fisher's brother's home.

"Richie and I went through footage from five dozen cameras," she said. "Two banks. One post office. But most of what we pulled was from consumer cams."

"Ring doorbells and Nest cams," Richie jumped in. "Better angles, but a lot of low-quality shit."

It was the first time I'd heard Richie curse. He and Shooter were gelling.

"You found a car driving there and back four times?" I asked.

"Not exactly." Shooter pushed the sleeves of her Duke sweatshirt back to the elbows. "So I started thinking—if I were him, would I go the same way each time?"

"No," Cassie said.

"We started cataloging every car and truck that drove near the house four times. It became this massive database. Too many variables. Too many shots of cars."

"Then you read Kagan's notes about the white RV," I said.

"Bingo." Shooter pointed at me. "There were nine RVs in the database. Five of them white. Four were families who live in the area. And then this—"

She turned her laptop, and I squinted at a picture of something dull and silver. Stuck to the metallic object was a torn piece of paper.

"Is it a sticker?"

Shooter zoomed in, nodding. The paper was aqua colored with white writing that read "ST" and "1974." To the left of the marks was a circle with a line coming down from it.

"It's from an RV's bumper," Richie said. "Most of it was peeled off."

I grabbed a plate and set a piece of meatball pizza on it.

"The vehicle didn't have plates?" Frank asked. The boss had a Coke in front of him and nothing else.

"Not that we caught in the picture on camera," Shooter said. "But RVs often have their plates higher up the back bumper. That way, they aren't blocked by whatever the RV's towing."

I nodded, and Shooter continued, "We found this RV near Fisher's brother's house four times, Gardner. And the timing looks good. Driving toward the house at 12:23 p.m. on Monday the thirteenth. Away at 1:36. Back toward the house the next day at 9:22 a.m. Then out again at 10:50."

These matched the rough estimates we'd made for Mad Dog's four trips. Two to get the body and cut it up. Two to bring it back in bags and then leave for LA.

"There's more," Richie said.

A piece of strawberry blond hair fell into Shooter's eyes, and she swiped it away. "The sticker read 'ST' and '1974,'" she said. "So we thought—"

"Established 1974," Frank said.

"Exactly," Richie said. He nodded at Shooter. "Agent Harris made some doodles to see what the other part of the sticker might be."

"The part that peeled off by the circle and line?" I said.

"I started thinking that the line was a hiking cane," Shooter said. "And the circle a stick-figure fist. Kinda like an old school graphic, you know?"

I stared at the markings. It was possible. Anything was possible.

"I researched hiking areas and national preserves founded in 1974," she continued.

"There must be dozens," I said. "The Leopold report came out in what?"

"Nineteen sixty-three," Cassie said.

"That laid the basis for wildlife management," I said. "National park growth."

"The Endangered Species Act passed in seventy-three," Cassie added.

"Sure, sure." Shooter looked from me to Cassie. "You two know all that bookish stuff and could go on for days. But you don't hunt or trap."

I stopped talking and focused on Shooter. "You've been there," I said.

She clicked forward on her laptop. On the screen was a picture of a T-shirt design from the 1980s. It read BIG THICKET NATIONAL PRE-SERVE. Below was an illustration of a hiker, made of bubble-like shapes, the fist holding a walking stick. Under the design it read EST. 1974.

"I hunted with some friends five years ago," Shooter said. "It's ninety minutes from Houston."

I stared through the glass window that looked in on the adjoining range area. "You shoot white-tailed deer there?"

"With a bow and arrow. Dressed them out in the field, just like that medical examiner described."

This was more than a piece of the puzzle about Mad Dog. More than where he liked to hunt. "If this is his vehicle, Jo, it's our first nexus between Mad Dog and Arrowhead. Them being one and the same."

"It also makes three times we've tied these cases back to Houston," Richie said. "The Oilers hat Arrowhead wore. The bookstore. And an RV, camping in a park two hours from the city."

In the next range over from ours, we heard a boom noise replacing a pop. Someone had switched from pistol to rifle.

"One more thing," Shooter said. "I called the park service. Those stickers haven't been sold in almost twenty years."

Frank squinted. "So if he's in his twenties," he said, "these other crimes that Agent Kagan uncovered a few years ago—how old was he then?"

"Late teens," Cassie said.

"So the RV was passed to him as an adult? Or he bought it used?"

"Either theory works," Shooter said. "He could've grown up in the area. His family camped there as a kid."

"In that case, the vehicle is old," Cassie said. "You got a make?"

"Quantico is crunching data based on the length of the bumper," Shooter said. "So far they say it's a class A. Thirty footer. Probably late nineties. Once they narrow that to two or three makes, they'll go through DMV databases, starting in Houston."

I finished my pizza and wiped sauce from my mouth.

"So our killer lives in Houston, and Tignon lived in Dallas. There's five hundred and fifty miles between them. How did one find the other?"

No one said anything.

I got up. Grabbed a glass and filled it with ice from a bucket on the side table.

"I don't have the answer to that," Cassie said, watching me, "but I've got something related."

"Related to Tignon?"

"It actually comes from using books." She looked at Shooter. "Being bookish and all."

Shooter tipped an invisible hat at Cassie to proceed.

"We still don't know how Tignon was located years later in Texas, amirite?"

"Correct," I said.

"I don't want to bore anyone to death, but suffice it to say that I've spent the day doing tax research. Anyone know what a ten–thirty-one is?"

"Property tax exchange," I said. "Ten–thirty-one is the section of the IRS code."

"Of course you'd know that." Cassie smiled. "Well, I followed a ten–thirty-one exchange in Beverly Polis's tax return. Worked backwards to a man named Credence Polis."

"Who's Credence Polis?" Richie asked. The rookie was wearing a golf shirt and slacks. Between him and Cassie, I wondered if I'd missed the email about casual day.

"Beverly Polis's grandfather," Cassie said. "And, as it turns out, the man who founded Ashland, Texas. Owned half the lakefront. Watersports. Bait shop. Grandpa Credence was like this OG fisherman slash real estate mogul." Cassie turned to me. "Now, you said Tignon was a big fisherman, amirite?"

"That was his passion," I said.

"I started thinking—what would *I* do if I faked my own death? Go somewhere familiar. Far from Florida, maybe. Someplace I could practice my favorite hobby."

Shooter squinted at her. "What *is* your favorite hobby?"

Cassie didn't answer. "So I followed Grandpa Credence's money," she said. "How it flowed out to his grandkids like Beverly. And their spouses, like Ross Tignon."

"You found a trust in Bob Breckinridge's name," I said.

"I did. But this may surprise you, Gardner. It was filed back in twenty thirteen. In January, specifically."

This smarted. January was two months before Saul and I found that burned body. Tignon had planned his move west before we'd even met him.

"The trust purchased a condominium in Dallas," Cassie said. "Tignon lived there for five years, presumably with Beverly. Then he bought in Ashland. After he stranded his wife at that hospital."

I dropped into my chair, pouring a Coke into my glass. Something was off, but I couldn't find the right string to pull.

I turned to Richie. "Did you find any crimes in Texas? Similar to Tignon's MO back in twenty thirteen?"

"One," Richie said. "Six months ago, in a place called Menet. Twenty-three-year-old blond woman. Her body washed up on the riverbank. Liver was gone, but locals figured the fish got it."

"And Menet is where?"

"Fifteen minutes from Ashland," Richie said. "But only five if you've got a boat."

Perhaps Tignon had returned to his old ways after his wife died. But he was smarter now. Dumped his victims in the water.

Was this how Mad Dog had found him?

My eyes moved to Frank's. "Do you have something, boss?"

"I do." He rose and stood behind his chair. "It's interesting that you and Cassie mentioned Aldo Leopold and the national park movement. People think of Leopold as a conservationist, but he was also a hunter. And a writer. Let me read you a quote."

Frank leaned down to his computer. "'A peculiar virtue in wildlife ethics is that the hunter ordinarily has no gallery to applaud or disapprove of his conduct. Whatever his acts, they are dictated by his own conscience, rather than a mob of onlookers.'"

"Oh my God," Cassie said. "He said that to Gardner. *My acts are dictated by my own conscience.*"

"That may be his mission statement," Frank said. "He's a hunter, ridding the world of bad people. But I was more focused on the second part of the quote. Him not worrying about a mob of onlookers. See, after LA, I thought Mad Dog wanted press. But everything he leaked out wasn't pointing at what *he* did."

"It was pointing at us," I said. "Our mistakes."

Frank nodded. "Then Richie said something to me on the way here today." He pointed at the rookie. "Tell them."

"I just said to Frank, a paper in Tignon's mouth? An insect in Fisher's heart?" Richie shrugged. "Those aren't clues. They're archeology. You put a normal team at the FBI on this, and you find those three months from now."

"A normal team," I repeated.

"Well." Richie smiled. "I just joined and all. And I get that you guys all got booted here 'cause you screwed up somewhere else, but . . . Listen, the way I see it, PAR is like a team of superheroes, all with different strengths. No one else would've gotten this far, this fast."

"You think Mad Dog's got a bigger agenda," I said. "That these were the breadcrumbs someone was supposed to discover later, after he completed some endgame."

"Does that sound too lofty?" Richie asked.

"Not for this guy," Frank said.

"He's also gone silent," Cassie said. "By tonight, it'll be three days without a kill. Almost four days since he's logged into Banning's account."

My phone dinged, and a picture came through. The digital composite, based on the bookstore photo: a Caucasian man, estimated at twenty-five years old, with wavy brown hair.

"Well. If this guy attended Banning's book launch"—I passed the phone around—"then he's most likely from Houston. We know what he hunts. And we might know what he drives."

I looked to Shooter. "Jo, what's our realistic timeline on that RV? I imagine in a state like Texas—"

"There's thousands," she said. "Right now, we're searching digitally. We can knock on doors, too, but either way . . . three days."

Three days was an eternity on a case like this.

"And we won't go out to the public," Richie asked. "Why?"

"We've got a blind spot," I said.

The rookie looked around for an explanation, and Frank obliged.

"Motive, kid. We have no idea why, and we have no idea why now."

These were the two big questions about Mad Dog. Why this mission? And what started him on it?

"If we drive him out," Frank continued, "we might be sending him on another murder spree."

Richie nodded, but I could tell he had something to say.

"Go ahead, Richie," I said.

"Nah."

"No one's gonna beg you, rook," Shooter said. "If you've got something, let's hear it."

"There was this work," Richie said slowly. "I was doing it before the Academy. And during. Took me three summers, going through data from the Bureau."

"This was the same study where you looked at Tignon?" I asked.

"Not just Tignon. I looked at every major case in Bureau history. When I was done, an analyst at Quantico took the project to some think tank. They've been building it out ever since."

I studied the rookie. Was this why his file was sealed? Had he developed some methodology the FBI deemed valuable?

"Let's hear about it," Frank said.

"It's a new approach to profiling," Richie said. "Instead of looking at killers as organized or disorganized and developing likely traits of the offender, it studies the connection between each offense and the offender."

"That approach has been used overseas," I said. "I'm familiar."

"Sure," Richie replied. "But mine was different. It focused on one criterion only—the offender's view of morality."

I hesitated, thinking of the intersection of justice and morality, both of which Mad Dog seemed obsessed with.

"Someone like Tignon," Richie said. "It predicted he would run. That's why I was studying that case. My model failed for him."

Except it hadn't failed. Richie was right. Tignon *did* run. We just didn't know about it.

"Have you taken our profile on Mad Dog?" Shooter asked. "Plugged it in?"

Richie nodded, but didn't speak.

"Do we need a drumroll?" Frank asked.

Richie sat up. Fumbled with his computer. Apparently he wasn't expecting us to take him seriously. He got something open and stared at the screen.

"Well. A guy like this is not trying to bring justice to an unjust world," Richie said. "He's more pragmatic than that. At his core, he's actually moralistic."

So what? I thought.

"Okay?" I said.

"So when he leaks information to the media," Richie continued, "he focuses on punishment and fairness, versus bragging about him being the author of that punishment."

"This is all in Frank's profile," I said.

"Sure," Richie said. "But here's something different. Mad Dog thinks PAR is compassionate to his cause. We solve puzzles. We correct wrongs. He thinks we're like him. But not just . . . kinda like him. When he wrote 'partner' on that bathroom wall in LA, I don't believe he was being sarcastic."

"Then what?" I asked.

"He thinks he was covering for you, Agent Camden," Richie said. "For you getting to LA so late."

I bit at my lip, my mind running through something.

"You got an idea?" Frank asked.

"Maybe we don't need to know Mad Dog's motive," I said. "Maybe we just need the right recipe. One part—driving him into the light. One part—telling him he's *not* one of us. And the last part . . ."

"What?" Cassie asked.

I thought of how quickly Mad Dog had become weary with me on the phone. Of Richie's theory that he was leaving breadcrumbs for some other team to find later.

"Rage," I said.

"The last part is rage?" Shooter asked.

"At how stupid we all are," I said. "The stories that have been running—the media wants to talk about incompetence, right?"

"That's what they're reporting," Frank said.

"So we tell them a different story. The FBI never gives up. You call them 'cold cases.' We just call them cases. We bring Kagan's files into the mix. Tell them we've made a connection. These serial killer murders were a travesty, but now we're close to solving three unsolved murders from years ago. And these other people—they were innocent. Not like Tignon. Not like Fisher."

"You're talking Arrowhead's victims?" Cassie said. "The people Kagan found?"

"I get it," Frank said. "We dress up these old victims as heroes, and Mad Dog moves from vigilante to murderer."

"Meanwhile," I said, nodding, "we feed the press some evidence. Information that'll drive him into the light. The sketch. The RV. The connection to Houston."

"And the rage?" Cassie asked.

"We make it clear he's not one of us. And the reason: he's unqual-ified. He's dumb. Reckless. Unethical." I hesitated. Turned to Richie. "What does your model say he'll do then? Will he run like Tignon?"

"No," Richie said. "He'll reach out to us. Real angry, too. See, he's on a course of action he planned a while ago, Agent Camden. A course he doesn't want to get off."

"Like a program?" I said.

"Exactly," Richie replied. "And this? This will disrupt his world-view. He'll have only one choice. To lash out."

"Good," I said. "That's when we catch him."

CHAPTER THIRTY-FOUR

BY 3 P.M. EASTERN TIME, DEPUTY DIRECTOR POULTON HAD arrived by helicopter at the Jacksonville office. We prepped him on what we had found on Mad Dog and on our strategy to draw him out.

By three thirty, the parking lot was crowded with news vans, the lobby full of reporters. Poulton and I spoke in a waiting room that Human Resources used. The walls were covered in flyers about employee benefits and discounts to area theme parks.

"That agent at the Houston bookstore who did research for Banning," Poulton said. "Her name is Lisa Yang. She's out of the D.C. office."

"I'll need to speak with her," I said.

"She'll be made available," Poulton replied. "In the meantime, I emailed you her file."

"We'll study it."

"Per the director, you'll study lightly, Camden," Poulton said. "She's highly decorated."

I nodded in understanding, and side by side, we moved out toward the ground floor's atrium.

"You asked me to come here, and I'm giving you an hour," Poulton said. "But I want to see action, Camden. Arrests, not analysis."

"Of course," I said.

We walked up onto a small dais then, with a blue curtained back-drop covered in tiny repeating FBI shield icons.

"Thank you for gathering on such short notice," Poulton said as the reporters quieted. "I'd like to introduce Special Agent Gardner Camden, who is going to review the details of our ongoing investigation."

He moved aside, and I stepped forward.

"Good afternoon," I said, introducing myself and spelling my first and last name.

Fourteen men and women with recording equipment focused on me.

"Twenty-four hours ago, we released a brief statement about the murders of Ross Tignon, Barry Fisher, and Ronald Lazarian. And as much as we regret the loss of any life, one of the advantages of a national law enforcement agency is our ability to make connections. I'm here to announce that, in the last day, we've linked three new victims to the same man that killed Tignon, Fisher, and Lazarian. And we have a strong description of the suspect in all six murders."

The FBI is not known for its transparency. Murmurs moved through the small group of reporters.

"We've built a profile of the man we're searching for," I continued, "and we're seeking the public's help in locating him."

I produced the digital composite supplied by Marly's team. Our production department had enlarged it onto poster-size foam core.

"Locating this man is a top priority of the Bureau, as we believe he's linked to several other cold cases. We know that he drives a white recreational vehicle and is most likely from Houston or the surround-ing area."

Camerapersons elbowed each other, trying to get close-ups of the sketch, and hands went up in the reporters' pool.

"When will you release more information on these new victims?" a reporter asked.

"By the end of this week," I said.

"Is there a vigilante on the loose?" a different reporter hollered.

"No," I said, "these are murders. There's a murderer on the loose."

"Would you categorize the suspect as a monster, Agent Camden?"

"I don't think of criminals in those terms," I said. "And I don't use language like that."

"If you don't call him a monster," the reporter continued, "how would you describe him?"

This was the moment I'd been waiting for.

"Isolated," I said. "Ignorant. Frightened. Reckless. Angry."

"So a dangerous idiot?" the reporter asked.

The crowd chuckled, and I considered how Mad Dog would react to these words. Then I said, "In plain speech, yes."

Poulton stepped up to the mic, knowing the goals were twofold: one, get the public calling into our tip line; and two, upset Mad Dog. The deputy director thanked the media for coming and reminded them that the goal was to get the sketch out immediately, so the public could provide help in getting a suspect off the streets. He dodged questions, circled back to our 1-800 tip line, and closed down the conference.

I waited sixteen minutes in the break room for the first news channel to go live. A plastic cereal bowl filled with M&Ms had been left on the table, a sign that Cassie had been there. I calculated how many hands had dug into that bowl. Sixteen employees on this floor. Four building maintenance staff. Visitors. I picked two red candies from the edge of the bowl and ate them.

A moment later, CNN went live with the story, a graphic running along the bottom of the screen. It read "Dangerous Idiot Killer." I turned the volume up in time to hear my own words, describing Mad Dog as ignorant and frightened.

Then I moved back to my cube. I had been in Houston while the others examined Kagan's file. Now I took a look at my copy, breaking each section apart and moving them into eight piles, each separated by a two-inch space on my desk. I sharpened eight pencils and placed one atop each pile, along with a single sheet of paper for notes.

As I picked up the first section, Cassie popped her head around the corner of my cube.

"We got a login," she said.

Mad Dog was using Banning's password.

I followed Cassie back to our conference room, where Marly from Quantico was on speaker. As we walked, Cassie told me the login had happened in Dallas.

"Are agents rolling?" I asked.

"Already dispatched," Marly answered on speaker as we entered the room. "The ISP gave us the location of a coffeehouse called Sparrow downtown. If you hold, we'll give you updates."

The Dallas office was 9.2 miles from downtown. A twelve-minute drive. Poulton had made the decision to hold off on involving local police, who could typically get to a location faster, but were less discreet.

In the background on Marly's side, I heard someone say, "We've got movement."

Mad Dog had been on the coffeehouse's WiFi, but was now on the run. Which meant we were tracking a phone. If he kept the device on, we could pinpoint him to a three-foot location via GPS.

Cassie and I waited five minutes until Marly informed us that agents had pulled over a cab on the side of Elm Street downtown. The phone they were tracking had remained on the whole time, but the cab was empty.

"Put us on with the locals," I said.

An agent named Jose Salmon came on the line.

"We got an empty yellow cab here, Agent Camden," Salmon said. "The phone was on the floor in the back. Cabbie didn't even know it was left there."

"Damn it," Cassie said aloud. "He knows we know about Banning's login."

"A short-term fare?" I asked.

"It ended three minutes before we got here. Taxi driver said the guy got in at Elm and Seventh. Rode two blocks and got out."

Leaving the phone inside the cab.

"Per the driver, he was late twenties," Salmon said. "Five ten-ish with brown hair. Brown or blue eyes."

"Circle back to the coffeehouse," I said. "Pull cameras from stores nearby. And be careful, Salmon. He's dangerous. He might be watching you."

We hung up, and I thought about Richie. We'd sent him to Dallas and Shooter to Houston, guessing that Mad Dog might be in one place or the other. Richie's plane had landed just minutes ago. If needed, we could have him coordinate with local feds.

I turned to Cassie. "Do we know what past case Mad Dog was looking at in our database?"

"A program was capturing every keystroke," she said. "But I told them to prioritize locating him. Give me five minutes, and I'll find out."

Cassie headed out of the room, and my cell buzzed. I glanced at the screen.

A number I didn't recognize.

I held it up to signal Frank that it might be Mad Dog. "Quiet please."

Then I answered on speaker, placing the phone on the table and sliding up a chair so I could speak closely into the receiver. As I did, I looked to Frank, who'd set up the trace with Quantico and my personal cell carrier.

We'd been expecting this call.

"Camden," I said.

"So I'm a monster?" Mad Dog growled. "That's the story we're going with?"

"That's not the word I used," I said. "But we can talk definitions if you want. Someone who threatens others. Who deviates from normal behavior. I think if we consulted a dictionary—"

"I. Am not. A monster," he said firmly. "I'm a monster *hunter*. I have rules. Ross Tignon was guilty. Barry Fisher—"

"Was punished," I interrupted. "Thirty-one years. No monster hunter needed."

Mad Dog went silent then, and Frank looked up from his laptop. He made a motion with his hand that meant "keep him talking."

"We have a picture from the bookstore," I said.

"Must be a bad one," Mad Dog replied. "Explains why your sketch is so bad." He paused. "I'm curious, Camden. Did you enjoy the director's book?"

"I'm guessing by your reaction that you did not."

"My reaction?"

"The page you shoved down Tignon's throat. Your questions at the book event. You thought certain crimes should have been included, but were not?"

He laughed, but it was forced.

"Crimes in places like Oklahoma, Texas, and Arkansas," I continued. "Were you upset that your early work went unrecognized?"

"My early work?" he repeated, his voice raised an octave. More curiosity than concern.

"You left an impression on people," I said. "Mainly people on the sides of roads."

Mad Dog made a chuffing noise then, as if what I'd said was insulting. "You saw what I did to Barry Fisher, Camden. Does it look like I'm going after degenerates who stole five hundred bucks from the church kitty?"

In my mind, I saw a riddle with no answer.

The reference to the church kitty was to Lyle Davis, one of the men whose roadside deaths Agent Kagan had investigated. But Mad Dog was not claiming it.

"People remember you," I said.

"Now you're just lying. Cops aren't supposed to lie."

"Your arrowheads," I said. "Perfect hundred-degree hertzian cones. People paid good money for them."

He went quiet then, and I glanced up at Frank. I had gotten this part right.

"Why didn't you go to LA?" Mad Dog asked, switching up the conversation. "You've got a calendar on me. I have one on you."

"I *did* go to LA," I said. "I saw your work in that bathroom."

"But not right away. When we spoke, you were in Dallas. You could've flown there that night. I was waiting for you."

I pictured the bloody bathroom in Brentwood. My name on the wall.

"You arrived the next morning," he continued. "It's curious."

I felt a line of sweat trickle along my neck.

I had flown to Miami that night to hide Camila. But my flight had been off the books. In no FBI database that Mad Dog could access.

"You mentioned a mentor when we spoke that day," I said. "I thought you had a helper. I stayed in Dallas to investigate if—"

Ahhnt. He made a buzzing noise, like a quiz show. "Lie again, and I hang up."

"So the word *mentor*?" I asked.

"Really?" Mad Dog snorted. "That's what you want to talk about? Are you going to ask about my mother next? Find out if I was breastfed?"

Poulton came into the room, his steps slowing as he realized we had Mad Dog on speaker.

"I know that you grew up reading 'The Paddock and the Mouse,'" I said.

Mad Dog was quiet.

"I know what it looks like when someone acts out a fantasy with a tainted arrow. Imitating Odysseus—unclear on what's real and what's fiction."

His voice became stern. "You shouldn't talk about things you don't know, Agent Camden."

"Except it wasn't fiction. Those were real victims."

"You shouldn't talk about *people* you don't know."

I blinked. Mad Dog had become defensive. But not in the way I'd expected.

I put the phone on mute. Looked up at Frank.

"He knows about these early victims."

"Check," Frank said.

"But he's not claiming them as his own."

Frank bit at his cheek. "Check again."

I considered what bothered me most.

"The victims from years ago were all people who committed petty crimes," I said. "Now, two years later, the same guy is after famous serial killers?"

"Well, you thought Mad Dog had a partner," Frank said. "Kagan considered it, too."

"Helllooo?" Mad Dog said. "Cat got your tongue, Camden?"

I ignored him, remembering my conversation with Kagan. My statement that the bow-and-arrow attacks, from setup to cleanup, seemed like a lot of work. A lot for *one person.*

"What are you saying?" Poulton jumped in. We were still on mute. "They're not the same guy?"

"One man is Mad Dog," I said. "His partner is Arrowhead." I looked to Frank. "And you wanted to know your 'why' . . . your 'why now.'"

"Something happened between the two," Frank said.

"Pfft." Mad Dog made a noise. "What am I—on hold? Is the genius brainstorming?"

"Then, it's 101," Poulton said. "Force a wedge between them."

I looked to Frank. There was nothing 101 about this killer. I took the phone off mute, thinking of the right words to use.

One of the drawbacks of my personality is I struggle with nuance. Fail at sarcasm. But I would try.

"You want to know what the worst part of this case is?" I said to Mad Dog.

"What's that?"

I searched for the sort of terminology that Shooter or Frank would use.

"Hunting someone as unoriginal as you." The words came out flatly. Without tone. But they were the right words.

"What did you say to me?"

"At least with the bow and arrow murders, there was some creativity," I continued. "These new ones . . . you're just copying old crimes."

Mad Dog was breathing more heavily now, and his voice shook as he spoke.

"There are words for the type of animal you are, Camden," he said. "You feign weakness, but advance in the dark."

Frank stood up from behind his laptop. He wrote "Lake Ashland" on a piece of paper in red marker. We had Mad Dog's location.

"This has always been about business," Mad Dog said. "Me, getting rid of scum. You people, fumbling along behind like you do. But now you've become disrespectful. You've made this personal."

I thought about Richie's notion of a program. Of Mad Dog being disrupted off it. And what he might do.

"I just want to understand," I said, "what you're after."

"You," he said. "That's what I'm after now."

Frank's eyes settled on me, and I felt the muscles in my forearm tense up.

"I'm gonna show you two more magic tricks, Camden," Mad Dog continued. "You liked LA? You enjoyed Rawlings? I'll go one better."

"Why don't we talk about—"

"I'll prove I can get to anyone anywhere. Out in the world. On trial. Man. Woman. Even someone locked behind bars."

The line went dead, and I looked up. The sun had dropped behind a building, and the room was darker.

"He's in a cabin in Ashland," Frank said. "West side of the lake."

"One road in, one road out," Poulton added, looking at Frank's map.

"We got a boat on the water and six deputies blocking the road, Gardner," Frank said. "Good job."

My hands were below the table, but my fists were in balls. Unusual for me.

Cassie came back into the room.

"Did you find out what he was looking at?" I asked. "When he logged in?"

"Personnel files," Cassie said. "Not case files."

"What's it matter?" Poulton said. "He took the bait. We're circling him."

But Cassie's forehead was crisscrossed with lines.

"*Your* personnel file this time, Gardner," she clarified.

I turned to the far window and stared out toward the south.

"What is it?" Cassie asked.

"His questions about me not going to LA," I said. "How did he know I was lying?"

"Did you tell anyone?" Frank asked.

"Just you," I said. "He also said that he could get to any man *or woman*. 'Even behind bars.'"

Frank paused before shaking his head. "No way," he said.

"Anything's possible," I told him.

"I don't understand." Poulton squinted. "What's going on?"

"Gardner's ex," Frank said. "Anna Camden may be his next target."

"We could get a release," I said. "I could drive down there."

"You're the lead. You're not going anywhere," Poulton said. "We got this guy!"

"And if he's working with someone? A partner?"

"We'll get her into solitary for now," Poulton said. "Get a release into custody by end of day."

"Thank you."

Over the next ten minutes, Frank got on the phone and made it happen. Favors were called in, and my ex was moved to solitary confinement.

As Frank got off the phone, Cassie came over, her lips still thin, but her voice steadier now. "They got a guy in cuffs," she said. "In Lake Ashland."

I exhaled, nodding. "Thanks, Cass. I needed that."

I got up and walked out of the conference room. Took the elevator down and stepped outside, my body tight in a way I was not familiar with.

I needed to hear my daughter's voice, so I called up Mitchell Hannick and asked him to put Camila on.

"Oh Daddy, I'm having so much fun," she said when she came on
the line a minute later. "I'm learning to ride a horse. And there's an
alpaca named Flaca, because he's so skinny."

Breathe, Gardy.

Camila went on about the bunny-feeding area, how Hannick's son
had given her a riding hat, and how she was learning on a pony named
Boba.

"Like the drink, Daddy," she said. "She has pink circles down her
side."

I knew I had to get back upstairs. "Daddy's gotta go," I told her.
"But I'm glad you're having fun."

I hung up and walked back into the building. As I got off on our
floor, I saw Frank standing beside Poulton in the conference room. I'd
thought the deputy director had left for D.C., but he hadn't.

"Wasn't Mad Dog," Poulton said.

"What?"

"In the cabin. Kid we cuffed was a teenager. His parents showed
up. Dad's a cop. Vouched for the kid's whereabouts at the time of the
murders."

"Mad Dog must have used a virtual location app," Frank said.

There were four different third-party phone apps that cost less than
ten dollars and allowed everyday citizens to "choose" the location their
phone identified as.

Mad Dog was in the wind.

Poulton's nostrils flared. "I'm heading back to D.C.," he said, clearly
frustrated. "Find this guy."

Frank and I nodded, and Poulton began walking away. Then he
turned.

"Incidentally, this thing with your ex-wife," he said. "I signed the release, and we'll hold her for a week. But it was a public matter, her getting sent away. I don't know how you figure this guy would need access to your personnel files to get at it."

My head was spinning. "He said he can get to any man or woman. 'Even behind bars.' Not sure if you were there—"

"No, I heard that," Poulton said. "But we got a lotta serials behind bars, and she's not one of them. So . . ."

Poulton looked more closely at me. I hadn't responded.

"You okay, Camden?" he asked.

My mind was chasing something. Something in my personnel file that wasn't anywhere else.

"He said 'behind bars,'" I said.

"Yeah, we all heard that, buddy," Poulton said.

"Not all bars are physical," I mumbled. "Some are in the mind."

Poulton squinted at Frank, confused.

I leaned over and hit the speaker button. Called Marly. "The GPS data can be fooled," I said, "but there's a CSLI that's generated for whatever app he's using to disguise his identity."

"Yeah, we tracked it down, but the cell went offline," she said. "Also it's not as accurate. It pinged off one cell tower, then went dead."

"Where?" I asked.

"West of Dallas," she said. "Woodrell, Texas."

I hit the button to hang up without saying anything. Grabbed my phone and dialed the number of my mother's cell.

It went to voicemail.

I called the front desk at her retirement home, but it rang endlessly.

My mother had no connection to me that could be found anywhere. Her anonymity was why I hadn't worried about hiding her when I'd placed Camila and Rosa at the ranch.

Except for one thing. Her married name and current address were in my personnel file, where she was listed as a beneficiary.

I tried the number again and was cycled back to hold music.

"What's going on, Gardner?" Frank asked.

I hung up and dialed Richie's cell.

"Richie, I'm texting you an address in Woodrell," I said. "Go there, stat."

"Woodrell?" he repeated. "Sure. What am I looking for?"

Mad Dog was never in Florida. He had no intention of going after my ex-wife.

He used WiFi in that café in Dallas. Then left the burner phone in the cab. Drove nearby, but not to Ashland.

"My mother," I said to Richie, my mouth suddenly dry. "You're looking to see if Mad Dog murdered her."

Poulton's face went gray, and Richie listened as I read off the address.

I hung up. Stumbled across the office toward my cube.

Didn't I already know what Richie was going to find? That the one person who supported me was gone. The woman who taught me how to channel everything that was strange about me. The endless facts. The stored memories. The odd logic . . . all transformed into something valuable. Something useful.

In nine minutes, I called Richie back.

"I'm in the parking lot," he said. "There are firefighters here. Some sort of grease fire in the kitchen."

A diversion.

"Ignore it," I said. "Third floor. Room 302."

I waited sixty seconds, then hit the button to switch to video. Richie accepted, and I saw him moving up a stairwell.

"Agent Camden," he said, breathing heavy. "Why don't I call you once I'm inside her roo—"

"Faster, Richie," I said, my voice hoarse.

He took two steps at a time. Rounded the corner near my mom's room.

I saw the door open.

"Mrs. Camden?" he called out.

"Maher," I said, using her married name.

The room was dark. My mother was turned on her side, away from Richie. A comforter covered her body, and Richie pulled it back.

"Mrs. Maher?"

I saw an injection mark on her neck. A drizzle of dried blood below her right ear.

"Mrs. Maher?" Richie repeated.

I waited.

"Come on, wake up, please," he hollered.

I squinted into the darkness of my phone. "What is it?" I said. "I can't see."

The phone shifted, and I saw the vague, unfocused look in my mother's eyes.

"I'm sorry, Agent Camden," Richie said. "She's been injected with something. She's not responding."

CHAPTER THIRTY-FIVE

I DON'T REMEMBER EVERYTHING THAT HAPPENED NEXT, which is unusual for me.

But it began with a stream of images, one after another.

- *The pitcher of water in my mother's room, the color of a robin's egg.*
- *The writing on the wall in the bathroom in LA. "Too slow, Gardner."*
- *Cassie's scarf in Jacksonville. A purple lipstick stain on it, four millimeters long.*

Then the images came faster.

- *The 10-31 exchange, something wrong with it.*
- *The deputy's Adam's apple on that first day.*
- *Richie, mislabeling Fisher's Cobelli's gland as his thyroid in New Mexico.*

Infrequently a frenzy overtakes me. The details that I cannot help but record become like crystals that are too beautiful, and they reso-nate, as if struck by some strange tuning fork.

When this first happened as a child, it was the result of a boy named Jarvis, who repeatedly flicked my neck in PE. I jumped on Jarvis. Didn't stop hitting him until an adult peeled me off.

I looked around the office.

Frank was staring at me, Poulton beside him. I turned and realized I'd wandered into a waiting area outside of a series of cubes.

- *A cut in Tignon's abdomen, sliced in the wrong direction.*
- *A burn mark on the back shoulder of Shooter's sweatshirt.*
  An odd location for a burn.

A lamp flew off a side table, yanked from the wall and tossed across the room. The lower panel of my cubicle bowed inward suddenly, then out. My foot against it.

The wall went down, and Frank headed over.

"Get away from me!" I screamed.

The door to the office kitchenette was suddenly there. I must've traveled fifty feet. I moved inside. The microwave flew off the counter. A hole appeared in the drywall and my hand was inside it.

Find somewhere safe in these moments, Gardy.

I leaned over and stopped, and the world of the office went quiet. But the facts kept coming. One after another. Burned into my mind.

I saw Cassie approach me, but moved around her, my hands wav-ing her and Frank away.

I pushed out of the kitchen, moved down a stairwell and out the emergency exit. I heard an alarm chirp as I left the building, but I kept going. Out toward a hedge of trees behind the building. Out into nowhere.

A squad car found me two miles down the road. A female officer got out. Blond. Heavyset. Pretty. I wish my mind did not track every inane detail, but it does.

"I'm just here to help," she said in a gentle voice.

I moved away from her. Into another field. Picked up my pace. Counting as I walked. Prime numbers.

"I can control my breathing," I repeated in between the numbers. "This is all temporary."

I moved farther away from the noises of traffic. Got to the number 7,841 and stopped. I was missing a shoe.

I sat down in a bed of alfalfa. The smell of dirt was strong, and my face was wet with perspiration, my knuckles bloody.

"C'mon, Agent Camden," the same officer said. "I'm here to take you home."

I turned. Had she been following me?

The officer drove me to my place. She never lifted her radio receiver. Never asked a question. Just silence until I was at my apartment.

I moved inside in the dark. Stripped off my clothes and found the bed.

I thought of the conversation I'd had with Mad Dog. But mostly I thought about my mother.

Never use your intellect as a weapon, Gardy.

On the call today, I had found Mad Dog's soft points and dug in. His childhood. His value system. Poulton had told me to break him, and I did. I caused him to lash out. To target my mother. I was responsible for this.

I found my cell phone and called my mother's physician.

"Is she dead?" I asked when he answered.

"Of course not," he said. "But she hasn't regained consciousness, so we have her on a ventilator."

Exhalation takes little effort, but inhalation requires multiple muscles to work. When respiratory muscles are paralyzed, the lungs are unable to breathe.

"We've taken blood samples," he said. "They tested positive for vecuronium."

This was a paralytic, commonly used by anesthesiologists. The same one I'd seen listed in the ME's report the night before. The chemical found injected in Ross Tignon's neck.

"What have you tried so far?" I asked.

"We've used other medications," he said. "To antagonize the muscles to relax."

"No effect?"

"With her age and condition," he said, "it's possible she won't wake up again."

I dropped my hand that held the phone. Stared into the darkness of my bedroom.

"We can call you as soon as—"

I hung up. Moved back to bed and felt the pillow, wet against my cheek.

CHAPTER THIRTY-SIX

AT 2 A.M. I AWOKE. SHOWERED AND GOT IN THE CAR. DROVE to the office. The building was quiet as I worked.

I laid out every part of the Tignon case from 2013 on the ground at the far end of the conference room. Atop the table, I placed Kagan's files, broken into the eight sections from my cube.

By 2:50 a.m., I had used all one hundred and twenty-two Post-its I had found between Frank's desk, Cassie's, and Shooter's. My own cube was a mess from earlier, and I avoided it.

Inside the conference room, I covered every inch of the window with a different color. Pink for a detail from Tignon's, Fisher's, or Lazarian's original cases. Blue for anything in Kagan's files. And yellow for the new murders in the last week. The deaths of the serial killers.

Evidence and questions surrounded me, and I exhaled. Then I opened the folder on Agent Lisa Yang, who had been at the bookstore in Houston.

Yang was thirty years old and attractive, with shoulder-length dark hair and wide eyes. She had done her undergraduate degree at Yale, before moving to Iowa to get a master's. She had been with the Bureau for six years, with one field assignment in the Philadelphia office before returning to a research role in D.C. Eighteen months ago, she had checked out Barry Fisher's file, but not Tignon's or Lazarian's.

I moved back to the conference room and started digging for details.

By 3:30 a.m. I had removed all but four of the Post-its from the window. I peeled off two of them and got in my car. Drove over to the Deerwood neighborhood in southeast Jacksonville and found a ranch-style home with strips of red brick and a covered front patio.

I knocked on the door, and eventually Frank opened up. He wore boxers and a white V-neck. The guy looked perfect, even while he slept.

Except he had a Heckler and Kotch .45 in his right hand.

"My God, Gardner. I could've shot you," he said. "Get in here."

I held still outside the front door. "I don't want to bother you too much."

"That's why you're banging at my door at four a.m.?"

"Four twenty-nine," I said without looking down at my phone. "Listen. Frank. I started from scratch. Every piece of data. Recheck. Brainstorm. Cross-reference—"

Frank held up his left hand, palm out, as if to say stop. He turned on the porch light, which he'd left off until then. Some security experts claimed that lights on at night only helped burglars.

"You're in shock, Gardner," he said. "Go home, right now. That's an order."

"Cross-reference," I continued. "Take the Post-its off the window. Classic approach—whatever's left up—no matter how unlikely—"

"This is a response to trauma," Frank interrupted.

"No matter how unlikely," I kept up, "has to be something we missed or didn't understand."

Frank popped the magazine from his weapon and cleared the slide.

He placed the gun on a cherrywood side table by the door. The look on his face was pity.

"She would've wanted this," I said. And Frank understood that I was referring to my mother. "Me working now. While the case is hot. In the least, she would have expected it."

He hung his head, and I waited.

"I'm not promising anything," he said. "But I need coffee if we're gonna talk. Get in here."

I followed Frank across the entryway and into the kitchen. He turned on the lights. I had picked Frank up twice from this house but had never been inside. The place was spotless.

The kitchen overlooked a koi pond in the back with a decorative wooden bridge. The counters were black granite, the cabinets a light oak. Off the kitchen, I could see a great room with a wall-to-wall fireplace. Cardboard boxes were piled against the wall.

Frank opened a drawer and took out a box of coffee filters. Found it empty.

"Son of a gun." He tossed the box into the trash.

I pulled out the two Post-its I'd brought with me. Both were yellow, which represented the words of Mad Dog or a piece of evidence found in the last week.

Frank leaned back against the counter. He'd given up on making coffee.

I stuck one of the yellow Post-its to his fridge.

"Fat old angler." Frank read the words on it aloud. "Okay . . . ?"

"Mad Dog said that to me when he called. He described Tignon that way."

"So?"

"You saw Tignon's body from the autopsy. Would you call him fat?"

"It's early, Gardner," he said.

I glared at Frank.

"He could stand to lose twenty pounds," he said. "Not my definition of fat, but some people are more discriminating."

"Tignon's Levi's were on the tray at his autopsy," I said. "Thirty-six, thirty-two. I remember thinking he must've lost a hundred and twenty pounds during the seven years since we thought he'd died."

Frank pointed at the Post-it, half following me. "The old Tignon," he said. "That's who he's talking about."

I nodded. "And let me ask you this. Would you even call him an angler?"

He squinted. "Uh—since he was fishing with *human liver*, I'd say that's a big yes."

"First off, that was a detail that only the FBI and the boat captain knew," I said. "Now, sure, he could've seen that in our files. But consider this . . ."

I took out the other Post-it and stuck it next to the first. It read "Ashland: no rod or reel."

"Richie went through the inventory of Tignon's garage in Ashland," I explained. "Or should I say, Bob Breckinridge's garage. There was no fishing equipment."

Frank scrunched up his face.

"The rookie was looking to see if Tignon was active again in Texas. In case there were victims with the same MO as back in Florida. Blond girls cut up, Tignon fishing with their livers. All this under his new name, Bob Breckinridge."

"Right," Frank said. "Except out west, he had no gear. So why would Mad Dog call him that?"

"There's only one answer." I tapped at the Post-it. "Mad Dog *knew* Tignon, Frank. Back in twenty thirteen in Florida. When *I* knew him."

Frank's eyebrows pitched upward. "You got proof of that?"

I held up my index finger, beckoning him to hold on.

"That's not all," I said. "There was a flaw in Cassie's logic yesterday. About the property exchange."

"The ten–thirty-one?"

"She found out how Tignon got to Ashland," I said. "But how did *Mad Dog* find Tignon?"

"He got into our files. Using the director's login."

"Except none of that information was in our files. Cassie worked backwards from Beverly Polis's tax returns, and from the name Bob Breckenridge. But that was a name we only knew *after* Tignon died. She started with the answer."

Frank nodded now, getting it.

"There's only one possibility," I said. "Mad Dog knew Tignon before Tignon left Florida. He knew Tignon before Tignon faked his death. Back when he was setting up that partnership. 'Cause after that moment, there was no way to find him."

Frank looked back at the Post-its.

"So?"

"How many seminars have you and I attended on the factors that influence killers?" I asked.

"Too many," Frank said.

"How a killer needs a warm-up act."

"Needs practice," Frank said, nodding.

"The theories," I continued. "Biological. Self-conflict. Functionalism. The elements that turn something *on* in these men. The way they first practice on animals. How they need—"

"Permission," Frank cut in. His jaw had loosened. "Oh my God, Gardner." He shook his head. "Your witness in twenty thirteen."

I nodded, thinking of the overnight drive I'd taken to Alabama to

find the man on the boat trip whom Tignon had confided in. To whom
Tignon had bragged about fishing with the girls' livers.

"Tignon didn't 'disappear' my witness all those years ago," I said.
"He inspired him."

"Your witness back then is Mad Dog," Frank said. "He was the
other man on the boat."

"And at some point on that trip, Tignon *told* Mad Dog about Ashland. About his father-in-law owning half that lake. That's how Mad
Dog knew where to look for him years later. Why he called him a fat
old angler. That isn't just some description from years ago. It's a description from *that boat trip*."

Frank opened his fridge and took out a sixteen-ounce bottle of Dr
Pepper. Flipping it open, he took a long drag. He was processing what
I had said. How Mad Dog could have been shaped by Tignon.

"You wanna go back to Alabama," he said.

"I do."

"But you went whole hog there years ago, looking for that witness.
Came up with jack."

"True," I said. "But maybe I missed something."

"You?" Frank raised an eyebrow.

He studied me. Was the look on his face pity? Was the look on
mine desperation?

"Craig Poulton stood there while you destroyed the office," Frank
said. "He told me, Camden's off of work until a doctor says different."

"Then don't tell him."

Frank glanced upstairs, considering it. "Give me twenty minutes,"
he said. "To get dressed and tell the wife. In the meantime, for the love
of God—go get us coffee."

CHAPTER THIRTY-SEVEN

ORANGE BEACH, ALABAMA, WAS A SEASIDE TOWN, FORTY-five minutes southwest of Pensacola, just west of the Florida line. Condos lined the white sand beaches, but Frank and I headed a few miles inland, where residential streets were curved and there were no sidewalks. Intermittently, between houses, a grassy area sprung up. In the center was a man-made pond with a sprinkler feature shooting water eight feet into the sky.

We pulled up outside a light blue cottage with a red door. There were white-framed windows to the left and right of the entrance, and a lawn that measured no more than ninety square feet, the edge of the grass lined with a low picket fence.

I had caught three hours of sleep on the drive, and it was after 10 a.m. My phone showed three missed calls from Cassie, and I presumed they were about my behavior in the office last night.

"This boat captain's gonna remember you?" Frank asked.

"People tend to."

"But you never met him here?"

"I met him on his boat," I said. "The *Lady Saint Jean*."

"Well, he lives on Easy Street," Frank said, glancing at the stop sign. "Literally—9087 Easy Street. You know what a red door means in these parts?"

"Mortgage paid," I said.

"I got ten years to go on a fifteen," Frank sighed. "Okay, let's do this."

We got out and walked along the path that bisected the tiny lawn. Rang the bell and heard movement inside.

The man who opened the door was white and in his sixties, with a patchy gray-brown beard and a baseball hat turned backward. He wore torn jeans stained with paint and a gray T-shirt that looked like it might've once been white.

"Aaron Pecun?" Frank asked.

The man glanced from me to Frank.

"This is Special Agent Frank Roberts," I said. "I'm Special Agent Gardner Camden. You and I have spoken before."

Frank was holding out his badge, but Pecun was studying me. The smell of dead fish hung in the air.

"Sure, I remember you," he said, taking a pair of eyeglasses that hung around his neck and putting them to his face. "It was some years back."

"Six years, three hundred and one days," I said.

"Now I definitely remember you."

Still, it was a long time. Fidelity on his memory was critical.

"You called your local police department about something you heard on a trip," I said. "Do you still recall what that was?"

"A fella was on the boat, bragging to a second fella about using human body parts for bait."

"Specifically?" I asked.

"A human liver," Pecun said.

Frank asked if we could come inside, and Pecun nodded. We sat down at a wooden table made of reclaimed wood, painted white. It wasn't clear whether seeing the darker wood under the white was an aesthetic choice, a sign of age, or a mistake.

"I followed up with my buddy at the PD a month later," Pecun said. "He told me you boys caught the guy. Or he died or something."

"We're here today about the second man," Frank said. "The one he was bragging *to*. What do you remember about him?"

"White guy. Paid in cash," Pecun said. "Met me down at the docks."

This was old information. Data points I already knew. I glanced around Pecun's home. The place was cluttered with furniture, the couch behind us threadbare.

"And the trip?" I asked.

"Early-morning departure, standard six hours. A hundred bucks a person back then. Plus fuel and tip."

"What about the man?" Frank asked.

"Fifties or sixties," Pecun said. "Knew his way around a boat."

Frank glanced at me, then back at the captain.

The detail of the man's age was consistent with my notes from the investigation years ago. But it was also a detail that had not matched with everything else last night as I eliminated clues. In fact, it was on one of the two Post-its I'd left behind, still stuck to the window in Jacksonville.

A Post-it I'd avoided telling Frank about, lest he not agree to take the trip with me.

In 2013, Pecun had consistently described the man Tignon told about the livers as in his fifties or sixties—and that was seven years ago. Same as he'd done just now.

We knew Mad Dog was much younger. Midtwenties.

"You're sure about that age?" I asked Pecun. "Could he have been younger and you confused him with another boat trip?"

"I don't reckon so," he said.

Pecun sat down across from us, placing his coffee cup on the table. It had been filled too high, and brown liquid spilled down the sides of the ceramic, onto the wood. I counted eleven other coffee rings on the table, the marks of each one eating away at the white paint.

"Any identifying marks you recall the man having?" Frank asked. "Scars and such?"

"None of the above," Pecun said. When he spoke, he used his hands, and the smell of cleanser wafted in the air, mixed with a briny odor.

My mind drifted. If the guy fishing was too old, then nothing worked here. I was out of ideas.

"What about equipment he fished with?" Frank kept up. "This guy supply his own?"

"Yup."

"Anything you remember about his gear?"

"It's a good question," Pecun said. "A nice rod I'd remember, more than a person. And I don't at all."

I was experiencing something unusual. I found myself unable to concentrate. I pictured my mother. A trip we took to the shore every spring when I was a child. Kiawah Island, South Carolina. I would sit on the berm of the sand and tell Mom I was going to count the whitecaps. She agreed that it was a good idea and crowded behind me, her legs extending around my small frame, staying silent while I murmured numbers into the hundreds.

"You can't count them all, Gardy," she'd say, "just like you can't count all the people in the world. Everyone's different. Everyone takes a different approach to get through life."

Pecun was still talking. "The equipment was pretty standard that trip. It was a small charter."

I blinked and was back. Pecun had previously described the trip as "two men on a boat." Now it was a charter?

"There were others?" I asked. "That day on the *Lady Saint Jean*?"

Pecun shifted his gaze in my direction, his hand in the messy curls of his beard. "I do a hundred trips a year, Agent Camden."

He got up and walked to the kitchen.

"Well, we take the information when we can get it and how," Frank said in a folksy voice. "If you recall something now that you didn't before, that's fine by us, Aaron."

Frank was trying to connect with Pecun. To build rapport.

The boat captain stirred sugar into his coffee. "The guy had a kid with him," he said.

"The guy Tignon bragged to?" Frank cocked his head.

Pecun nodded, and I bit at the edge of my lip. This is how Frank must have felt, being surprised in that hotel room in New Mexico by Cassie's interview with Fisher's brother. Of asking the same question and getting two different answers.

Except I was not Frank. I had grilled Pecun years ago. We'd talked for three hours back in 2013.

"If I didn't mention it before," Pecun said, "it was probably because I was referencing the specific conversation about the liver and all. Which was between Tignon and the older man."

"Do you keep records of your charters?" I asked.

"I did," Pecun said.

Past tense.

"Couple years ago Hurricane Michael made landfall close to here. Flooded basements, tore down homes. We didn't get hit," he said, "but the city encouraged everyone to clean up. I took most everything in the basement and tossed it."

"Maybe we could take a look at what's left," I said. "Just in case—"

"I'm sorry, Agent Camden. All that paper got hauled out of here. I rented a dumpster for the week."

I studied Pecun. I was not ignorant that different people achieved rapport in different ways. But was the boat captain locking up on account of me?

"Mr. Pecun," I said. "Like Agent Roberts mentioned, it's okay if you didn't say something before. I'm not sore, I promise." This came out stiffly, but it was the best I could manage.

"Well, I appreciate that," Pecun said. "From what I remember, the kid was a teenager. And kinda acting like one around his dad."

"In what way?" Frank asked.

"At first, the kid followed the old man around like he was his shadow. I remember 'cause the dad got upset. Hollered at the kid to give him some space. That's when the kid went down and hung out with your guy fishing with the liver."

"The boy was fishing as well?" Frank asked.

"As much as he could. His shoulder was in some sort of . . ." He motioned with his hand against his chest.

"A cast?" I asked.

"More like a homemade sling. Fashioned out of stuff you'd have in your hunting tent."

"How old was this boy?" Frank asked.

"Nineteen, maybe?" Pecun guessed.

I looked to Frank. A nineteen-year-old would be midtwenties when Kagan was investigating. The right age.

And suddenly it hit me. Their connection.

"Arrowhead and Mad Dog," I said. "Father and son."

Frank met my gaze.

"That's why there were two MOs," I said. "Years ago and now. It's also why Mad Dog knew about Arrowhead's crimes, but didn't take ownership of them."

"He told you that you shouldn't talk about people you don't know," Frank said.

I nodded. When I had spoken about Arrowhead, I had been talking about his father.

"The RV," Frank said. "The family vehicle. And the son is the one who interacted with the buyers. Who sold the flint-knapped arrowheads at the fairs."

It was also why he'd gone after my mom. When we went to the press and insisted the crimes Kagan had uncovered were the acts of a cold-blooded murderer, I'd insulted his dad. And Mad Dog had snapped. Devolved from an organized killer to a disorganized one. To a state of chaos.

Pecun could tell we'd discovered something, but wasn't sure what.

"This is good?" He squinted. "You guys figured something out?"

I pulled out my phone and showed him the sketch we'd presented at the press conference. "Could this be the boy—as an adult?"

The boat captain stared, his shoulders turned up. "I'd just be wild-ass guessing."

"Poor?" Frank asked. "Rich? Maybe based on how they spoke?"

"They weren't poor," he said. "But I'd remember if they were loaded. I get those types, and they let you know it."

"Did Dad have any tattoos?" Frank asked.

"I don't remember."

"So the boy was with Tignon?" I asked, clarifying this point. "You said he left his dad and—"

"Yeah," Pecun said. "I guess both he and his dad spent time with your suspect, just at different times during the trip."

I considered what we knew of Mad Dog. If he and his dad were from Houston, it would be a seven- or eight-hour drive to Orange Beach.

"Your charters leave at six a.m.?" I asked.

"Uh-huh," Pecun said.

"People who come from far away," I said. "Do they stay the night before . . . somewhere in town?"

"Back then," Pecun said, "the Red Horse was clean and close to our dock. They're kind of a mom-and-pop place, so not sure how good their records are, but you could check."

We asked him more questions, but got nowhere.

Ten minutes later, Frank and I hurried out to the car. The late-morning air was brisk, and I was doubtful that the hotel lead was strong. But something important had clicked for us. The theory I'd concocted in the middle of the night was accurate. Tignon and Mad Dog had intersected years ago, just differently than I'd thought.

Frank turned on the ignition, and I spoke before he could.

"I'm okay," I said.

"I doubt that's true, even for you, Gardner," he said. "But it doesn't matter. You can't be here with—"

Before Frank could finish, Pecun was rapping on his window. Frank rolled it down, and the captain leaned his head in.

"You need a license," he said, out of breath. "If you catch something. The kid did, so I sold his old man a license on the boat. I'm authorized to issue the paperwork. I turn the money over to the county once a quarter."

"So the county would have records," I said.

"I couldn't tell you. But it's a duplicate form, and my copies are in my attic. Some old boy downtown scared me into thinking I'd be fined if I didn't hold on to them, so I never stored them in the basement."

Frank turned off the car, and we got out.

"It's a mess up there," Pecun warned. "But I didn't toss nothing—I can tell you that."

We followed the boat captain back to his house. In the kitchen, he pulled on a cord, and a makeshift ladder folded down, revealing an opening twenty-four inches square that led up to his attic.

Frank and I put on gloves.

"Somethin' else," Pecun said. "The dad was kinda old for a dad. I don't think he was his grandpa. I didn't pick up on that. But he was a bit old to have a teenager."

"Okay," Frank said. "Appreciate that."

I moved up the wooden ladder, peeking my head around as I got to the top. Pecun had built a catwalk from plywood to store file boxes. I counted sixteen in total.

I pulled my body up and crouched, my hair brushing against the angled pine that made up the inside of the roof.

Frank came up behind me. He glanced around, looking from his pleated four-hundred-dollar slacks to the dirty catwalk, before giving in and sitting down on the wood.

We got to work, opening boxes, many of which were filled with personal tax returns and receipts. Others held the fishing licenses.

"I don't see dates on these," Frank said.

I had the second box open and was holding up a stack of three-by-eight-inch slips of paper. They were canary-yellow in color and looked like the third copy of something that was originally triplicate. "It's on the individual permit," I said. "Upper corner."

The slip I held read February 2016. I put that packet back in the box. The top back on.

About eight boxes in, I saw a ticket with a March 17 date in the right year. From there, I found a permit for March 24, 2013, the day before I'd arrived to talk to Pecun years ago.

Under persons, it read: 1.

I moved to the top of the ladder and glanced through the open hole at Aaron Pecun, who was washing his dishes in the kitchen below.

"Anyone else catch anything that day?" I asked.

"Tignon may have, but he had his own permit already," Pecun said. "So if you find the ticket, it'll say one person."

I moved back onto the catwalk and held the ticket out for Frank. Under NAME was scribbled "itc nolan." The ink was faded and barely legible on the yellow duplicate. No other information was listed. The address line was empty. Beside the name, it read PAID.

I pulled out my phone to call Cassie, then stopped. Stared at Frank. I wasn't supposed to be working. I was suspended or worse.

Frank took out his cell and put Cassie on speaker. "Where are you?" he asked.

"Houston," she said. "Shooter was running down a few leads, and I joined her."

"I might have something," Frank said. "I need you to look into the name itc nolan."

He spelled the letters out, with the name break.

"Is that a first name or . . . ?"

"I don't have more than that," Frank said.

Behind him, I stayed quiet.

"Well, where'd you get it from?"

"I'm sorry, Cassie," he said. "Can you just trust me and check it out?"

She agreed, and he told her he'd call back in an hour. We got through the last box of permits and found nothing else.

"Let's head to Texas," I said. "Everything's pointing to Texas."

Frank put the top back on the last box. "I agreed to go with you to Alabama," he said. "Which is more than I should've. And we're in Alabama."

"I could just observe," I said. "Throw out ideas."

Frank stood up. Brushed the dust off his pants. He grabbed a Ziploc we'd gotten from Pecun to preserve any prints on the fishing permit, and we headed out to the car.

"I've never pulled rank once," I said as we walked. "I got sent to El Paso years ago and took it like a man. At PAR, I never demanded credit when I cracked some big case for the LA or New York office. But after what happened to my mom, Frank, I've earned this."

I opened the door. Got in the driver's seat. Not taking no for an answer.

Frank opened the opposite door and got in. He pulled out his phone and found a photo on it. Laid it down for me to see. "Look," he said.

I stared at a photo of the office kitchenette. Paged forward to the next photo.

There were holes in the walls from a fist. Not the single hole I remembered making, but three or four. A toaster oven and microwave lay broken on the floor.

"I'm sorry," I said, staring down at the cuts on my knuckles.

"This guy here"—Frank pointed at Pecun's house—"he doesn't know anyone we know. But I can't show up at a real crime scene with you right now, Gardner. Poulton'll have my head."

I lowered my chin, nodding. Realizing this might not just affect me, but the future of PAR.

On a more personal level, though, it could also end my chance to find Mad Dog.

"Now in the time it takes to get a charter flight—or fly commercial—I could drive to Houston," he said. "If you want to join me on the road, we can talk more. Think about this "itc nolan" clue. If we figure something out, you gotta trust that I'll follow it up. But at some point, I need to drop you at an airport, Gardner. You need to go home. Take care of your mom. See your little girl. Clear your mind."

It was seven hours to Houston, presuming Frank averaged seventy-five miles an hour.

"Okay," I said. "I'll stay on as long as you'll let me."

I fired up the engine then, and we got onto the Baldwin Beach Expressway out of Orange Beach.

Around us, the cypress trees slowly gave way to farmland. Which gave way to horse ranches and back to cypress. Then cotton and peach farms. Frank moved my shield and weapon to the center console and laid his head on the side window.

"I did this," I said to Frank.

"Did what?" he mumbled.

"I had a witness in a box," I said. "March twenty-fifth, twenty thirteen. And in comes this lead about Tignon fishing. I sat on it for a day."

"Why didn't you send Saul?"

"It was my first time leading a case," I said. "I had to do everything myself."

"And you think what?" Frank smiled. "You woulda come to Orange Beach years ago? Said some magic words to this kid and stopped him from doing what he was gonna do?"

The road began to curve in a northwest direction. Out the window, stalks of corn filled a field.

"I'm gonna say something," Frank said. "And I don't mean any harm by it, Gardner."

"Okay?"

"The level of intelligence you got . . . the confidence that comes with how you are . . . there's an arrogance there, too. A feeling that knowing something equals solving it. That logic . . . equals truth. Those two are not the same, Gardner." Frank paused, then said, "Now I don't know what the future holds for you. But if you don't ever learn what I'm saying, you're never gonna realize your own potential."

I nodded, but couldn't speak. It was the kind of advice my mother would give.

"If that kid is following his dad around that boat," Frank continued, "after he's seen Dad shoot people with an arrow? Hell, maybe he even *sent* the kid down to collect the arrows after he shot those guys. Either way—that process was underway. That boy was being trained to kill."

I wondered about Mad Dog as a boy, being sent away by his dad on that boat trip. I pictured a teenager with a homemade sling on his shoulder. Had something happened between father and son, causing the boy not to want to spend time with his dad? Sending him to eavesdrop on Tignon, who spoke of fishing with human liver? Did the boy hear Tignon discuss other places he'd fished? Like Ashland, Texas?

Had he been inspired in some new way?

I went quiet, and Frank put his seat back. Soon, I heard him snoring. I picked up speed, bringing the Crown Vic up to eighty-five.

Within an hour, the Mississippi Sound was on my left. After that, I passed Gulfport.

As I drove, I thought about Arrowhead. I had taken apart Kagan's file, but nothing in it indicated how the father got started. Arrowhead's crimes began out of nowhere. A vigilante, avenging petty offenses.

Eventually, Frank stirred. I'd been trying to let him sleep, but we were below an eighth of a tank of gas and would have to pull over soon.

He glanced around, rubbing at his face. "Where the heck are we?"

"Over the border into Louisiana."

"Jesus," he said. "You gotta make yourself scarce."

We drove northwest to Baton Rouge, and I followed the signs to the airport. I thought of asking Frank about the future of PAR. About my future, with or without PAR.

"What are my chances?" I said finally. "Give it to me straight."

"If the case gets solved?" he said. "Happy ending all around. You explain about your mom, and we stand up for you . . . Fifty-fifty maybe? Otherwise, I dunno, Gardner. I dunno."

I pulled off the interstate and onto a highway that looped around the airport. As I did, Frank's phone chirped with a text.

"Cassie?" I asked.

Frank nodded, studying it. "Nothing on itc nolan."

A minute later he dropped me at the airport, and I walked inside. I had my ID with me, but no badge and gun. For the first time in years, I felt like I had no identity.

I stared at the board of flights and wondered if I should make my way to Miami for Camila or fly to Dallas and see my mom.

In the end, I found a flight to Dallas and bought a ticket at the desk. Walked through the airport without a suitcase or a carry-on.

Settling in at my gate, I stared at the planes taking off in front of me. Maybe it was the fatigue of so many days without sleep, but I felt like I was in a trance state, watching as the metallic birds lifted off and landed.

Time passed. An hour. Then ninety minutes. When I broke free of it, an idea was blooming in my head.

I used my phone's browser to look up something. Then took ten minutes to do more research and make sure I was right.

I called Frank. "I have his name," I said.

"You need to stand down, Gardner," he said. "Listen, I just got off the phone with Poulton. He told me you'll get a chance to explain yourself. A review board."

"I could catch up with you," I said, "tell you what I found out."

"I'm hanging up," Frank said.

"Creighton Emwon."

"The name Mad Dog used when he posed as that realtor?" Frank asked.

"Emwon is the clue. Literally becomes M dash one."

"M one?"

"As in the tank," I said. "Also known as the Abrams Tank. Named for Creighton Abrams."

"Okay?" Frank said, a question more than an answer.

"Creighton Abrams was the commander of U.S. Forces in Vietnam, from sixty-eight to seventy-two. He implemented the strategy to win the hearts and minds of the rural population."

"What the heck does that tell us?"

"It's part of a puzzle," I said. "Come back, and I'll tell you the rest."

"I ain't coming back, partner," Frank said. "But if you have a good lead, I know you're gonna tell me, so I can get the hell after it."

I exhaled loudly. Frank wasn't going to turn around.

"The Creighton Abrams detail told me that Mad Dog's father was military and served in Vietnam," I said. "From there I realized it was not itc nolan. It was LTC Nolan."

"Lieutenant Colonel?" Frank said.

"Specifically, Lieutenant Colonel Jack Nolan of Houston, Texas. Two tours in Vietnam between sixty-seven and seventy."

"Son of a gun," Frank said. "You looked him up?"

"He has a son named Ethan Nolan," I said. "Twenty-six years old."

"Anything on the kid?"

"I'm just working off a phone browser," I said. "Only thing I can find is some hackathon in Houston when the kid was twelve. He's some sort of tech prodigy."

"Get on a plane," Frank said. "You rest up, partner. We got this."

I flashed to a moment two days ago in Georgia. Agent Kagan telling me his whole life was the Bureau. Was I any different?

More than that, could Frank do this alone?

"Frank," I said. "Doing the detail work I do—it's not something you can just tack on to the big picture work you're so good at."

"Funny," he said.

But I wasn't joking.

"I'll do my best," he said. "Channel my inner Gardner."

Frank hung up, and I watched two more planes take off.

Why were we being left these clues? I thought of Richie's statement—*a paper in Tignon's mouth—an insect in Fisher's heart . . . put a normal team at the FBI on this and you find those three months from now.*

I stood up and left my boarding pass on my chair. Walking downstairs, I found the rental car center past baggage claim and got a car from Avis.

Out on the interstate, I pushed the sedan to eighty. Soon, I was more than halfway through Louisiana. Signs for the Sabine National Refuge directed traffic south, but I kept west, crossing the border into Texas.

After a while longer, I made the decision to call Cassie. I needed to know if Mad Dog had been caught.

"It's Gardner," I said when I heard her voice.

"Oh my God," she said. "I've been calling you. How are you?"

From her tone, I could tell that Frank had not mentioned our visit to Orange Beach.

"I'm fine," I said. "You know . . ."

Cassie made a noise with her nose. "I do."

I swallowed. "I'm trying not to think about her, but . . ."

"Yeah."

There was a long pause, and then Cassie jumped in to fill the space. "It was weird, but I thought you were with Frank earlier," she said. "He called and had this lead. Then he called again with more information."

"Where are you?" I asked.

It was her turn to hesitate.

"Cassie," I said. "I just want this guy to get justice. Jail time."

"Shooter and I are at a house, east of Houston."

"Owned by the Nolan family?"

"So you *are* with Frank?"

"No," I said. "But I know about Nolan. Did you arrest them? The family?"

"Ethan Nolan was gone before we arrived, Gardner," she said. "A neighbor confirmed the family owned a white RV. But there's no *them*. The mom died in childbirth. And the dad is dead. Had a heart attack last year."

"When?"

"December first," she said. "There was a mass card under a magnet on the fridge."

I added this event to the timeline in my head.

Two weeks later, Ethan Nolan showed up at Banning's book launch in Houston. The killings started twenty-six days after that.

"Per the neighbors, there were lights on in the house last night," Cassie said. "They heard the RV come in around one a.m. It left an hour or so later."

"What's their property like?" I asked.

"Marshy," she said. "Forested. It's a bit . . . off-the-grid cable show. They have their own water storage. Two dozen solar panels. The neighbor down the road told me he kept thinking Nolan Senior was about to start a farm."

"Based on what?"

"One year the old guy would use his tractor to create giant dirt berms. Dam up the stream. Next season he'd pile up logs. There's trails, too, Gardner, moving through this whole place. Kinda sus. Two feet wide, five feet high. More like tunnels with heavy growth around them. Like some kind of maze."

A place to hunt. To play chase games.

Cassie had used present tense when she first answered. She'd said, "you *are* with Frank."

"Frank is on his way there still?" I asked.

"No," she said, her voice suddenly registering concern. "He told us he was chasing a lead. Said he'd check in an hour ago. We figured you two were together."

I considered the last twenty-four hours. At four o'clock yesterday afternoon, Mad Dog had been in Dallas at the Sparrow coffeehouse, logging into our system. By five o'clock, he'd been in Woodrell, with my mom. By two in the morning, he'd left Houston and made his way somewhere else.

Where?

"Did Ethan Nolan live there with his dad?" I asked.

"Oh yeah," she said. "The kid's got a shrine to his father. There's also a roomful of computers, taken apart and half built. Puzzle and riddle books. Volumes on computer coding."

In our first conversation, Mad Dog had said he liked me. Had he read up on PAR? On me?

"What do you mean 'shrine'?" I asked.

"Pictures of the two of them," she said. "Some hand-drawn maps. They're weird, though."

"Weird how?"

"All the maps have a red L on them, Gardner. As in 'loss.' Except for one. The son covered the walls with them. Shooter called them a mix between a hunting map and hide-and-seek."

Ahead of me, in Beaumont, Interstate 10 turned south toward Houston, where the team was.

Except Frank was not there.

"Text me pictures of those maps, will you?" I said. "I'm going stir-crazy not working on this."

Cassie told me she would, and we hung up.

A minute later, my phone dinged. Then dinged again. The maps were hand-sketched, as Cassie had said. Topographic.

An interstate sign loomed ahead, indicating a turn for Route 287. I was nearly past the off-ramp when I slammed on the brakes. Swerved to make the turn.

I steadied the rental car.

I knew where Ethan Nolan had gone.

And so did Frank.

CHAPTER THIRTY-EIGHT

BIG THICKET NATIONAL PRESERVE WAS LOCATED TWO hours east of Houston. It was called a preserve, as opposed to a national park, since it permitted hunting, which I was sure Mad Dog and his father went there for. It was also the national preserve whose sticker Shooter had found on the RV in Rawlings, New Mexico.

I made my way up Highway 287, past Lumberton and Kountze, the navigation on my phone telling me I was minutes from arriving at the preserve's visitor's center.

My goal was to get there before the place closed. I pulled into the parking lot at 4:58 p.m.

Inside, the center was part gift store and part educational facility. A woman in a National Parks uniform stood by a desk to my right. Along the wall behind her was a rack of books about the ecology of Big Thicket.

"Can I help you?" she asked.

"I'm a federal agent, and I'm searching for my partner," I said. "He took off after a suspect, and I haven't been able to locate him."

The woman hesitated, and I took out my phone. On the drive over,

I had gone onto my cloud server and retrieved images of my FBI badge, which Frank had kept. I showed these to her, explaining that my credentials were with my partner.

"Is your partner real handsome?" she asked. "Late forties? Black?"

I nodded.

"He showed me a sketch," she said. "Told me he was on the lookout for a vehicle."

"A white RV," I said.

"That's the one. He wanted to drive through the parking lots at the trailheads, but I told him we're not set up that way."

"I don't understand."

"The preserve is spread out across a hundred miles. A lot of these trails are hard to find unless you hunt here. There aren't really formal parking lots or trailheads like you see in other national or state parks. I recommended two or three spots for him to start with."

"Where?" I said.

She unfolded a map on the counter. "First one was Turkey Creek, east of Warren. Next was Lance Rosier in the opposite direction, south of us." She pointed to the far right side of the map. "Lower Neches was the last. Jack Gore Baygall Unit."

I stared at these names. The different hunting units of the sprawling preserve were separated by dozens of miles of private roads, houses, and the tendrils of the oil and gas industry. Small cities, even. I had driven past parts of the preserve along the way and hadn't even noticed.

"What direction was he headed first?"

"Turkey Creek," she said.

I found it on the map, north of the visitor's center, and hustled back to the rental car. Barbed wire marked the edges of private property, and the sun was dropping. The phone's navigation was on, but the volume was down. I missed the turn for Turkey Creek and flipped a U-turn in the parking lot of a restaurant. On their storefront, the word *country* was spelled with a *k*.

In a minute, I found my way along a road with four-story beech trees leaning at angles so close to the pavement that it felt like driving through a downtown. Three miles farther, I turned in at Turkey Creek and slowed. Right off the highway was a parking area, where I saw Frank's Crown Vic.

The driver's side door was swung open.

I cut my engine and glanced around, weaponless. Under the trees, the light was fading, and the night was getting cool. I backed the rental car in beside the Crown Vic, ready to gun the engine if a shot rang out.

But no shot sounded.

The only noise was the hum of insects.

I moved into Frank's car.

Atop the dash were his car keys.

But Frank was gone. Taken by Mad Dog.

I examined the inside of the sedan. My Glock was missing, but my badge and phone remained on the center console. Left for me to find.

An invitation to come after him.

CHAPTER THIRTY-NINE

I CALLED UP CASSIE AND TOLD HER ABOUT FRANK.

"I can't believe he didn't call for backup," she said.

I thought of my warning to Frank—and his response. He was trying to prove something to me.

"How far away is Richie?" I asked.

"Four hours," Cassie said.

"And you and Shooter?"

"Little under two."

I thought of the games Mad Dog and his dad had played. The Ws and Ls. How much time did Frank have? Was daybreak too late? And how long would it take me to find them, if I could?

"I need a game warden," I said to Cassie. "We have a liaison to National Parks. A place this expansive . . . there's gotta be someone on call for emergencies."

Five minutes later, Cassie rang back. She couldn't get a chopper for three hours, but Shooter would start driving my way.

"Poulton said to wait 'til daybreak," she said. "After he told us you shouldn't be there at all. That you're suspended."

"And the game warden?" I interrupted.

"Yeah, I had better results with that. One is driving down from a place called Beech Woods. From what they tell me, she's worked there twenty years and will be at your location in fifteen minutes."

I thanked Cassie and used the time to inspect the rest of Frank's car. But nothing else was out of place.

I studied the map I'd taken from the visitor's center. The trail at Turkey Creek was twelve miles long. Nearby signs described carnivorous plants, and I deduced that this was one of the draws of Big Thicket: a place with plants that ate insects in the night.

A few minutes later, a white truck with a Big Thicket logo pulled in and a woman got out. She was tall with light brown skin and a thick head of coarse black hair, pulled back in a ponytail. She was dressed in casual clothes, not a uniform.

"Tallulah Terradas," she introduced herself.

I explained how I'd found Frank's car. "It's likely Agent Roberts was taken by our suspect. How well do you know the hunters that come here?"

She shrugged and nodded at the same time. "I've worked here for two decades, Agent Camden. Supervised every unit, from Menard to Beaumont. If they've been coming a while, I might know 'em."

"Two men," I said. "The younger one is twenty-six. Caucasian. The dad is a veteran. Their last name is Nolan."

"That could be a lot of fellas," Terradas said.

"Most likely they've been hunting here since the younger man was a boy. Eight or nine."

"You know what they hunt?" Terradas asked.

"The father is an expert archer. My presumption is deer."

"Well, we're shotgun and bow-and-arrow for deer. Kids can start shooting at nine if they're accompanied."

"The older man may have looked too old to be the boy's dad," I said.

She nodded, her brain cranking away. "Like a grandpa, maybe?"

I nodded. "You limit the number of permits, right?"

"Depends on the unit. Some areas top out at fifty. Others, nine hundred permits per year."

"Do you regularly drive the hunting areas?"

"We do," she said. "Check licenses. Firearms."

"They own a white RV," I said. "Twenty-plus years old."

Her eyes lit up.

"I think I might know them fellas," she said. "The old man is rigid with his son, but polite to us."

I called Cassie, and she sent me a picture, which Terradas verified.

"Back at the office," Terradas told me, "we'll have permit information on them. Tomorrow, I could pull—"

"Ms. Terradas," I interrupted. "I've got a situation tonight. I'm looking for where they hunt. Where their special place is. A place others might not know about."

The warden pulled out a map similar to the one from the visitor's center. Spread it over the hood of her truck and used her phone as a flashlight.

"If it's the guys I'm thinking, it's gonna be a little hard to find at this hour. You want that I go with you?"

I considered this. Shooter was on her way. Two hours out, probably. And I was working without a badge. If I waited 'til sunrise, someone from the Bureau would stop me for sure. Shut me down while they did a confab on how to approach the issue. I was guessing Frank didn't have that long.

"No," I said. "My team knows where I am, and they're sending someone. I'll keep them abreast."

"Well, this particular spot is in Jack Gore," she said. "A baygall unit? You know what that is?"

"It's a clay layer that traps water," I said. "A poorly drained marsh."

"Exactly," she said. "So it's pretty dark in there, and not just at night. Tangled vines. Tannin from rotting plants. You gotta be careful."

She gave me directions, east out of Turkey Creek. "You're gonna come off of Ninety-Two onto Craven Camp Road," she said, marking her map with a red Sharpie. "From there, you find Franklin Lake Road."

I glanced at my phone. Time was passing, and I needed to go. "Franklin Lake has a campground?"

"Franklin Lake doesn't even have much of a lake," she said. "But if it's them two and you want their secret spot . . ."

"Yes."

"Then there's an old Union Gas depot. Place has three or four tanks, but mostly it's a vacant lot. The hunters aren't supposed to park there."

"These two do?"

"Sorta. I've seen them pull that white RV under some scrub brush nearby, probably to keep would-be thieves away while they're gone. There's a field over there with a dozen hunting blinds. That's where they begin. From there it's on foot—toward the river. That's the best I can tell you. Their spot's in between the thicket and the water."

"Do you have a topographic representation of this area?" I asked.

"On my laptop," she said.

She retrieved her PC from the truck and fired it up. Punched in variables to bring up the Franklin Lake area.

I studied the digital topographic map. The screen showed a mix of blues and greens in one area. Reds and yellows in another.

Terradas moved an errant hair off her face. She had dark brown eyes and a perfect aquiline nose.

"Deep blue is thirty feet above sea level." She pointed at the screen. "Green, sixty. Yellow, ninety. Red, a hundred and ten."

Near Franklin Lake was a swarm of dots that I suspected was a river.

"Can you zoom in on that?" I pointed at her laptop.

She did, and the area magnified. "This is the dead end by Union Gas?" I asked. "The parking lot?"

"There's a little turnaround there," she said. "And nearby is Franklin Lake. It's a puddle, really. John's Lake below is larger. Leads into the Neches. But those two men head in a more northeast direction. Away from John's Lake."

I pulled out my phone. Studied the hand-drawn maps that Cassie had texted me, the curving lines I felt were indicators of topography. There were two with an L on them and one with a W.

Down at the bottom of each was a date, and I stared at the date below the W.

March 22, 2013.

Two days before the fishing trip with Tignon.

Was this the one time Ethan Nolan had beaten his dad at their game? Was it then that his father had exacted some punishment that put Ethan in a sling?

I examined the river of dots in the hand drawing, then motioned at Terradas's laptop. The curve was identical. "These blue dashes are water?"

"No." She shook her head. "That's the thicket. Before you get to the water, you gotta get through the pines and live oaks. Beech trees. Then comes the water, thick around your boots. Then swampier still. There's water elm. Cypress. Tupelo. What we call the backwater slough."

Was Mad Dog hunted as a child as part of some game? Did he cover his wall in maps that showed where he lost to his father?

"You don't have a weapon to spare, do you?" I asked.

Terradas gave me a look. "I came straight from dinner." She reached into her truck and produced a pocketknife. "This is the best I can do."

"Appreciate it," I said, taking the knife. "I'll get this back to you."

I hurried over to the Crown Vic.

Mad Dog was baiting me to chase him onto territory that he and his dad knew better than anyone else. With his father dead, he was now the expert, and the night was growing darker by the second. At any minute, Mad Dog could end Frank's life.

I got in Frank's car and pulled back onto the county highway, heading east, the ranger's map on the passenger seat and the dome light on so I could glance at it.

In a few minutes the road became dirt, and my hands jerked at the wheel. In the dark, I could not tell how soft the road was, and I regretted not accepting at least an escort from the warden.

Gravel crunched under the Crown Vic's tires, and the constitution of the road changed again. Soon I turned south. Slowing, I swerved left onto a small road that headed toward Franklin Lake.

I let off the gas.

Out my window, the silhouettes of hunting blinds stood, eight feet by eight, built on wooden platforms raised ten feet above the saw grass. A place for a hunter to wait for deer.

Looking east, I studied the line of trees I'd seen on the topographic map. The same ones that looked like a river of dots in the hand-drawn diagram. I kept up my speed so as not to get stuck in the dirt, my headlights the only thing illuminating the bumpy road.

Beyond the thicket, the water grew deeper, until you were in the Neches River. Up ahead I saw what looked like four large tanks, almost like grain silos, with a catwalk mounted to the front. I clicked on my high beams and saw a sign that read UNION GAS OPERATING COMPANY, 1000 ACRES. The red metal listed a registration number and a date.

I steered around the circular parking area. Nothing.

Then something caught my eye. The edge of a white vehicle, parked under a tree's bough a hundred feet away.

I followed the circular road I'd come in on, heading back out as if I was done with my search. When I made my way to the gravel road, I shut off my lights.

In a perfect world, I would approach the RV from the rear, examining the doors and evaluating the best path. But I had no weapon other than a pocketknife, and the night was pitch-black.

I had come up working with several people at the FBI who were referred to as mavericks. Saul was one. And I'd noticed two things that made him different. One, he thought differently than others. A skill I had in spades. Two, he acted unexpectedly. Chose instinct over rules. Justified his disruptive behavior later. And was rarely wrong.

Think like you do, Gardy.
Act like other people.

I turned the Crown Vic around. Pointed it back toward the area by the round tanks, evaluating the danger to Frank versus the element of surprise.

I accelerated in the dark, my eyes barely finding the edge of the dirt road. I was moving at twenty miles an hour. Then thirty. Bouncing over small dirt ruts. When the gas tanks and the catwalk came into view, I swerved right through the underbrush and put my foot to the floor.

I hit the RV at full speed, the center of my car as far from the gas tank as I could to keep the vehicles from bursting on impact.

My airbag popped on, a sharp pressure thrusting against my nose.

The white recreational vehicle pitched back, caught on a downed log, and went airborne, flipping onto its side.

The Crown Vic plowed into it as I swerved, and the combined mess of us came to a stop.

I knew I could've hurt Frank if he was inside, but Mad Dog might do worse, and I needed the element of surprise.

I undid my seat belt. Cut away at the airbag with the ranger's pocketknife.

Putting my hand to my nose, I found it bloody and likely broken. I got out fast. Climbed onto my hood and from there, on to the RV. One of the two doors was facing up; the other was pinned to the ground.

Standing on the side of the RV, I swung the door open.

Silence.

I dropped down into the hole of the door and found that my feet were traversing the side wall. I used my flashlight to scan the vehicle, hoping to find Frank. Or Mad Dog. Or a weapon he'd left behind. But no one was inside.

Was Frank ever here? Or had Mad Dog killed him in Turkey Creek and left his body in some unknown location?

My light raked the inside of the RV. I was about to leave when I spotted something familiar. My light came back to it.

A bullet hole in the side of a briefcase. Frank's.

Mad Dog was close.

If I was lucky, so was Frank.

CHAPTER FORTY

I CLIMBED OUT OF THE RV AND MOVED BACK TO THE PARK-
ing area. Walked over to the thicket of pine and hardwood trees that
formed the curve I had seen in the hand-drawn map.

The dust and debris from the crash were settling, and my neck
throbbed with pain. I stared out at the swamp. At the tendrils of branches
to my right. Half of the trees had fallen down naturally or were rotten,
and getting through them would be time-consuming.

I began moving, inching my way through the dense vegetation,
foot by foot. The night was black, a waning crescent moon above. Insects bounced off my arms. Mosquitoes. Horseflies. The weather was
cooling, but in the trees above, an orchestra of noises resounded.

My mother had taught me the songs of katydids and crickets. I
heard both, along with the low vibrating croaks of bullfrogs, whose
voices bounced off the palmetto.

After a half hour, the ground became muddy beneath my feet. I saw
the bank of a river, first to the west, then curving north around me.

Take one step and pause.

Listen. Be silent.

The water in the preserve was suffocating in its ubiquity. The shoreline was flat enough for it to seep into the marsh grass and duckweed, soaking the ground without one even noticing.

I edged along the waterline, at times stepping furtively into three inches of water. At others, ten inches. In my memory, I saw the hand-drawn topographic maps in perfect detail, sensing the rise and fall of the land beneath my feet.

As I walked to higher ground, I counted off the distance from the shore, then adjusted to halfway back, my mind placing the squiggle of hand-drawn lines one below the other as I moved.

The two maps had an X drawn through them, each about twenty feet from the shore. If I understood the notations about elevation correctly, there would be some hole in the ground there, perhaps a natural divot where Mad Dog had hidden in the mud as a child.

Was he hiding there now, holding Frank hostage?

By 4 a.m., I had walked most of the map, moving in a quiet circular pattern, inch by inch, steering clear of the areas with the X until I absolutely had to, wanting to come up on that area last and furtively.

Finding higher ground, I caught my breath. The night was nearly devoid of light, and my footsteps were silent.

But something had been splashing in the water, and the rhythm of it felt purposeful, like a fish caught in a net.

Effort, then rest. Effort, then rest.

I counted in my head, waiting for the splash again. The area of noise in the water was ten yards from the shore. Directly back from that point, on land, was one of the Xs.

I held my phone to the ground so no light shone and set the timer for five minutes, the alarm noise set to a piece of music from my library.

Before I heard the splashing noise again, I drew my arm back like a quarterback and threw the phone through the night. It landed just as the splash sounded, perfectly concealing the noise of the phone settling into a dense grouping of sweet bay magnolia, halfway between the shoreline and the X mark.

I quietly stepped backward then, away from the water and into the thicket and higher ground. Stopped there and lowered my body so it was prone to the dirt.

Then I crawled back toward the water, moving slowly on my stomach, my hands pulling my body along and my stomach gliding over dirt berms and wet grass.

Sixty feet from the X.

Forty.

Twenty feet.

I froze.

Something was there.

Someone was there, the shape of a head barely visible in the night.

I moved closer.

Sixteen feet.

Twelve.

I stopped again, counting the seconds in my head. Then I scooched slower still, inch by inch through the mud, my body prone.

Ahead of me, the outline of the back of a man's head became visible. If I was seeing him correctly, he was on his stomach, the back of his boots one body-length in front of me.

I counted. Ten seconds left. Five.

A light came alive, ten feet away in front of the dark shape. Then came music.

Older fans of Dixieland jazz would call the ring tone "Tiger Rag," but most Louisianans knew it as the song the LSU Tigers play after every touchdown. LSU: the place where I'd gotten my master's degree.

The shape in front of me rose up on its elbows and shot with a rifle. Bam. Eject. Bam. Eject. Bam.

"Tiger Rag" kept playing, and the phone skipped through the air.

I inched closer in the dark.

Four feet.

Two.

The man tossed the rifle and sat up, pulling out a handgun.

As he did, I leapt into a crouching pose and knocked the Glock from his hand. He dove for it, but I pushed him off balance and got to it first.

I swiveled around, and we were face-to-face.

Me, holding my Glock. And Ethan Nolan, pointing Frank's weapon at my chest.

"Agent Camden," he said.

My muddy hand gripped the Glock, and I moved into a crouched position.

"Where's Frank?" I demanded, my finger on the trigger.

"Frank could be in a lot of places pretty soon." Nolan motioned over his shoulder. "See that tower?"

I flicked my eyes toward the shore, my gun still held on Nolan.

Twenty feet away was a hunting blind, except this one was built into the Neches River. Reflective tape along the legs of the structure indicated the depth of the water.

Something was moving there. The sound I'd heard earlier.

"Can you see him?" Nolan asked. "Your boss? Tied up?"

I focused on Nolan, my left hand moving up to support the Glock in my right.

Firearms experts will tell you that striking first is essential because action beats reaction. They will also inform you that, statistically speaking, experienced criminals can point a gun and fire it in less than nine-tenths of a second. A solid eight seconds had already passed, and neither Nolan nor I had discharged.

"I thought you were the good guy," I said. "The vigilante, holding us all accountable."

His finger was on the trigger. If I fired, I would receive a shot to the chest in return a moment later.

"Well, you know how it is," Nolan said. "Even Batman has to go dark sometimes."

Behind Nolan, I heard the splashing sound again. A bubble popped in the water.

"I think Frank's time is up," he said.

CHAPTER FORTY-ONE

I GLANCED AT THE WATER.

At the top of the hunting blind, a windsock hung lazily. Along the side of the structure, the shape of an arm reached for something, then fell back into the darkness.

I looked back at Nolan.

"When I was younger, we'd play survival here," he said. "Rule was, sun comes up, and I win."

I wanted to shoot him dead.

"I'm sorry your dad did this to you."

Nolan laughed. "Dad did nothing but raise me with honesty and fairness. You really don't know anything, do you?"

He straightened his arm then, and Frank's Glock nearly touched my shirt. "You're gonna let me walk out of here, Camden. 'Cause if you don't, we're gonna kill each other. Or we'll stay like this all night. And Agent Roberts doesn't have all night."

An insect was crawling on my face. The wind had grown colder.

"Can I add a complication?" he said, smiling. "See, I like playing games with you. And you know I had Banning's login. Kind of a nice view. You can see anything. Like what was going to happen to PAR next month."

He moved from a crouching position to a standing one, and I mirrored him.

"PAR is getting disbanded," he said.

"I know," I replied. Even though I had not been sure about this.

"That's why they didn't care when you were assigned this investigation. Frank is dumping you to run Dallas. So maybe you want to take a shot at me after all. Let your boss die."

I said nothing.

"Cassie Pardo is being sent to Information Services in Clarksville," he continued. "Jo Harris to Omaha."

I recalled Richie's comment about a one-month trial at PAR, after which Frank would decide where he'd go next.

"Wanna know what was gonna happen to you?"

"It doesn't matter," I said. "I'm suspended right now. So I'm gone anyway."

"Interesting," he said. "So whadaya say? Wanna wait here all night 'til backup comes? Let Frank get what he deserves for not telling you all?"

"No."

"Then I'm backing up," he said. "And maybe there's a chance you save your boss."

I thought of Nolan's smashed RV, a half mile away. I could get Frank and still go after Nolan.

He took another step back into a grove of hardwood, his gun trained on me the whole time. And mine on him.

"Last chance to shoot me," he said.

The moonlight on the tree trunks showed off how enormous they were. One moment, Nolan was beside them. The next, he'd disappeared.

I heard footsteps. The crashing sounds of palmettos being pushed aside. When the noise faded into the distance, I turned. Picked up the rifle and slung it over my shoulder. Headed for the hunting blind.

"Frank?" I called out.

I heard a muffled sound and saw the tail of a gator slide into the water.

Alligators are apex predators, related to beasts that lived 150 million years ago. Shooter once told me they were easy to kill—if you were an expert shot. You simply had to place a bullet behind the rectangular plate on the top of the reptile's head.

I pointed in that direction and emptied my Glock in a tight pattern. In the light of my flashlight, the water went a reddish brown.

"Frank," I hollered again, the hunting blind now twenty feet in front of me.

I moved into the three-foot-deep swamp, my eyes darting left and right. I'd already lost my mom. I couldn't lose Frank.

I saw a shape along the east-facing pylon on the tower and trudged closer. The ground dropped, the water rising to my chin. I held my gun above the surface.

Frank was tied to the pylon, his head barely above water. I cut at the rope with Terradas's pocketknife, and he broke free.

"C'mon," I said.

We turned back through the greenish-brown water, and I heard a splash north of me. Jammed a new magazine into my Glock and fired blindly.

As the water level got lower and the shore drew closer, I saw Frank's face was cut. As were his legs.

"Faster," I said.

In a minute, we'd made it to shore. Frank dropped to the ground, and I scanned the thicket for Nolan, my Glock held out.

Nothing.

Above us, a bank of trees was covered in Spanish moss. I remembered my mother teaching me as a child that the plant was neither moss nor from Spain.

Frank lifted his leg. The cuts there had shredded his slacks, and he was bleeding badly. I presumed Mad Dog had cut him to draw in the alligators, but this could also have happened from moving through the thicket. Either way, I had to get him to a hospital.

"I'm not sure the tailor can mend these." He motioned at his pants, half laughing. "And you know *I* got a good tailor."

Frank was in bad shape. Dehydrated. Bleeding. There was no way I could leave him here and chase Nolan. And there was no way Frank was in any shape to join me.

"Tell me you killed that son of a bitch," he said.

I had never heard Frank curse before, and I shook my head. Smacked at a mosquito.

"No," I said.

I walked past the muddy divot where I'd surprise attacked Nolan. Found my iPhone in a bush nearby. The face was cracked, but no bullets were in it.

"I wrecked his RV," I said. "But he knows this area. And he's got a head start."

I held up my phone. One bar. Cassie picked up on the first ring.

"You got him?"

"Frank, yes," I said. "But Nolan is in the wind. Send an ambulance for the boss. And have that game warden meet me by the Union Gas turnaround."

I hung up and dropped onto my back, exhausted.

Frank turned to me. "Thank you," he said.

He started crying then, and I reached a hand over. Put it on his shoulder.

"I didn't deserve this," he said. "You coming to rescue me."

And at that moment, I knew Ethan Nolan was right. PAR *was* being shut down, and Frank was leaving us behind.

CHAPTER FORTY-TWO

BY 5 A.M., WARDEN TALLULAH TERRADAS HAD ARRIVED AT the turnaround where I'd crashed the Crown Vic into the RV. Frank was in an ambulance, heading to Houston Methodist. Terradas had my map of east Texas spread out over the hood of her truck.

At her side, I studied the lay of the land.

"We faced off here," I said, pointing to an area in the Jack Gore Baygall Unit. "These rivers run north to south, correct? Eventually they ferry you down, east of Beaumont and out into the Gulf of Mexico."

"Yes, sir," she said.

"I passed a sign for canoes."

"Those trips are educational, mostly. We've got boaters, though. A lotta them."

Before Terradas had arrived, I'd examined the back of the crashed RV in the predawn light. It sported a hitch with a two-inch ball, suitable for hauling.

Nolan had a boat stashed somewhere.

A white truck pulled up beside the game warden's vehicle, and Shooter got out.

"How you doin', Gardner?" she said, her face more serious than usual.

I introduced Shooter to Terradas, and the warden estimated how far Ethan Nolan could have traveled in the three hours it had taken for me to get Frank to the road. She broke her numbers down by canoe and motorboat. If he was in the former, he could still be on the water.

"If I was him," Terradas said. "I'd put out somewhere near Rose City. It's close to the Louisiana-Texas border."

I glanced southward on the map. At the Beaumont area I'd driven through last night.

"The current takes you there fast." She tapped the map. "And you're right near Interstate Ten. From there you can go west toward California or east toward Florida."

Meaning he could be anywhere.

Shooter looked at me. "We got a bird coming in twenty, Gardner. You make the call."

"The logical thing for Nolan to do is float down that river," I said. "But he's been countering our logic for days. I'd bet he went upriver instead. Put out to the north."

As our eyes moved in the opposite direction, Shooter's phone chirped. It was Cassie, and Shooter put her on speaker.

"Guys," Cassie said. "I found something at the Nolan house. Kinda low-key weird."

"Weird how?" I asked.

"It's a picture of Nolan Senior from nineteen sixty-eight," Cassie said. "Vietnam."

"Yeah, he served," I said. "Sixty-seven to seventy."

"We know that," Cassie said. "But in the photo, he's with a group of soldiers. Gardner, I swear I recognize one of them."

"How do you mean?"

"I could be wrong," she said. "But I think it's a young William Banning."

CHAPTER FORTY-THREE

I PACED IN BETWEEN THE WARDEN'S TRUCK AND SHOOT-er's, my head and neck throbbing from the car crash and from carrying Frank out of the swamp.

"Like I said, I could be wrong," Cassie said.

In my head, I thought of Ethan Nolan's words to me just hours earlier.

You really don't know anything, do you?

I turned to Shooter. "What did you guys report in so far to HQ? Last twenty-four hours?"

"Just that we'd found the Nolan house, but no one was there," Shooter said. "That Dad had died in December, and the son was in the wind."

I looked east to the swamp, then back to Shooter.

"We need to call Marly," I said. "There's a question we haven't followed up on."

I urged Cassie to keep looking around and hung up. Phoned Quantico.

"Marly," I said when she came on the line. "The information Ethan Nolan looked at when he accessed Banning's personnel file in December. You go through it yet?"

"Haven't had a moment," she said.

"Can you?"

Marly pulled it up, and we waited. As we did, she explained that the system left a timestamp whenever an item was inspected.

"Huh," Marly made a noise.

"What is it?" Shooter asked.

"There's a letter here. Apparently, a Lieutenant Colonel Jack Nolan applied to the Bureau and used Banning as a reference."

"The letter's from Nolan?" I asked.

"No," Marly said. "It's from Banning. Nineteen eighty-three. An internal memo, suggesting the Bureau double-check Nolan's psychological fitness."

"Jesus," Shooter said.

I was starting to get a bad feeling about this case.

"When was the director's login used?" I asked, "To inspect that document?"

"At one twenty-one a.m.," she said. "December eighteenth. It was Nolan Junior's first login."

This was early in the morning, just hours after Banning's book event had ended.

I blinked. Something didn't fit. Based on the video from the event, I'd assumed that if Nolan had gotten into any account, it would be Agent Yang's.

"Can you access an agent's case history for me?" I asked.

"If it's relevant to the case," Marly said.

"Agent Lisa Yang," I said.

When I looked at Yang's résumé, a pattern had bumped. She'd

gone from Yale to Iowa. An odd move for a smart daughter of East Coast immigrants.

But the Iowa Writers' Workshop was top 5 in the country.

This was probably the same detail that William Banning had noticed when she'd applied to work on his team in 2016.

"Tell me something, Marly," I said. "How many files does the average agent check out per year?"

"Fourteen," she said.

"And someone in the research group?"

"Maybe twice that."

"How many files did Lisa Yang check out in the last four years?"

I waited, and Marly came back. "In the teens, most years," she said. "But in June of twenty eighteen, Yang checked out thirty-three files."

"All in one month?"

"Uh-huh."

"What about Banning?"

"Director Banning?" Marly asked. "The director doesn't do research, Gardner."

"Can you look?"

I heard a few keys being punched. "Huh," she said. "Between July first of twenty eighteen and April twentieth the following year," she said, "Banning checked out a hundred and twenty-one files."

I recalled Freddie's comments about Agent Yang jumping in during the book talk. And Frank's note about Banning knowing the cases cold, but not the way they were described in the book.

Yang had ghostwritten Banning's biography.

That's why her case activity was so high. She had done the research, back before Banning retired.

More than that, she'd done most of that research using Banning's login. Which she still had.

When Nolan captured the keystrokes off the 360-degree fan video, he didn't log in to Yang's account. He logged in to Banning's. He must've felt like he'd hit the lottery, seeing the note about his dad.

Or maybe he felt something else. Like rage.

I had gone silent, and Marly cleared her throat.

"What is it?" she asked.

I wondered if it was normal to travel with your ghostwriter.

"Lisa Yang," I said. "On December seventeenth, she was traveling for the Bureau. Did she submit for reimbursement?"

Marly typed for a moment, then answered. "Yup. Flight and taxi."

"What about lodging?" I asked. "In Houston."

"None," she said. "She stayed overnight, but—no—nothing for lodging."

Yang and Banning, I thought.

What had Poulton's advice been? *Tread lightly. She's highly decorated.*

But I had seen no such decoration in her file.

I knew what had happened now. More than that, I knew what was about to happen next. I thanked Marly and got Poulton on the line.

"Where's Banning?" I asked the deputy director.

"Houston," he said. "The director figured your team would catch Nolan today, and he wanted to be close by. Make a big splash with the announcement."

Or maybe control how much of the splash got on him.

"I got word about what happened with Frank," Poulton said. "That will go a long way for you. But as far as I'm concerned, you're off the clock still, Camden. Why are you calling me?"

"When's the last time you checked in on Banning?"

"I don't make a habit of babysitting the director."

"He served with Nolan Senior in Vietnam," I said.

"What?" Poulton's voice spiked.

"They know each other."

"I don't believe for a second that—"

"Agent Lisa Yang has no Bureau-paid lodging in Houston on December seventeenth," I went on. "The night of the bookstore event. Do you find that unusual?"

Poulton hesitated before answering.

"You might've saved an agent's life today, but you're skating on thin ice, Camden."

He knew.

"Nolan was at that bookstore," I said. "He watched Yang enter *Banning's* password."

"Bullshit."

"Then he followed Yang and Banning back to the director's room at the Lancaster Hotel," I said. "After they went to bed together, he logged into Banning's account. And you know what he read, Craig? Not a serial murder file. He read the director's *personnel file.*"

"What?"

"The director blackballed Ethan Nolan's dad with the Bureau. Three decades ago."

Poulton had gone quiet. I knew how his brain worked. He was calculating how he could use this.

"Take me off speaker," he said.

I did this, holding the phone to my ear.

"That mess you made in the Jacksonville office, Camden . . . most people, that's the end of their career."

"But not me, huh?" I said. "I'm lucky?"

"You're more persistent than I imagined. I see your value now."

Poulton was scheming. Deciding how he'd use this information against Banning. The affair, which he probably already suspected, he now had proof of. Plus the connection between the director and our suspect. Maybe he could push Banning into an early retirement.

"If you're trying to put an ace in your pocket, Craig, I don't think you'll have much time to play it."

"What's that supposed to mean?"

"Why do you think I was asking if you'd checked in on Banning? If I'm right, the director is long gone."

"Wait a damn second, Camden," he said, putting me on hold.

As I waited, I thought of "The Paddock and the Mouse." About the difference between being virtuous and acting virtuous.

That clue was never about the FBI.

It was about William Banning.

Poulton came back on the line. "The director took off two hours ago," he said. "Left his cell phone, badge, and key card, but took his weapon."

Banning knew where Nolan was.

"Tell me what you're thinking," Poulton said. "Is this kid gonna expose Banning as a fraud?"

The head of the FBI lying about writing a book was one thing. But being the trigger for a madman going on a rampage? The bloody pictures that had been pushed into the public eye during the case had both horrified and captivated the media. And all the while, the director would look like he was too busy to care, sleeping with a subordinate.

Then there was that ad campaign. I recalled Banning's lines from it: "The world's brightest in behavioral sciences work at the FBI. People like me."

The media would pull clips from that campaign and eat the director alive. And Banning knew it. Knew he'd be portrayed as incompetent.

"Politics aren't Nolan's concern," I said. "He wants revenge. He's going to find Banning and kill him."

"And Banning?" Poulton asked.

I contemplated a showdown between Banning and Nolan Junior. An aging bureaucrat versus a twenty-six-year-old on a property that Nolan knew well. Had hunted on. Had maybe even *been hunted on* himself.

"Banning wants the same thing Nolan does," I said.

"And wherever they're meeting . . . you think you can get there first?"

"I can try," I said.

And suddenly Poulton surprised me.

"Well, maybe you get there a little late, but still take down Nolan."

I blinked. "Late?"

"Then when I'm in charge, you can call your own shots. Set up your own shop."

I hesitated, unsure of what to say.

Could I save PAR?

"Jesus, for once in your life, Camden, read between the lines. Think like the rest of us."

Before I could ask a question, the phone went dead. Poulton had hung up.

CHAPTER FORTY-FOUR

SHOOTER GOT NEWS THAT THE HELICOPTER WAS MEETING us in nearby Tyler County, and Warden Terradas offered us a ride.

I looked to Shooter, who had driven here. "The warden knows the area," I said, and we both climbed into the cab of Terradas's truck.

"You got any idea where Ethan Nolan went?" Shooter asked.

My mind was spinning, stuck on what Poulton had offered. Could I prevent PAR from being shut down? Run it, even? Did I have the skill to be Frank, if Frank was "dumping us," as Ethan Nolan had put it?

"Not yet," I said. "But wherever it is, it's faster to get there in a bird."

As Terradas fired up the truck, Shooter's phone buzzed. It was Cassie, and Shooter put it on speaker.

"Nolan Senior was Special Forces," Cassie said. "Part of SOG."

This was the Studies and Observation Group. They placed soldiers in Vietnam for secret missions. Tunnel clearing. Long-term reconnaissance. Assassinations.

"Apparently he was embedded with a team of locals in Central Vietnam," Cassie said.

I had studied every detail of the Vietnam War for my master's dissertation, a dual degree I'd received alongside one in information sciences. To me, the study of data and the study of war were closely related.

"The Montagnard Bowmen," I said, my brain immediately going to work. "They lived in Vietnam's Central Highlands and were experts in archery. Nolan may have shot with them. Maybe even learned about poisons from the group."

"He also earned a silver star for saving the life of a soldier," Cassie said. "Now go ahead, Gardner. Ask me who."

"William Banning," I said.

"Winner, winner. Chicken dinner."

And Banning had repaid Jack Nolan by blocking him from the FBI. I shook my head.

Warden Terradas made a hard right turn, and we were back on the state highway.

"Cassie," I said. "The house you're at—how well have you gone through it?"

"I'm still underway."

"These guys are more than casual hunters," I said. "You see any indication of places they visited, other than Big Thicket?"

"There's a den with a bunch of photos on the wall," she said. "The same place is in a lot of them."

We waited a moment while Cassie moved to this room.

"It's a ranch," she said. "In eight or ten pictures."

"What kind of ranch?" Shooter asked.

"The kind you'd like," Cassie replied. "Has a shooting range. Bows. Rifles. Ethan is decked out in camo pants. Same with his dad."

"The terrain in the photos," I said, thinking of Big Thicket, "is it swampy?"

"No," Cassie said. "It's hilly. A few high points. Ethan is a preteen in some of these. Then a teenager. There's a bunch of guys around them."

"Weekend warriors," Shooter said. "Must be some sort of training facility. Maybe a hunting preserve the family ran?"

Cassie didn't answer; for a moment, it sounded like we'd lost her.

"Guys, there's a big framed photo that was taken off the wall. It's on the table in here. Older men in it, sixtyish. A reunion. Banning and Nolan Senior in the photo. Looks like five or ten years ago, maybe. Everyone's got the same logo on their shirts. A circular shooting target with crosshairs, then the letters NTX."

"He's headed there," I said.

"Nolan?" Cassie asked.

"Banning too," I said.

Shooter looked shocked. "The director wouldn't do that," she said.

"Banning came back to the FBI for a farewell tour, Jo," I said. "The Bureau is his life. His identity. And Ethan Nolan's whole game is to make a fool of him."

"How would Banning even know where to go?"

A synapse fired. In Banning's office, there was a glass table. A piece of wood under it. Texas black gum with a carving on the side. NTX.

"That reunion," I said. "Wherever that is, that's our location. Banning came to it. Took back this giant piece of wood to make a table in his office."

Terradas's truck hit a bump, and I lifted the phone closer. "Check Nolan Senior's records, Cassie. Property taxes. Former addresses the military has on file. We need the location of that ranch."

We hung up, and Terradas slowed into a concrete lot where three helicopters sat. Closest to us was an MD 530, its blades whipping at the wind.

Hopping out, Shooter grabbed her gear from the back of the truck, including a long duffel that held her rifle. We lowered our heads and moved across the open space.

It took the pilot five minutes to fill up the tank. We waited in a single-room building next to the helipad and checked in with Richie. He'd stayed the night in Dallas and was following up on the murder in Keller. The one that matched Tignon's MO from Florida.

"I've been trying to confirm if Ethan Nolan knew Tignon was active again," Richie said. "But there's nothing definitive here."

A memory came to mind. "There were ten glasses on a bar cart in Tignon's home," I said. "Two were turned upright. An inch of water in the bottom."

"Ice cubes," Richie said, solving the riddle. "They melted. What does that mean?"

"He's a talker," I said.

"A talker?"

"Nolan Junior spoke with Tignon before he killed him. He wanted to know about the girl. Wanted to confirm Tignon was active again."

"Justice," Richie said, repeating the theme that had been consistent with Ethan Nolan. "Same as why he sent that priest to visit Fisher in prison. He wants to talk to his victims before he kills them."

Richie was on speaker, and Shooter jumped in. "You think he'll want to do the same with Banning? Have a chat before he tries to take him out?"

"Wait. He's going to kill Banning?" Richie's voice spiked. He'd been out of the loop for the last hour.

"He'll want to talk even more," I said to Shooter. "Banning is personal."

Outside, the helicopter pilot removed the fuel hose from the copter. I thought of what Poulton had said to me. Wondered again if it was within my power to save PAR. To keep us all together. And what the cost would be.

"Our problem," I said, "is that we might not get there in time."

Shooter's nostrils tucked in, and her eyes pinched to a point. "Wait a sec," she said. "When Poulton took us off speaker, he didn't offer that, did he? For you to slow-play this? To keep PAR open if you did?"

The helicopter pilot waved at us, and I told Richie we had to go.

"Wait," Richie said. "Guys, I know what's going on with PAR."

I glanced at Shooter, and she silently shook her head from left to right, letting me know she hadn't told him what we'd heard in the elevator.

"You can't let Poulton do this," Richie continued. "I know Banning's a hard guy to like. He's curt. Arrogant. But underneath it all, he's a good man. I know this about him."

Richie, defending William Banning. Why?

"Richie?" I said.

"He's my grandfather, Agent Camden."

CHAPTER FORTY-FIVE

"THIS IS WHY YOUR FILE IS SEALED?" I ASKED. "YOUR GRAND-
father didn't want anyone to know?"

"It's a little more complicated than that," Richie said.

He explained how his sister Vanessa was supposed to be the agent
in the family.

"She was a natural athlete. Smart. Funny. The kind of person people
are drawn to without knowing why."

I noted the past tense in Richie's speech.

"One day, we woke up and found her. Hung in the garage." Richie's
voice broke as he spoke. "Those bastards did it to her. My dad. My
grandpa. All their pressure."

And suddenly it made sense. Richie wasn't a volunteer. He was a
recruit. A replacement for his sister.

This also answered the question of how he'd gotten access to
Bureau data to do his research project for three summers before the
Academy.

"So the reason you chose PAR?" I asked.

"Let's just say I looked at the team," Richie said. "All of *your* mistakes. Shooter's. Frank's. I figured—here, everyone flames out. I will, too."

We went silent for a minute, and then Shooter spoke. "Don't worry, rook. We'll do our best, all right?"

We hung up, and I looked to Shooter. The helicopter was ready, but Cassie still hadn't found us a location.

"You're getting sent to Omaha," I said.

She took this in. "Where are you going?"

I smiled. "If we do this, where I'm going is the unemployment line."

My phone buzzed with a text. A location from Cassie.

"Well, shit," Shooter said. "Neither of us were ever really good at politics, were we?"

"No, we were not."

"Maybe Nebraska isn't so bad." She extended her hand. "It's been a pleasure, Gardner."

"Same," I said, shaking. "Let's save the old man."

We ran across the tarmac and climbed into the helicopter.

The location Cassie supplied was a twenty-three-acre plot of land on the edge of the Angelina National Forest, some fifty miles away. A place we could get to in twenty minutes in the MD30.

If our theory was correct, Banning had left the Dallas safe house more than two hours ago. Which put him at the property sometime in the last fifteen minutes.

Ethan Nolan, meanwhile, had probably headed south to the Y in the Neches River this morning around 5 a.m. If he took the water north from there, he would have beaten Banning to the hunting compound by a good hour.

Shooter turned to me as we lifted off, speaking through the headset. "You think Banning brought his cuffs with him?"

"Doubtful," I said. "But we know he brought his weapon."

I reminded Shooter about the steps that Nolan had taken with Tignon and Fisher, how he'd needed some sort of conversation with them before he killed each man.

"So what do you do if you're Ethan Nolan, Jo?" I asked. "He's a hunter. You're a hunter. He needs to talk."

She thought for a moment. "If I could get there first, I'd get to higher ground. Use a bow and arrow."

"Take Banning down," I confirmed. "But not kill him."

"Not right away," Shooter said. "Once I neutralized other threats, I'd come out of my hiding spot and question Banning. Make him explain to me why he screwed over my old man."

The helicopter shifted, its blades picking up choppy wind. "Let's pull up a lay of the land," I said. "Of this compound."

In a minute, we were looking at a satellite map on Shooter's phone.

"Higher ground looks to be here." I pointed.

"True," Shooter said. "But if Nolan is trying to hit the director with an arrow, that point is too high to be accurate with a bow, Gardner. You'd shoot a rifle from that elevation."

I pointed at a gray area to the south. "And this?"

"Call that the opposite of high ground. Most likely an old mining quarry."

I looked at the brown Beretta GTX shoes that Shooter had on. "Good boots," I said.

"Always."

"Then we'll put you down here." I motioned at a dip in the valley. "You hump it the rest of the way on foot. Get up to that peak."

We gave directions to the pilot on where to drop her, and Shooter and I went back to the map. A fire road circled the property, running from the quarry over to a cabin. Halfway along it, the road came to a T and cut south, down the mountain toward Highway 63. This was how Banning would arrive. The ridge below the T was where I would be dropped.

CHAPTER FORTY-SIX

BY 10 A.M., I HAD HIKED A HALF MILE FROM WHERE THE chopper had dropped me and found my way to a small cabin on the hunting preserve.

Tire marks from a sedan were visible in the gravel beside the structure, and a hundred yards to the right, I saw a white Buick LeSabre, parked under a bough of shortleaf pines. A government sedan.

I tried the knob to the front door of the cabin, and it turned. I pulled my Glock and let the door swing open on its own.

"Director Banning," I called out. "It's Gardner Camden."

The place was one large room with a kitchenette and dining area. A hall led into what I assumed was a bed and bath.

The door swung closed, revealing Banning, dressed in a blue suit, as he was a few days earlier. He lowered a Remington 870 that had been clasped tight in his hand.

Was he simply lying in wait? Hoping Nolan would walk in?

"You alone?" Banning said.

I could've asked him the same question, but I already knew the answer. "For now."

He made his way to the kitchen and laid the rifle on the counter. There, he had a stack of newspapers he was placing tape on.

Looking around, I saw he'd covered all but one window. He was blocking Nolan from seeing into the place.

"Ethan Nolan is assuming you'll come here," I said. "We gotta go."

"I'm not going anywhere," Banning said, taping the newsprint over the last window. "I'm counting on that little shit coming here."

I leaned my body into the hall. Made sure no one was hiding in the bathroom or bedroom.

All this felt like bad news. Just as they had in their Houston or Big Thicket property, this preserve was probably a place in which Ethan and Jack Nolan had squared off, the father chasing the son.

"So what's the plan?" I asked.

"The windows are blocked," the director said.

"With newspaper."

"Which removes sightline," he countered. "You take that away, you take away the advantage of hitting me from afar."

I blinked.

The Bureau had a history of face-offs with men held up in cabins, and most of them had ended badly. The problem with Banning's strategy was that he was thinking like the FBI. Not like Nolan.

"You're a by-the-book guy, Camden. I'm sure you already called for backup, right?"

I nodded.

"So what do we got?" he asked. "A half hour before an army descends? If anything, that'll force him to run for cover and hole up in here. When he does that, the four of us will be here to greet him."

"The four of us?"

"You. Me. Remington. And Glock."

Under the polished veneer, Banning was a cowboy. Except he

hadn't drawn up an operational plan since he was in the field fifteen years ago.

I thought about the clues left behind by Ethan Nolan and the riddles he'd told me. The *Helleborus* that was a nod to his dad's crimes, the signed paper in Tignon's mouth.

Ethan Nolan was going to escape somewhere far away or take himself out as he killed Banning. That had always been his endgame. The clues were meant to be an embarrassment, a stain on Banning's legacy.

One that would've been slowly teased out months later if PAR had not been on the case.

I eyed Banning's rifle. "When's the last time you shot here?"

"Maybe twenty fifteen." The director shrugged. "I'll tell you what—the place was kept up better back then."

My face must've shown something, because Banning scowled at me.

"Don't give me that look, Camden," he said. "You don't know these people. Jack Nolan . . . he saved my life, all right. By burning down a village. Women. Children. They were like stains on the ground."

"Sir, I need to get you into that car and off this land."

"Not a chance," he said.

"What if Nolan uses some sort of heavy mortar?"

"Heavy mortar?"

"Tosses a grenade at the cabin?"

"A grenade?" Banning repeated, smirking at me.

"What if he—"

Before I could finish my thought, we heard a popping noise, and Banning turned his head.

The sound of a CO_2 cartridge being discharged rang out, and one of the windows shattered. Tiny pellets tore through the cheap newsprint and bounced off the walls, creating a powdery haze.

The director moved away from the smoke, pulling his jacket in front of his face. But more pellets followed. The newspaper on the other windows was sealing us in, rather than airing the place out. The dust began to build up: a mix of salt, tear gas, and capsaicin, the element found in pepper spray.

Outside, heavy glass shattered, and I knew that Nolan had shot rounds into Banning's car. The powder would coat the seats and dash, making it impossible to drive.

"Shit," I said.

I pulled my shirt over my mouth and found Banning by the door, ready to flee.

"Wait," I hollered. The shooting sounds had come from the south. If Banning was making a run for it, he could do better than simply sprinting out the front door.

I glanced through the haze and found a dining table, the top of it a wooden round, four feet across.

"Let's roll this out as you go," I said. "As cover."

The director nodded, helping me get the table onto its side. I kicked at the circular piece of wood twice, and the round top separated from the base.

"Three, two, one," I said, flinging open the door and shoving the round wood out the doorway. It rolled, end over end, and Banning ran behind it, a perfect device for concealment.

I took off after him, my eyes burning, the powdery haze moving out the door behind me. We cut behind the cabin and headed north, away from where the gun had been fired.

We didn't stop running for five minutes. When we did, Banning's chest was heaving.

"Let's head toward the fire road," I said. "Get there, and we can start down the mountain."

"I need to sit down," Banning huffed. "Rest a second."

He removed his suit jacket and bent over, his hands by his ankles. Began coughing and spitting.

The forest was too quiet. "We gotta move," I said.

But Banning held up his palm, as if to say wait.

As he stood up and turned to me, I heard a sound.

Thit, thit.

I ran at Banning, tackling him behind a downed log, its circumference over three feet. It was a giant green ash, and I dragged his body behind it.

Two arrows were stuck into the ground nearby.

"God damn it," he barked. "I'm gonna get this kid if it kills me."

Banning pushed me away and scrambled over to where he'd dropped his rifle. He cocked it and stood, aiming at the hillside. But even as he found Nolan, an arrow whizzed down and struck him, right through his slacks, deep into his upper thigh.

"Gahh!"

Banning fell to one knee, his rifle discharging into the air.

I pulled him down, wondering if the arrow was tipped with *Helleborus*. I took out Warden Terradas's pocketknife, and Banning's eyes got huge.

"I gotta cut that out," I said.

"No." He shook his head. "No, no, we can wait. We can wait for backup."

Now he was interested in backup?

He didn't have that much time. From the length of the shaft, I could tell the arrowhead had broken through his flesh and buried itself under his skin.

"I have a plan to distract Ethan Nolan," I said. "But you need to stay put. Can you do that?"

Banning nodded, but glanced at the rifle at the same time.

And I knew he was lying.

"I want to thank you," I said, "for believing in me. For giving me the chance to lead this case. I'm gonna get him now, okay?"

The old man nodded then, happily believing that Ethan Nolan would be dead before backup arrived. That's when I turned and hit the director with the heel of my palm as hard as I could, right along the jawline, one inch below his ear.

Knocked him out cold.

Then I shimmied down his leg, cut away at his suit pants, and inspected the arrow. Cutting into the thickest part of his thigh, I sliced at the skin around it. Dug the tip of the knife in and flicked the arrowhead out, scraping at the muscle around it.

Blood surged from the wound, and I tore a strip of fabric free from my shirt, winding it around Banning's leg to slow the bleeding.

He was out cold, and the forest had gone quiet again. I popped my head up for a second. Saw movement in the brush thirty yards up the hill from me.

I'd have four seconds to get to a new location, so I used my hands and knees to crawl behind the log, sixteen feet to its conclusion.

I made sure the safety was off my Glock and rose.

Pop. Pop. Pop.

Right at the spot where I'd seen movement.

I fell to the ground, ducking as an arrow cemented into the dirt nearby. A second one landed in the ash tree, an inch from my body.

I was cornered. No way out.

But five seconds later, I heard a cracking sound and saw the impact in the dirt and trees where'd I'd aimed.

Shooter had climbed throughout the morning until she was at the peak that I had first identified as higher ground. Too high for Ethan Nolan to be targeting Banning with an arrow. But the right elevation for Shooter to have an advantage over Nolan if things went bad.

And now Jo Harris, the pride of the 2012 Olympic shooting team, was laying down fire along the ridge where Nolan was.

I took off in that direction. As I ran, I heard the shots continuing. But not aimed at me.

Shooter had eyes on Ethan Nolan, and she was directing me like a quarterback leading a receiver. I heard the sounds shift south and adjusted course. Then lower in elevation.

He was running. I was running. And I was on an intercept course.

I leapt over the brush, popping a new magazine into my Glock and letting the old one fall out as I pumped my fists.

I was heading down a trail that widened onto the fire road. Ethan Nolan erupted from the bushes, just ahead of me. But I was moving faster. I smashed into him with my body, and he hit the ground hard, his arrows and bow flying into the bushes.

I steadied myself and pointed my Glock at him.

"FBI. Stay down."

Ethan Nolan lifted his head, staring at me. "You're not gonna shoot me, Agent Camden," he said. His hands found the ground. Pushed up. "We've been through too much together."

Behind Nolan was that giant pit in the ground, the mining quarry. From my angle, the drop-off looked to be eighty feet.

I steadied my aim. "You run, and you die."

He nodded, as if understanding, his eyes as big as moons. "Then my mission is complete," he said. "Banning is dead. Or soon will be. I don't care if I die."

Nolan wore a black T-shirt and camouflage pants. He'd changed since last night.

"Oh, you hit the director," I said. "But I cut the arrowhead out."

"No." Ethan Nolan squinted at me. "No, you're lying again." He took a step backward.

"He'll be on his feet in a few days," I said.

"But that's not fair." He stared at me, outraged. "You're a fair person. My dad saved Banning's life, Camden. And you know what that son of a bitch did in return?"

"He blackballed him from the FBI," I said. "We found the letter."

Ethan Nolan glanced back at the quarry.

"My pop was a force of positivity," he said, almost as if he hadn't heard me. "He opened a shooting range. Taught people to defend themselves. He even arranged this get-together for the old crew from 'Nam. And Banning came."

"You were there?" I asked. "Is that when your father realized what Banning had done?"

"Realized? No, no. He never realized, thank God. No, my dad hosted them all. And afterwards he was inspired. I came home from camp that summer, and he told me."

"Told you what?"

"That it's a calling, Camden. Law enforcement. It doesn't matter if there's a paycheck. So Dad did what he was born to do. He took out the trash."

Nolan had been moving backward, little by little. I watched him, calculating his distance to the edge.

"How did you know to look?" I asked. "In Banning's file."

"I sent him an invitation to the funeral," he said. "Did Banning attend? No. Did he send flowers? No. How about a card for the man who saved your life?" His eyes locked on mine. "What do you think, Camden?"

"No," I said softly, suddenly thinking about my mother. I hadn't even begun to think about a funeral.

"Dad always talked about how great William Banning was, and I believed it. Saw those ads on TV. But after my dad passed, I started to wonder. I reached out to his office to ask if he could send some letter of recognition to read at the funeral. His secretary called back. Said he didn't feel like he knew my father well enough to do that."

And this was when Ethan Nolan's rage had begun.

"A month later he's on this book tour," Nolan continued. "Bragging about some book he obviously didn't write. I follow him back to the hotel bar. He's married, but having drinks with this young girl. And then he goes to his room with her?" Nolan threw up his hands. "It all became clear. He's above the law. And he's not gonna respond to anything less than a public shaming."

I thought of the high-profile killers Nolan had eliminated. He'd applied his dad's approach to a man his father was too ignorant to know was his nemesis. All to make the Bureau look foolish, with Banning the idiot at the top. The least bright person in the field of behavioral science.

"You can't be mad at *me*," he said. "I did what you couldn't, Camden. I removed the worst of society for you."

"And my mom?" I asked.

Nolan put his hands up, palms out. "I regret your mom," he said. "There was no reason to do that except . . ."

Except I'd angered him. He worshipped his dad. And I'd made the man into a monster.

"I'm gonna rush you now," Nolan said. "And you're gonna shoot me dead."

The grip on my Glock was rock solid, my aim at Nolan's head. I heard my mother's voice.

Don't do it, Gardy.

I lowered my aim to his abdomen. To injure, but not kill. "No," I said. "You rush me, and you'll get a shot to the gut. Another to the leg. You can limp around a concrete cell the rest of your life."

Nolan glanced back at the quarry again, changing his tack. "I talked to your mother, you know," he said. "I thought she was buying time at first, chatting me up. But then her questions got personal. My father. My childhood. My mother."

I flashed to that phone conversation at the airfield, just days ago.

The expression "serial killer" is just a convention of man, Gardy, she'd said to me. *At the end of the day, every killer is just a human, searching for something.*

"She was trying to understand you," I said.

He took another step toward the quarry. "She told me what she did for a living. How you showed her pictures of Tignon."

I made eye contact with Nolan, remembering the first night of the investigation.

"I asked her," Nolan said, "if I did bad things . . . did she think I could change? Maybe . . . be someone like you?"

"And?"

"She said I'd never be like you. That you were special. Then she told me to get on with it. That she got forgetful. She didn't want to have an episode and think I'd just gotten there."

A single tear ran down my right cheek.

"That's when I did it," he continued, "as a courtesy to her."

He was baiting me now. Angling for a quick ticket out. But my shooting hand didn't waver.

"It wasn't a life for her, Camden," he said. "I killed her *for you.* As a mercy."

Nolan was twenty feet from the edge now.

Eighteen feet.

Sixteen.

"You better stop moving," I said.

He turned and ran. Out toward the lip of the canyon.

If I didn't shoot him, he was going to swan dive, right into that hole in the ground. A glorious end to his mission. He would kill the serial killer who'd killed serial killers.

I took aim at his running leg. But inside, I wanted him dead, and I knew the fastest way was not a trial. It was me, letting him make that leap.

And I took my finger off the trigger.

CHAPTER FORTY-SEVEN

A NOISE CRACKED THROUGH THE SKY LIKE THE SOUND OF A jet airplane making speed.

Ethan Nolan went down mid-stride, his hand grabbing at the fibrous cord that connected the muscles in the back of his calf to his heel bone.

I looked up. I had not taken him down. I hadn't had the strength.

But Shooter had. And she got him right in the Achilles' heel. Nolan got to one knee but screamed as he attempted to get up. As he switched to the other foot, a second shot rang out, and I heard the snap of the same tendon in the other leg.

Blood poured from the back of both feet, just above his heel, and Nolan howled in pain.

He began crawling toward the edge of the quarry, grunting as he did.

I walked closer, but kept out of Shooter's eyeline.

Blackish-red blood was pooling in the dirt behind him. A gate was nearby, a fence surrounding some electric equipment that fed path lighting around the quarry.

"She's gonna take off your wrists if you keep moving," I said.

Nolan glanced up toward the mountain, using the edge of the fence to pull himself closer to the quarry. "What the fuck?" he said. "Who shoots someone like this?"

"It's your Achilles'," I said. "Greek mythology. That Oedipus arrow thing you and your dad were doing. She's got an odd sense of humor."

I grabbed Nolan by his left hand and dragged his body southward.

He screamed in pain, and I took out my cuffs. Locked them onto his wrist. Then clicked them onto the metal fence.

I turned, and he yelled, "What the hell? You gonna leave me here?"

I reholstered my Glock, unsure what I was capable of if he began speaking about my mother again.

"You're going to prison, Ethan, and you're never getting out. Someone'll come get you."

Five minutes down the trail, I found Banning, sitting on a log. He looked groggy.

"It's over?" the director said.

"Yes."

"You kill him?" he asked.

I shook my head. And Banning looked in the direction from which I'd come. An old bull, perhaps thinking he'd go after Nolan still.

But I heard the sounds of a mechanical bird, coming up over the ridge where Shooter had been. Jo would help the agents get Nolan onto a chopper and off to a hospital.

I assisted Banning back to a picnic table outside the cabin. An ambulance arrived sometime after. Took him away.

I sat alone then. Waiting for Shooter. When she arrived, we cleaned the pepper dust from Banning's car and headed back west.

•   •   •

I got to the intensive care unit at UT Southwestern Medical Center in Dallas four hours later and met with my mother's physician on the fifth floor, in an office looking out over a green lawn covered in curving walking paths.

There was no new news, and after a few minutes of the doctor speaking, I stopped hearing the exact terminology that left his mouth, focusing instead on the words that he placed particular emphasis on: *endotracheal tube* and *informed decision.*

I thought of something my mother had once told me when we were discussing religion. She had grown up in a faith household, but had not raised me in that way. "Still," she'd said to me, "a lot of things are faith-based, Gardy. Love, for instance. It's hard to prove. But you know it when you feel it."

I stood up, and the doctor stopped talking.

"For the time being, I'm not going to withdraw care," I said. "I owe it to her. To see if she comes around."

"Of course," he said.

I moved back to the elevator and took it to my mom's floor.

In her room, the sheets were pulled up around her arms. I heard the sound of whirring machines. My mother hated hospitals.

Richie and Cassie stood outside the door, and Shooter was a few feet down the hall. I nodded at them and entered my mother's room while they held the door open.

"Let's give Gardner a minute," Cassie said, and I heard the door shut.

I leaned over my mother's body, smelling the soap she used.

"I remember everything," I said. "Not just what you said, but what you meant. The lessons."

I stayed close to her for ten minutes, holding my hand against her cheek. "Wake up," I said. "I need you."

Then I stood up and wiped tears away with my wrist.

Cassie came in and hugged me.

Then Shooter.

I stood there, arms against my sides, unused to being held this long by so many.

When Richie joined in, I slowly put my arms around everyone. My mother was not my only family.

An hour later I drove over to my mother's nursing home and found my way to the main room. Residents gathered, and her friends told stories about my mom. They described her as the resident analyst, advice columnist, and sometime shrink. She got a nurse to leave her cheating boyfriend and helped an orderly reconcile with his wife.

"When your mom was with us," her nurse, Flavia, said, "I mean really with us—there was no one like her."

CHAPTER FORTY-EIGHT

THE FBI HELD A PRESS CONFERENCE ANNOUNCING THAT we'd caught Ethan Nolan. A special guest attended, one Burke Kagan, formerly of the Oklahoma City office. Kagan was given an honorary citation for his work in advancing the case.

The rest of PAR stood in the wings, except for Richie, who chose not to attend. He didn't want to give his grandfather the satisfaction of seeing a legacy on the podium. Frank came, too, although he was still healing up from the cuts along his legs and arms.

Oddly, he still hadn't told us anything about the fate of PAR. Maybe he couldn't bring himself to face the decision. But I could see it on his face when he avoided my gaze.

An informal ceremony happened a week later, thanking William Banning for his twenty-five years of service to the country. I was invited, and took Cassie as my plus-one.

As everyone expected, Craig Poulton had taken the director's spot at the top of the FBI. That night, he stood quietly in the wings, letting Banning have his moment.

Cassie and I milled around the edges of the party, which was mostly attended by bigwigs from D.C. and Bureau alumni, none of whom we knew. Cassie wore an orange dress that ended past her knees and a peach-colored sweater atop it.

"You look nice tonight," I said.

"This little 'fit?" She motioned at herself, smiling. "Why thank you, Gardner."

After a couple drinks, my partner turned to me. "So," she said, "would you consider this a date?"

"Every day is a date," I said. "Today is the nineteenth."

Cassie glared at me.

"We're partners," I said. "This can't be a date."

"Sure, sure," she said. "But, you know . . ."

"What?"

"You could be Shooter's partner. Richie's pretty sweet on you, too."

"Or I could be no one's partner."

"Yeah, I heard about that," Cassie said. "PAR closing. That would make it real easy. Then again, we'd both be out of jobs."

We left the notion alone for a moment and ate some finger foods. Listened to a couple speeches. I was thinking of a movie I'd seen, where the man turns to the woman and says, "You wanna get outta here?" Takes her back to his place.

Could I pull that off? Say those words to Cassie?

As I turned to face her, I felt a hand on my arm.

"Camden," a voice said.

Craig Poulton stood in front of us, a cigar hanging from his mouth.

"Sir," I said.

"Let's take a walk." He looked to Cassie. "You mind?"

She put up both hands, palms out, as if to say "take him away," and we walked into a side garden. Once out of sight, Poulton tossed the cigar into a trash can. The edge of it was unlit. Like so many aspects of Craig Poulton that I observed, the cigar was a prop.

"I read your report," he said. "One pop from you, and Banning went down, huh? From someone else, I'd think that was an exaggeration. From you . . . no way."

My report was twenty-two pages long, single-spaced. It covered every moment, from PAR's perspective, as well as Nolan's. And this was Poulton's takeaway?

"What can I do for you, sir?" I asked.

The last time we'd spoken, Poulton had told me to get to Banning late, and I hadn't. The only other official communication I'd received was an email, saying that in lieu of an accommodation for saving the lives of Frank and Banning, I was reinstated as a special agent.

"Very direct, right," he said. "There's things in your report, Camden." He offered me that same sharkish grin. "Maybe they didn't happen exactly that way."

I stared at Poulton. "You haven't filed it yet?"

"I'm still dotting i's and crossing t's."

In my mind, I considered one fact that I'd received directly from Nolan and taken as truth without checking.

"Were you not disbanding PAR?" I asked.

"We were," Poulton said. "Frank was moving to Dallas, to run that office. That was decided two months ago. With his injury, we'll hold the spot. Give him time to recuperate."

So Ethan Nolan was right.

Poulton grinned. "There are *other things* I'd like you to take a second look at." He pointed around, at the remains of Banning's retirement party. "There's no reason to smear the reputation of a good man, is there?"

Banning.

His affair. His book. Maybe even getting knocked out in one punch. Poulton didn't need Banning to be pushed out anymore. He was already in charge. So now he'd collect a different favor, by removing anything that slandered Banning's legacy.

I thought of Anna and Saul. Of the decisions I'd made in Miami seven years ago. Of how rigid I was.

And I thought of what Frank would say.

"I serve at the whim of the director of the FBI."

Poulton nodded, pleased. He put his arm around my shoulder. "I'm glad you said that," he replied. "I know you'll figure out what to edit. How to tell the story better. I also think there's a real need for a team like yours."

I squinted at Poulton. "Permission to speak frankly?"

"Wow." Poulton smirked. "You mean you're learning how to turn it on and off?"

"When you say there's a real need," I said, "you mean to say that, now that you're in charge, you want a safety valve, correct? A bunch of . . . what did you call us . . . brilliant freaks?"

Poulton's smile faded. "I'm offering you something real, Camden. You see anyone else with their hand out?"

"I'm tired of staring at the parking lot," I said.

"Take Frank's office, then. It looks out over the lawn."

"My daughter is in Miami."

"So we put PAR in Miami." He shrugged. "You think I give a shit where you're housed?"

I blinked.

I had met the previous night with Rosa. Told her that I was taking Camila with me when school began next year. But if Poulton's offer to put PAR in Miami was real, it meant that Rosa would not have to travel to Jacksonville to see her granddaughter. Camila would not have to switch schools. And my daughter could see her Nana whenever she wanted.

Perhaps things were turning up.

Just that morning, I'd received a text from a nurse in Texas. My mother's right hand had begun trembling, a positive sign in coma patients.

"I'll give you one year in charge as a test," Poulton offered. "Maybe two. Let's see how many times we come to blows after you throw some insult my way. Tell me I'm obtuse. Or unintelligent."

"Just those two words?" I asked.

He stared at me.

"That was a joke," I explained.

"You'd report directly to me," Poulton said. "So . . . I don't know what Frank told you in terms of me being some asshole. But the guy tried to sleep with my wife at an FBI function. Not sure what you'd do in a situation like that, if you were me."

Poulton hesitated, and his smile got bigger. "At least I can be sure that if I invite you to one of those events, you're not gonna make that mistake. I mean—you wouldn't even know how to hit on someone, right? Part of your whole . . . living inside your head thing."

I thought of Cassie, back at the party. *Let's get out here*, I'd say when I got back to her.

"So?" Poulton asked.

I didn't like Craig Poulton. But I didn't like William Banning, either. Neither was as brave and committed as the 226 agents I had interacted with over my years with the FBI. Those men and women, despite any personal flaws they might have, represented the best of America.

Poulton put out his hand. "We have a deal or what?"

"Yes," I said.

"Good." He patted me on the shoulder. "I'll have Olivia call about a relocation package. We'll cover your moving. But I want you set up in a week, Camden. Ready to go."

"Yes sir," I said.

"Congratulations," Poulton said. And then he was gone.

I stood there by myself, thinking about my mom. How proud she'd be of me. And of the Head Cases, a real unit, no longer stranded in a satellite office.

As I turned to head back to the party, my phone buzzed with a text.

Cassie.

> I grabbed an Uber. Two drinks and I start saying crazy shit.

> See you Monday, partner.

I stared at the words. Maybe it was for the better, especially if I was the new boss.

I turned and moved out to the parking lot. Used FaceTime to call my daughter. As I got in my car, she came on the line.

"Daddy," she answered on her iPad. "It's late. I'm in bed."

Camila was in her PJs, her face illuminated by a pink nightlight I'd bought for her.

"I've got news, honey," I said.

"Good news?"

"Great news. You are talking to the head of the Miami office's . . . brand-new association . . . of very, very, very significant agents."

Camila started laughing then. Louder and sweeter than I'd ever heard anyone laugh. And a tear came to my eye. Strange, I thought. A tear. Rare for me.

Miami, here I come.

ACKNOWLEDGMENTS

I WOULD LIKE TO THANK ALL THE READERS WHO MADE THE jump over from my P. T. Marsh series, as well as new folks who discovered this book. I love to hear from readers, so please send me an email and let me know what you think at McMahonJohn@att.net. And, if you enjoyed this book and don't know about my other series, please check out *The Good Detective, The Evil Men Do,* and *A Good Kill* (best read in that order). *The New York Times* listed them as "Top 10 Crime Novels" of the year twice, so hopefully I am not steering you wrong and you'll enjoy.

This book took a longer journey to get out to the public, so before anyone else, I want to thank Kelley Ragland at Minotaur, for bringing the book to market. Equally as important has been my team at Writers House, who made it happen: Simon Lipskar, Genevieve Gagne-Hawes, John Schline, and Laura Katz. Shout-out to Amy Berkower for making a great intro and Tom Ishizuka, Michelle Kroes, and Cecilia de la Campa for all your help bringing this to Hollywood.

I have an incredibly supportive family, which seems like a prerequisite for any success at writing. This starts with Maggie, Zoey, and Noah, but goes wider to my brothers and sisters, Andy, Kerry, and Bette. A big thanks to all the McMahons, Archbolds, Carlsons, Gmelichs, and Thomasys for your continuing support.

Several incredible authors read early copies of my last book, *A Good Kill*, and were nice enough to offer quotes on it. So a very delayed thanks to Karen Dionne, Brian Panowich, and William Kent Krueger. Their books are stunning. Also, thank you to Jess Lourey, J. A. Jance, and Karen Dionne for reading advance copies of this book. Appreciate you all.

I am grateful to writers and editors who provided notes on this book. That begins with Jerrilyn Farmer, but also includes B. J. Graf, Alex Jamison, and Andrea Robb. A shout-out to the folks who assisted on my research road trip in Texas (especially my friends McKenna and John at the *real* Murder by the Book) pictured within this book.

After finishing my last book, I switched agencies, and my friend Marly Rusoff was so professional and hospitable in this changeover that it reminded me that gracious and generous people still abound, the kind who believe in art and friendship over sales. And speaking of publishing, I am just getting to know the team at Minotaur/St. Martin's, but I know it takes a village to get a book out—from editorial to proofing to sales. So thanks to the ones I've met so far like Katie Holt, Mac Nicholas, Stephen Erickson, and Sarah Melnyk—and the ones behind the scenes, too.

People email a lot, "When's the next book coming out?" The reality is that it's harder than ever to get a book deal, but as readers, you can help. Here's what I recommend: the giant authors (we all know their names)—check them out from your local library. The up-and-comers like me and hundreds of others—spend your money and buy them wherever you buy books. That's how we keep this thing going. And as to the question about a next installment, this book is part of a two-book deal, so look for the next Gardner Camden/PAR novel sometime in early 2026.

Writing is a strange and solitary craft. You are pulled into a story by some unconscious force and spend years hosting and reforming it until you no longer own it. It leaves home, like a child off to college, the only remains some echo of the room they once lived in. In truth, its only real home is in the hands of a reader, so thanks for taking it in. And onto the next . . .